T0196925

JACK DILLON:

THE SPACE DRONE

J.T. SPEARS

iUniverse®

JACK DILLON: THE SPACE DRONE

iUniverse books may be ordered through booksellers or by contacting:

iUniverse
1663 Liberty Drive
Bloomington, IN 47403
www.iuniverse.com
1-800-Authors (1-800-288-4677)

ISBN: 978-1-5320-8698-4 (sc)
ISBN: 978-1-5320-8699-1 (e)

Print information available on the last page.

iUniverse rev. date: 12/18/2019

Dedicated to:

My grandmother Myrtle Lillian Gilkes,
Aminah Gilkes,
and much thanks to the entire Tonsil Family

EXPEDITION ONE

CHAPTER
ONE

THE LAST THING he remembered, was falling out of his air-coupe, nearly 2,000 feet to his death.

He didn't fall as far though, because he's now laying in this bright room strapped down to a levitating mag-gurney.

The air was cold, wet smelled incredibly clean---not the slightest hint of an odor anywhere. A positive sign that someone had the room burned...not with actual fire, but with light. A very bright, blinding light. Hot enough to singe the hair off a man's skin, and totally devastating to any micro-bacteria within its range. Hence, the odorless air. There was (literally) nothing to smell.

He'd bet all of his globe-creds, that whoever snatched him out of the sky, had something to do with him being shot. How else would they know where to snatch him? It's no easy thing, you know. Nearly all snatches are done on solid ground, and most likely while the unsuspecting victim's still stationary. Worked well on crooks. But it was a kidnaper's tool.

The Whorganians brought that technology here; but then someone got a good look at one of their Teleportation Chambers and modified the whole thing down to a wrist-band and a door-frame. Illegal of course, and very expensive on the black Market.

His new friends must've operated on him, because a patch of itchy synthesis was covering the wound in his chest where an Ion-blaster, had vaporized a nice chunk of flesh. Had it not been for his armor, there wouldn't have been a scrap of him left anywhere to fixed.

What the hell is this place...?

He didn't appreciate being strapped down like this.

Or was he paralyzed? Drugged...?

He couldn't move an inch. His vision was limited to just his eyeballs shifting about inside their sockets. Two long tubes of blood were sticking out of his arms. He must've needed a transfusion to save his life.

Phmph!... He thought fretfully to himself.

A blood transfusion. Ion-blasters.... Snatchers!

He'd spent forty years as a Private Detective; used his weapon no more than five or six times. Sixty years as a Federal Agent before that---snatched a handful of bad-guys, but that was all. Most corporate crooks aren't killers anyway; you investigated'em, build your evidence, then snatch'em up and toss'em in jail....

That been his life for the past 100 years. He wasn't qualified for a wife, nor was he engineered to have children. The sole purpose of his creation was to uphold federal law. He had very few interests besides sports, comedic halo-plays, and policing. His life-span expires in the year 2231 AD: about 75 years from now, And up until eight hours ago, he looked forward to living out his entire 210 years in total satisfaction.

But he wasn't too sure about any of that now. He'd killed more people in the one day, than during his entire

60 years as an agent; broke more laws than be cared to remember.

Phmph...!

Aliens....

To hell with'em all!

CHAPTER
TWO

HE THOUGHT IT would be a simple enough thing to deal with, this case. Some stolen alien relic, swiped from the holds of one of their fancy interstellar cargo ships. A worthless looking thing (from what he could tell), as the fuzzy hologram of a metal cube appeared above the tiny glowing cavity of his desk-com projector.

"What am I looking at here?" he asked his new client. He was genuinely confused. There weren't any distinctive markings, or designs, anywhere on the relic. Just a plain old solid cube. His Elemental-reader detected neither silver, nor gold, nor any other of the known elements in the Universe--alien or otherwise. In fact, the metal from which the cube was made--according to his Reader--didn't exist. And this confused him even more, you see, because the world's become so shrouded with alien technology, our lives now revolved around them. From the Snatch-frames, to Ion-blasters, his desk-command Elemental Reader, were all the wondrous marvels of some alien mind. But yet, he'd been hired to find some metal box, made from materials unknown to both of their worlds. That should've been his first warning that this case consisted of more sinister implications than just mere theft. Maybe this so-called relic didn't belong to his client in the first place.... But he was way ahead of himself back then. He wasn't even close to begin thinking along those lines.

"It's called the Jhusrot," his client said. "Or 'Unknown' in your language."

"That much is pretty obvious," the Detective said, irritated by the creature's simpleness. Despite its apparent lowly status in the alien's version of a caste system, it pretended to be the owner of the relic, instead of something that was hired by something else, hired to hire something to hire him. But he was still confused, and intrigued at the same time, so he played along with the foolish game. "I mean...what is it? What's the significance of this Jhusrot? Why was it made?

"It's a work of art." Was all his client said.

"That's it? Just art?

"Same as your sculptures and paintings."

It went without saying, that our extraterrestrial guests are far more intelligent creatures than us Humans. They were said to be at least 3 millennia ahead of us, by our own estimates. And yet., they were surprisingly naive.

Through some unfortunate missing-link during their own evolutionary process, they were unable to detect deception. The notion that someone could be lying right to their faces---about anything--was incapable of registering in their otherwise super-intelligent minds. They were notoriously easy to trick, manipulate, and seduce.

Not so much the seduction part, though. He doubted anyone could be desperate, or sick enough, to couple with one of those things. For one, their sexual organs resembled nothing that we're used to seeing here on Earth.

And for another, they were worms...literally.

Maybe not the squirming through the mud, early-bird fish-food kind. But worms nonetheless. A Symbiot, as a matter of fact. Or, what he liked to call them: parasites. Galactic parasites, visiting worlds to find suitable hosts (those with no kind of common-sense, as far as anyone could tell), to assimilate themselves into the life-form's central nervous system, commanding complete control over their bodies. From there, they go on to achieve incredible things. They built their cities, conquered their worlds light-years away, and do as they please (as far as Jack was concerned).

So, it wasn't just one alien species that invaded...visited... our planet. They came in many forms. From the goat-looking, to the dragon-lizard-looking, down to the more humanoid ape-like creatures.

But there's one species within their ranks that was more common than the rest. These were a bit more humanoid in appearance, but still pretty ugly. Very tall and slender, with tiny heads no larger than the size of a human fist. Green skin, pigeon-peas for eyes, two pin-pricks for nostrils, and one slit for a mouth where a pig's tail of a tongue occasionally slid out. Seven long digits (what they called fingers), very elegant and graceful, stretched like tentacles from each bony hand. Their feet were as flat as a diver's flippers, which bespoke of the creature's home-world as being somewhat aquatic.

They called themselves, Whorganian's (swift as dolphins in water, these Whorganian's). They were chosen by their Symbiot masters as vessels of supreme intelligence, which was why there were so many of them. The lesser creatures, as they became known, served different purposes in the Symbiot's thirst for conquest, galactic relevance, ultimate survival, or just plain old bragging rights to the other

Symbiot conquerors, that they too can hold their own in the galaxy.

That's what his client was: a Whorganian. The humblest of their sort, from the looks of it. A long tunic was all that covered its lanky body as it sat in one of his chairs. The afternoon sun shone through the window to reflect off the sleek metallic plating that covered its tiny head and encased its slim neck within a pipe of brilliant gleam. Like a pellucid tunnel, a glass tube trenched from the back of the creature's skull, where the metal plating covered its green scalp, wrapping itself once around its neck. Lemoncolored liquid swished around within this tube, often revealing the brown, slimy Symbiot inside.

"Okay," the Detective said, as he began a metal recording of the creature's own version of events. "I need to know everything about this Jhusrot. Who created it? What's its origin?"

"No one knows."

"No one knows...what? It's creator, or where it came from? Because, I see here, that this thing's made from an unknown metal."

"It is."

"Then what about its origin?"

"That too's unknown. Very little's known of the Jhusrot, except that it fell to our world from the sky, a very long time ago. Longer than it took you Humans to evolve."

"The Whorganian's home world?"

"No, Detective. Our home-world."

"You mean...the home-world of the Symbiot's?"

"Yes."

"Okay..." He needed time to think. So far, he wasn't getting anywhere with the dull creature. Most folks would be eager to offer any information they can, in order to help retrieve their lost items. But Whorganian's lacked the intuitive sense for such things. He wondered if the Symbiot's took away some of their smarts? He could hardly believe such intelligent creatures would be so naturally dim at the wits. "So...the Jhusrot, is a Symbiotic relic of unknown origin, with unknown metallic properties."

"A work of art."

"In which the creator is also unknown?"

"Yes."

"Which makes it more priceless than any other thing in the galaxy."

"Yes."

"Then what's it doing on Earth? Why's such a cherished item being zipped across the galaxy in star ships, instead of being heavily guarded in one of your museums?"

"We don't have muse---"

"Never mind that. Just tell me how this Jhusrot came to be stolen."

"No one knows."

CHAPTER
THREE

RIGHT THEN AND there, he should've chased it out of his office.

But he didn't.

He allowed it to take him to their ship instead: a wonder of grand edifices in its own right, casting a dark shadow over most of the city while it hovered above the skyscrapers, downtown. It was just one of their many cargo vessels, stationed in every country's airspace around the world. The real ship--their Mothership--remained somewhere in the thermosphere, orbiting the planet.

So big, it could be seen at any time during the day and night.

With just a few days on the alien's armlink, they were gone, snatched from his office in a subtle display of sprinkling lights, then dropped somewhere in their vessel downtown.

The first thing you'll notice upon entering any Whorganian's ship, is the smell. A rancid odor, more pungent than piss--very offensive to the Human nose. That was the natural air the Whorganian's breathed on their home planet. Toxic to us Humans. Which why he always carried a special filter with him. A small device, the size of a baseball, that latched itself securely over the nose and mouth, allowing only oxygen to enter through the filter's computerized sensors.

Some years ago, our baffled scientists discovered that the Whorganian's didn't breathe--at all---once they left their ships. It was obvious that Earth's atmosphere lacked the proper gases necessary to sustain their complex anatomies far too long. And yet, they wore no helmets, nor used any visible breathing apparatus. They didn't need to, however, for the Symbiots injected all the necessary nourishments right into their bloodstreams.

It was so with all the creatures they possessed as well. Each life-form wore the same metallic plating on their heads, and the same glass tubes around their necks. However, different color fluid filled the tubes that kept each creature alive outside of its own natural atmosphere. For instance, red fluid filled the tubes around the necks of the goat-things. Black for the dragons, while the other humanoid species wore either blue or green.

The second thing you'll notice right away aboard any Whorganian ship, is the endless streams of art, etched into the inner hulls of the entire vessel. Intricate carvings of symbols, planets, galactic maps, exotic life forms, and alien writing, all engraved in minute detail. And it was all around; from the desert and forest worlds that seemed to pop right out at you from the ceiling, to the bone-chilling tales of black holes and exploding stars that threatens to consume you as you strode across the ship's smooth glossy floors. Even the lights that illuminated the vessel were things of sophisticated make and invention, for they weren't the glowing things encased in light bulbs and tubes, but flat strips of pure light that stretched endlessly in one long glowing band.

So efficient was this single sheet of radiance, no shadows survived, yet so gentle, you can put your hand through and feel the warm energy filling you up inside.

The corridors teemed with all forms of intelligent life. Some he'd never seen before outside the vessel: mere Drones of the Symbiots attached to their necks, as they walked by without giving the slightest glance in their direction. There was a busy air about the place... a sense of urgency perhaps.

It made him wonder---as he often did---of their true purpose of coming to our world. Their claims of trade, and sharing knowledge, never sat too well with him. Though they were incapable of telling lies, he wasn't quite sure if they were incapable of hiding the truth. These creatures (their hosts) were slaves, carried off from their natural worlds. He doubt if their intentions for us weren't the same.

The Whorganian led him to a different section of the ship; he guessed it was part of the vessel's extended wing, because of all the porthole windows they were walking past. He'd seen these same portholes everyday from the ground, the ship's wings stretching at least six miles from tip to tip; the sun's light reflecting off metal glass. Chills slipped down his spine as he realized he was walking down these same wings. He never once imagined he'd be up there, looking down at his own world. He couldn't help but think that our days as a free species were being counted. What was taking them so long to make their move, was beyond his comprehension. Maybe the wiser Bureaucrats of our race, convinced them that we were nothing like the Whorganians...and indeed, we weren't. All of our defense-systems were aimed up at their ships---including the hulking Mothership, orbiting above our satellite---just in case they ever wore out their welcome.

Maybe all they really wanted to do was to be our friends---cosmic relatives of a sort. But he doubted it.

He was grateful for the short walk that led to the room where the Whorganians kept all their priceless artifacts. And what a treasure-trove they possessed in this immensely large room...larger than any museum we have here on Earth.

"This is the Chambers where the archives of all of our allies are held," said the Whorganian, as they entered this 'Chamber of Archives.' "Each of these races, we have assimilated at one point in our history. we each share a common bond, and their place in these Chambers represent very important periods in both or our histories."

The Detective couldn't possibly cover the entire area in a single week, much less inside the five hours before his filters became clogged. "Where'd you keep the Jhusrot?" He would have to work fast, despite his desire to explore the vast history of our galaxy that this room contained. There were so many sculptures, species of plants, animals, and other life-forms, it was impossible to take it all in at just one glance.

These are the things that share our galaxy that he was seeing! Humanoid beings, as large as twenty feet tall, stood frozen in time by some means of suspended animation. Countless artifacts and relics, created by beings we couldn't begin to imagine exists. It aroused the most fascinating and intriguing emotions inside him.

"I'm the keeper of these Chambers," said the Whorganian. "It's my responsibility for the safe-keeping of all of these artifacts."

"And where were you exactly, when the Jhusrot was stolen?"

Follow me." It took them through this maze of ancient alien relics and artificial habitats, until coming to what the Detective believed to be the center of the Chambers. There, encircled by a thick band of light, stood some kind of podium in the form of a levitating sphere. "I was right here Detective.

"It was stolen right before your eyes?" He thought this odd. Most thieves would rather wait until the area was clear before they made their move. "And what were you doing here?"

"Protecting the Jhusrot."

"So you knew it was in danger of being stolen"

"It's always in danger of being stolen."

"That much is believable. I can understand why such a priceless piece of art would be a highly coveted item in our galaxy... Do you know who would want the Jhusrot bad enough to risk being seen?"

"I know of no one, Detective. At least, not on this ship. I couldn't imagine what they'd use it for anyway."

"Okay." He began to circle the area, looking for clues he wasn't too hopeful to find. "Are you sure you weren't zapped with anything? Stunners? Flash-screens? Trane-guns? Or any other weapon that would knock you senseless for at least five seconds?"

"I assure you, Detective. I was thoroughly scanned for such injuries.

I was very much conscious when the Jhusrot was taken."

"So, it just vanished, right before your eyes"?

"Yes. It was here one moment, and gone the other."

"So it was snatched." He was confident he'd solved the first half of this puzzle already. How else could it have disappeared?

"Such transports are impossible with the Jhusrot, Detective. A Teleporter must have precise information on an object's genetic, elemental make-up, in order to successfully transfer that information from one place to another.

And since the Jhusrot is made up of unknown---"

"Yeah, yeah. I know." With his only possible guess shot down so quickly, he was forced to rely on more artificial methods. "Stand back, please," He said to the creature, tapping into his arm-key to retrieve the only other device that can shed light on this case.

A few years before the Whorganian's ships first entered our atmosphere, man had stumbled upon one of his greatest inventions since the lightbulb.

A device inspired by the common video camera, to allow him to bring forth events of the recent past right before his eyes. A technology, appropriately called: Ghost Recall.

It was long discovered, that vibrations---however minute---surrounds us at each and every moment of the day, all throughout our lives. Like the keys on a piano, once struck, will produce a lasting sounds long after the action had taken place; so too, do our movements produce the same effect. such events remain unseen to the naked eye, however, with the right equipment that can scan and then map the succeeding motions, a vague picture of the past moment can be created.

Yet, no matter how vague the picture of the past, it did provide enough information to from the right idea into one's mind. From there, the rest of the missing pieces can easily be filled in. Thus, a baseball game---due to different levels of so many vibrating tones all merging together at once-would appear as a jumbled mess of a sport. It might appear that the actual game was taking place in the crowd, and one might confuse a home-run for a low bouncing grounder, flying right through a serve-bot's hotdog stand. But nonetheless, one can still see that a baseball game was being played...

Man's made great advances in the technology since then (especially when these Whorganian's first came to our world). With the introduction of some very powerful electrical nodes, called Vibrods, we can now isolate past events as they happened, regardless of whether they overlapped each other or not. No longer did we have to sift through countless pedestrians over several interwoven days, to find just one man crossing the street. The Vibrods recorded each moment daily---the same way a camera would---then store the images into a database for later use. But unlike any camera, a single Vibrod can cover an area of ten square miles, recording the vibrations in people's homes, cars, buildings, and even under the ground.

They worked wonders when it came to fighting crime. Though violence and corruption is still a problem in our world, they're nowhere near the levels they once were before the 'Ghost Recall Act' was signed into law. Since then, a person's right to privacy had been virtually rescinded.

Even in the sky, the vibration of helicopters, airplanes, and alien space ships---especially alien space ships---are recorded. Tall, powerful Vibrods stood towering atop the tallest buildings, recording the flight-paths of everything that moved in the air---even blown dust.

As a part of our Galactic Treaty and Alliance, the Whorganians had to allow us to record the events that happened on their ship (even though nothing could stop these rods from penetrating their hulls). And in return, they were allowed to conduct trade.

"So, you say this theft happened this morning?" The Detective asked, tapping some calculations into his arm.

"Yes, Detective. About 3 hours before I came to see you."

"Stand back." He took about nine paces from the artifact, not yet sure what to expect when he recalled the ghost from this Whorganian's past. Their technology is way more advanced than ours, and only God knows what freaky devices were used to bypass the ship's securities and grab the Jhusrot right before this Whorganian's eyes.

With six of his scanner-chips, each the size of a small coin, he placed them around the artifact in a wide circle. Now linked within their own electromagnetic field, the chips glowed red then sneezed to life in a sputtering display of lights. Just random dots and lines at first, then real figures and shapes began to form. First, the Jhusrot, floating effortlessly above the artifact. Then, the thief. It had the same metal plating on its tiny head, and wore the same long tunic that dropped to its feet. It approached the relic casually, with no concern at all for its own safety, then took the object before retreating past the chips' electromagnetic field.

He spun around to meet the Whorganian's astonished gaze. At that instant, he believed they shared the same thought. The resemblance of the ghost, and this Whorganian's standing before him, was unmistakable. In fact, if he didn't know any better, he'd say they were both one and the same.

16

CHAPTER
FOUR

"I...I..." THE poor creature was at a lost for words, after seeing its own self sneak away with the most valuable piece of art in the history of its kind. "I would never do such a thing. You must believe me, Detective. That couldn't have been me. It's not possible. I would've remembered taking it."

"But it was you," the Detective said, even though he believed the Whorganian was somehow innocent. The face recognition software, implanted in his temporal lobe, read that the alien's expression of confusion and fear were genuine enough. It also told him that the height, weight, and signature gait of the ghost was a perfect match with this Whorganian standing before him. But common sense betrayed implications that something far more sinister was afoot. And this sparked his interest even more. It's been years since he'd dealt with someone clever enough to use the ghost of another to execute a successful theft; whether he be man, or alien.

But no Whorganian was that deceptive.

"It couldn't have been me, Detective."

"Was anyone else here to relieve you? Maybe they might've stolen the Jhusrot while you were gone."

"No one else was here, Detective. I'm the only one trusted with guarding the Jhusrot. And like I said before, I would never do such a thing, then come to you to investigate my own crime."

"But it was you."

"It was not---" The creature paused in stunned silence as the truth of the matter finally dawned on its mind. It realized this now. "Yes, Detective. It was me. But how---"

"This is what I'm going to find out. Does anyone else know about this?" "No. They cannot. If my superiors ever get the faintest word of this, I'll be dropped lower for sure."

"Dropped lower?" He was vaguely familiar with the term. But how can you get any lower than being stuck on guard-duty in a room of alien relics on a highly sophisticated intergalactic starship, conquering worlds, and enslaving other intelligent beings? he thought.

"Dropped lower to an inferior species," the Whorganian said. "That's how they punish us. Unlike your penal system, I think ours is more brutal. Just imagine, living in a body, completely alien from your own, the way we Symbiots do. Then imagine being assigned to the body of one of your pigs, to live in mud and filth. Or a bat, or a mole, to live in darkness and feed on worms and such things. But you couldn't possibly imagine living in the body of insatiable Llenaak, or the blind and deaf Twaboon. Just the thought of adjusting to the bodily functions, sleep cycles, and adapting to the nature of such beings is a dreadful thing to me."

"Which is why you came to me as soon as you discovered the Jhusrot was stolen."

"And a good thing too. My Captain would've investigated the matter for sure. And if it would ever come to light that the Jhusrot was carried off by my own hands, then I'll be banished."

"And by banished, I'm guessing you mean that you won't be assigned to any other life-form?"

"Yes. I'll die within hours, without the body of a host to sustain me."

He felt pity for the poor thing. They both knew it was being framed. Sooner or later, the others of its kind was bound to discover their secret, and it was certain to take the fall for the Jhusrot's disappearance. And because of this... or some need to fight for the sake of justice, buried deep somewhere within the contents of his genetic makeup, he decided right then and there that he would help clear its name. "You'll need to replace the relic with a replica of some kind, while I conduct my investigation."

The Whorganian looked confused at first; puzzled as to why they would need a fake Jhusrot to replace the old one. But after a round of hasty explaining, it caught on to what the Detective had in mind.

He figured since the relic was nothing more than a black cube, replacing it with a fake wouldn't be too difficult of a task. The Chambers didn't expect any serious visitors anytime soon, so it should provide a long enough cover until he located the real one.

While the Whorganian went about its task, the Detective conducted his own, tapping new commands into the keys implanted in his arm. Still linked to their own magnetic field, his scanner-chips rose slowly from the ground and reduced their size to just four feet in diameter. With the stroke of a single key, he beckoned them toward him, away from the illuminated sphere. As they neared, the

Whorganian's ghost reappeared, but only briefly as it strode out of the glowing circle once more. He readjusted the speed and the chips accelerated, catching up to match the long strides of the Whorganian's ghost.

He followed the ghost through the maze of ancient relics all throughout the Chamber, holding the Jhusrot in its open palms as though preparing to offer it up to some Whorganian god.

The Detective was anxious to know what could've possessed the creature to commit such a dishonest deed. And when it finally slowed to a stop, he thought he would get his answer soon. But, not soon enough, as it would turn out....

For ten long minutes, he just stood there with the Whorganian's ghost, waiting for their guest to arrive. And when he finally did, the Detective swore at himself for expecting anything different---from a Human, that is!

The man's ghost was very hazy, draped in a hooded rubber cape that cloaked his vibrations. He took the relic from the Whorganian and sent it an its way, but not before retrieving a device that was latched on to the metallic plating on the creature's scalp. He must've used it to scramble any communication between the Symbiot and the creature, all while transmitting his own commands.

He was disguised as a diplomat, this man. The hooded cape hung low over his head, so the Detective couldn't see his face. He strode quickly, and with purpose, vanishing from the scanner's field as he left the Chambers.

Reluctantly, the Detective came to a stop---at the corridor's threshold---where the ghost of a thief awaited just two feet away outside the Chambers. He couldn't risk being found holding his own private investigation on the ship, lest the Whorganian authorities discover their priceless relic was gone. So he was forced to let it go....for now.

He shut off the Ghost Recall's magnetic field, then watched the chips slide themselves into a single roll as they floated gently back into his palm. Luckily, the man's ghost appeared to have been heading toward the ship's exit---so his best move was to follow it there.... And, until he got off this metal island, hovering high over the city, he would have to rely on plain old Detective-works: by looking for things that aren't even there.

CHAPTER
FIVE

IF HE WANTED to tail the ghost any further---without alarming the Whorganians---he had to get back on the ground and position himself directly below the ship's docking ports. With any luck, he might be able to spot him through the window of his air-coupe.

To avoid detection, he had to make a slight change in his surveillance equipment. Special goggles, called Nocters, were needed for the outdoor use of Ghost Recall, lest the spectors of a thousand milling phantoms of the past, distract the pedestrians and motorists of the present. It was also difficult to view the electronically charged event during the day, where certain parts of the picture tend to hide behind the sun's glare at times.

Remotely linked to the scanning-chips, the Nocters enhanced the visual of the Recall one hundred fold. They were capable of zooming in at great distances, digitally mapping faces to determine age and sex; distinguishing moods to determine possible intent and motive; and capable of seeing through any disguise.

The device, to say the least, was virtually foolproof, but useless indoors (especially in dark places) without the ability to provide an adequate amount of light on its own.

Seated in the safe confines of his air-coupe, the Detective stationed himself at the southern end of the Whorganian's ship. From there, he had a direct visual right into the docking port where every vessel made its entry and departure. His chips were already up there, rotating outside their own magnetic field of 1,000 yards. He had to make sure he gave this ghost enough room, in case it turns out to be elusive, which he suspected it might.

In a normal video recording, the footage can be slowed or speeded up at a single command. However, when recalling an event from the past, the image can become distorted if the vibrations are manipulated in any way. Upon recall, the event will replay itself as it naturally would when it first occurred. In order to retain that image, the frequency of its vibrations must always remain the same. Thus, the vibrations of an image in motion, such as a man walking his dog, is never slow or fast...it'll simply lessen or increase in vigor. As the man's feet touch the ground, he'll create a strong vibration, but when he lifts his foot again, the friction weakens. This is how the motions of the picture comes to life. If slowed or speeded up at just a fraction of its natural frequency, the image will simply disperse.

It was his only regret of the technology's short-coming. You wouldn't believe how fast those sky-bikes and air-coupes shot out from the back of that ship, as if a hive had suddenly farted out a swarm of bees. Spotting the right ghost would've been nearly impossible, had it not attempted to travel in a cloaked vehicle. The Nocters infrared picked up on the coupe's heat signature easily enough, proving that too much caution----as is often the case---can bring about the most disasterous results.

He commanded the chips to lock on to the heat source, canceling out every other ghost within range. Only the thief remained in the sky---along with the vehicles of the present while he followed it through the city. But this was no easy task in itself, either. He had to deal with the present day's traffic, in which the ghosts of five hours past wasn't burdened with.

And there's another problem with following ghosts in fast moving vehicles. Though each scanner-chip's propelled by a very powerful but tiny fan, their max-speed is only as fast as the fastest man can sprint. Hardly any match for an air-coupe, or a sky-bike, zipping through the sky at 250 mph. The ghost will be in and out of the scanners' range in less than 30 seconds. Which meant that he would have to time the recorded event precisely, freezing the ghost before it flew out of range, then pick up from where he left off at that point. He could've only hoped they wouldn't have to travel too far.

He switched the air-coupe's automatic functions to manual, waiting just a brief moment for the steering wheel to slide out from its hidden compartment in the dashboard.

"As a pleasant reminder, agent Dillon. It is statistically proven that when utilizinig the city's Automated Guidance Systems as a means of travel, reduces the risks of auto-accidents by 100. If you wish to log the vehicle's controls back into the Department of Transportation's database, please do so now." That was the car's computer, telling him that he might crash once he took this thing on the skyway relying solely upon his 20/20 vision and snake-sharp reflexes.

"No, no, that's fine," he replied, staring at the computer's pretty face on the steering wheel's screen. "Just let me know well in advance if I'm about to hit something...auto-straps, please."

Four leather bands shot out from the back of his seat, strapping him in as they interlocked themselves to the shiny hooks attached to their buckles. "Auto-straps successfully engaged."

Without another moment to waste, he swung the air-coupe around and shot it up toward the ship, in pursuit of the ghost that was already zipping down the skyway through traffic.

"Virtu-ramp, in four, three, two, one...."

At such high speeds, the green runway of the elevated ramp approached like a stiff jab from a long-armed boxer. Nothing solid about it just a huge laser-light in the shape of a hundred-foot slide with bright yellow arrows flashing upward. He'll fly (harmlessly) right through it if he didn't make the computer's countdown. But nothing more.

He tugged back lightly on the steering wheel as the count reached "one." It wasn't the smoothest of take-offs onto the skyway, but when you've been fighting crime for as long as he has, it's the only way to get those intense juices flowing. At 200 mph, the city's buildings whizzed past his side windows in a blur. With the Nocters linked to the computer's mainframe, he uploaded the goggle's data into the windshield's screen where oncoming traffic, and the infrared image of the ghost, were on full display. He was now fully interactive with both machines, as well as preoccupied with having to pay attention to too many different things at once. On the one hand, he had a complete view of the skyway ahead of him, with fast approaching vehicles in different lanes in which he needed the computer's precise timing to past without crashing into one of them. On the other, there was the image of the ghost, still far up ahead with its current speed and distance displayed in small red numbers below. He'd only been on the skyway for ten seconds, and they'd already traveled 700 yards. He'll have to pause the event very shortly before he flew out of---

"Oncoming sedan in current lane.... Veer left in three, two, one...."

He turned just in time. His air-coupe made a graceful hop into the next lane, briefly filling the cabin with the sedan's buzzing engine as he flew by.... There was only five seconds remaining, so he paused the event. The hazy image of the ghost sat frozen in mid air while the oblivious motorists flew right through it.

In another second it was behind him. He instructed the computer to navigate them to the nearest off-ramp while he waited for the slow moving scanners to catch up.

They repeated the chase five more times, which amounted to no more than a two minute flight, just a little ways outside the city in a quiet suburban town. The reddish-orange smudge of its infrared image slid through the streets on auto-pilot, cruising heedlessly through other cars and pedestrians.

It eventually crept up to its present-day self a sleek late-model Cadillac, the color of midnight, parked in front of an old twentieth-century building.

But then, something very odd happened...

Instead of parking and merging into its present day self (he expected that), the ghost stepped out of the car---from the passenger's side---and hurried into the building. The Detective was now left with a dilemma of whether to pursue his original suspect, or continue following the air-coupe that was now on its way down the street. A strong hunch told him the ghost no longer had the Jhusrot. It made more sense that it was heading back up to the skyway, destined to only God knows where. But yet, the present car remained, which meant that the driver had returned sometime during the day. Or it could've simply been a trick, for the ghost might've programmed the car's auto-pilot to another destination in order to confuse any would-be followers. Or the air-coupe pulled in front of the building might not be that of the ghost, and the one driving down the street had no plans on returning at all. The only thing he did know for sure, was that the cloaked image of the hooded figure that stole the relic on the Whorganian's ship, was the same as the one who entered that building. So that's where he decided to go.

The building's entrance was secured by a very unique security system that required a retinal scan of all its residents---unless of course, you were a seasoned hundred-year veteran, and trusted agent of the law.

Thanks to an impressive record, he had access to all public, and a few private establishments, without the need of a signed warrant. Each building was programmed with a specific code that allowed the entry at the request of certain high-ranking city, and law enforcement officials. He, was one of those officials.

Inside, the building was as much twentieth century as it looked on the outside. Shabby walls; loose boards on the floor covered with dingy carpeting, doors that weren't automated into the building's security systems; antique light bulbs that still used filament coils; and rickety stairs that looked too dangerous to climb. From the dusty looks, moldy smells, and absent sounds, he guessed this building had been long condemned by the city, then perhaps recently purchased by some odd individual for whatever reason. A good enough reason (he would bet), to hide a priceless alien relic.

The ghost appeared the instant he turned the scanners back on. He followed it up the rickety staircase, all the way up to the third floor, where it entered one of the two apartments. Faint sounds came through the door from where the ghost entered, but the Detective couldn't determine exactly how many occupants were inside. He could hear the incoherent words of a man's voice, then approaching footsteps, then a hesitant pause---and before he knew it, the wall exploded, pelting him with centuries old bits and pieces of wood and sheet-rock. Had it not been for the Nocters, still strapped to his face, he would've been temporarily blinded and at the complete mercy of whoever was behind the trigger of that Ion-blaster.

Old instinct preserved his awareness as he threw himself to the ground. The Nocters picked up three infrared images through the gaping hole. Another blast...the wall exploded behind him, pitching his body forward with expelled energy.... That one stung!

He scrambled out of the way as another blast blew the door to cinders. On his arm-key, he tapped frantically into the screen, linking the Nocters back into the air-coupe's weapon systems, outside. Historic building or not, he'd rather see it come down in a pile of rubble, than have one of those blasters turn him into a puddle of gore.

He switched the Nocter's sights to x-ray vision, then locked on to any heat source that was bigger than a cat's. The instant he tapped on the firecommand, a wicked laser shot up from the air-coupe's gunport, straight through the brittle bricks of the building and into the first man that came through the threshold of the door frame to end his life. The man wailed in agony as the blue beam---hot as the surface of the sun---shot through his side and continued up the ceiling. He dropped his weapon (as a conscious effort to plea for his life, perhaps). But even as his Blaster hit the floor, the laser had already sliced him in half. In another moment it cut into the wall on its way into the apartment, causing the Detective to lay as flat as a coin as the "blue beam of death" swept an inch above his nose. Inside, it found its targets in mid stride, though their death-screams hadn't lasted as long as that of their comrade's. The sounds of their sawed-up carcasses hitting the floor, brought as much relief as the dread he felt of nearly sharing the same fate as his would-be assassins....And yet, it wasn't the worst way to die.

The Detective rose painfully on trembling lets, wincing from the sting of shrapnel that had bit into his back. The blood was already beginning to dampen his undervest, but he felt lucky as he stepped over the bloody heap laying near the door.

He wasn't surprised to find the most state-of-the-art equipment---both Human and alien---inside the apartment. The laser had made a mess of things in there. Everything that stood in its path was sliced up like butter. Daylight, from outside, shone through the ceiling in a hazy glare where the laser made long swerving lines all the way up through the roof. On the front wall, it made something that resembled a rockstar's squiggly signature. The blinds and windows---though not broken sliced diagonally; the molten glass was still hot.

He peered out the window at the air-coupe parked downstairs. Though the laser's cannon had long retreated back down into its port, trails of smoke still whiffed through the creases of its covering-panel.

The Jhusrot was nowhere to be found in the apartment, and to his most despairing discovery, the Nocters weren't working, either. The heat from the laser must've fried its circuits. An x-ray scanning would've definitely reaped better results, even though he had a hunch that the Jhusrot might not have been there at all. He'd left a wide gap in his investigation when he chose not to follow the ghost outside the Chambers on the Whorganian's ship. From there, it could've changed many hands. And now, considering where this ghost had led him, he realized that it would never have ended up here. These guys were henchmen, hired thieves, that hid in the shadows. But when he finally do confront the mind behind this theft, he had a feeling that he wouldn't have to worry about being shot at by any Ion-blasters in the halls of some shabby building....

Doubling back toward the apartments' entrance, he stooped down beside the ghost (now dead). His upper torso laid face-down with the hood's cloak still covering his head. The Detective spun him around, trying his best to ignore the severed guts that spilled from the wound. The thief was a young man. Bald. His right arm was sliced off at the elbow where the---no....

Something was very wrong with him....

He was still alive!

His mouth twitched, and his eyes, fluttered open to give the ceiling a blank stare....He was trying to say something. The Detective brought his ears closer to the man's mouth, but couldn't quite make out the quivering words. "Where's the Jhusrot?" He felt silly, but it was the only thing on his mind just then. "What....?"

"....Time....has come," the thief struggled to say.

"Where's the Jhusrot? Who'd you give it to?"

"Your...time has come."

The Detective rose up to get a good look at the man, who would breathe his last breath right then and there. The whole scene didn't sit right with him. And then he noticed the man's neck: the long tube wrapping itself around it. A slimy worm laid stiff in the clear liquid inside.

Chills ran down his spine! He could no longer feel the sting on his back.

He understood then---as he do now--what the Drone was trying to tell him. Our time(us Humans)have come! The thief didn't say it, for he was long dead.

Those words, were the last threats of a dying Symbiot.

CHAPTER
SIX

ANGRY, CONFUSED, AND more frightened than he could ever remember, he zipped through the skyway in a great hurry on his way back to the city. He called up an old buddy, who still worked for the Bureau. The only person he thought he could trust---They often spoke of the likelihood of something like this happening many times---he agreed they should meet at a location of his choosing right away. That's where he was rushing to now.

Those stinking parasites were playing us all along! He knew it. Any fool could've guessed that something wasn't right with those slime-sticks. Trade? Phaa! What practical use would our meager metals and stones be to any superior race that's been across the galaxy? He saw their Chambers of priceless artifacts, and what they deemed as cherishable. Not a single article of gold, or silver, laid among these things. They possessed gems, made up of elements that don't even exist on our planet. They considered our precious oil and coal the most primitive means of fuel, as much as we consider the ancient use of wood for cooking and heat. What need would they have of our resources---unless we, ourselves, are the resource?

Why couldn't anyone else see that? he thought, as he whizzed his aircoupe down the skyway.

"Upcoming off-ramp to the South Pier Harbor, to your right, in 3, 2,1...."

He could've barely contain his anxiety as he flew over the Harbor, past the countless droids, busily tending to their tasks of loading and unloading the giant ships that bobbed in the shallow, oily waters of Lake Michigan.

A green light flashed on the transparent map displayed on his windshield. It was his contact's signal, just 50 yards up ahead.

He switched on the auto-pilot and commanded the computer to ease the coupe down. As he neared, the Detective spotted his man, tapping into his own implanted arm-key upon the coupe's descent.

The Detective was still too shaken to have noticed it then, but his friend's whole disposition appeared rigid (now that he can better recall). He hopped out while the coupe was still two feet in the air, nearly scorching his own feet under the base-thrusters, and ran up to him like a little boy with exciting news.

The man, for his part, didn't regard the Detective's clumsy maneuver. He was more interested in what he had to say that was so important. "World war 4?" he asked, with the most inquisitive, yet sarcastic expression, as he gave the Detective's dusty clothes, and bruised face, the once-over.

"Not even," the Detective said, after a brief handshake. He silently wondered what he was doing there (at the Harbor) when he called him. The Feds never detailed these kinds of places anymore. Droids and machines don't commit federal crimes. But maybe he was already near the area, because he could see his own air-bike behind him. "You'd wish it was that simple after you see this, Nolan"

"What's going on, Jack?" Nolan was now concerned. Probably smelling the dry blood on Jack's back, with his enhanced sense of smell.

"We were right, man," Jack said, already hurrying back to the coupe. "Come take a look at this. You wouldn't believe what these stinking parasites are up to."

Jack led Nolan to the back of his coupe, where he popped open the trunk. He paid close attention when Nolan's eyes nearly popped out of his head upon seeing the three severed torsos all piled up together. "Look at what these aliens are doing, man!" It didn't matter that Jack said this out loud. Robots are even dumber than aliens.

"What aliens are you talking about, Jack? These aren't Whorganians, or Trofloons. They're men. Dead men. Are you saying that aliens killed these man? Is that what you're trying to tell me?"

"No. I killed'em."

"What!?"

"They were trying to kill me---" Jack had to pause as he realized that his good friend of the better part of 90 years, wasn't following him correctly. No fault of his own, however, that Jack's heightened emotions caused him to carry on with borderline incompetence. So, without saying anything further to insult his own intelligence, he removed the Drones' hoods and exposed the glass tubes around their necks. "They use clear liquid for us," he said, watching Nolan's speechless face turn white. It was his turn to be struck senseless. "Remember how we used to wonder what color our liquid would be if they ever enslaved us? Look! See for yourself....it's clear. Probably some kind of oxygenated fluid to help us breathe when they take us outta here."

"How'd you...." Nolan faltered, searching for the right words, but found none better that his first thought---so he continued. "How'd you ever come across something like this, Jack? What the hell kind of private work are you involved in these days?"

"No time to explain now," Jack said, closing the trunk. He rushed back to the coupe and opened the door, half-expecting Nolan to already be at the passenger's side. But when he turned around he saw Nolan still standing at the back of the coupe, staring down at the trunk in astonishment, as if he could see through the trunk in the dark. "You comin'?" He called over to him, in an effort to break his fearful spell. "I'll tell you all about it on the way."

When Nolan finally looked up at him, it was with a new face; uncertain, doubtful. "Where're we going, Jack?"

"Where else do you think we should go?" said Jack. He felt like an idiot, but he had to excuse Nolan's new dumbfoundness then, considering the situation, and what it implied to both of their futures. "We're going to see your boss, Nolan.... Now get in."

CHAPTER
SEVEN

IN ALL HIS years, it never ceased to amaze him how much the night differed from the day in this city. So amazing, it was the simplest of things that brought it to life---powered it, like an animated toy. Just the one thing, that caused the looming sky-scrapers to appear as if rising to battle the sweeping strobes of the alien's ship above. It made him feel safe, nestled, hidden within a vast forest of glass, steel, and concrete.

It was the lights.

Every hue, shade, and color. Blinding, glimmering, dazzling. They grabbed your attention with enticing ads as you drove by. They confronted you with tricks and illusions, taking on many shapes and forms. They beckoned. They excluded. Up close they showed courtesy, with welcoming invitations to fancy meals, good entertainment, and a place to sleep when you had your fill. From a distance, they shied away and clustered together in a speckled sea of glitter.

Even at the height of 2,000 feet, the skyway appeared as a solid road against the star-lit city below. Green bands of opaque light, some as wide as having eight lanes, stretched and twisted themselves all throughout the, sky like the mad strokes of an insane painter's brush. He'd often imagined them as thick bridges of ice, where the vehicles slid in countless droves each night.

".... As much as I can make of it so far...." They were halfway to their destination, and Jack had already spilled most of what he knew to Nolan, who'd sat in silence for most of the ride----holding on for dear life to his auto-straps---as Jack swerved the air-coupe through the lanes like a rebelracer. "There's some kind of division going on between the Whorganian....I mean....the Symbiots' ranks. Why else would they steal the Jhusrot from their own kind? I'm guessing a secret insurgence against the higher ups. And they're using Humans to help fight in their cause.

"But...." a concerned Nolan began. "Why do you think the rebellion's---if there is a rebellion---against the Symbiots' leading class? Why not the other way around?

Just think about it, Nolan. Why would the ruling party need to hide anything---"

"Oncoming sky-van, in the, three, two, one---"

"Why hide anything from a subordinate?" Jack continued, after hopping to a different lane to avoid a collision. "I learned a lot about these parasites from my client today. And trust me man, it ain't no fun being a leech-worm if you're stuck living as a lesser life-form. Anybody---I don't care what species---would get fed up with kind of shit eventually. But it's all guess-work for now. For all I know, half the God-damned city, or the world for that matter, could already be walking around with those things, sucking on their necks.

The traffic was beginning to thicken, so he hunkered down and focused on his flying until it gradually slowed to a snail's crawl. He swore at himself for not taking the last exit onto the local lanes which were much slower, but never congested with traffic.

He hated not being able to get where they needed to be. But what else could he have done? With a heavy sigh he engaged the coupe's auto-pilot and looked over at Nolan, still gripping tightly to his straps. For as long as Jack knew him, Nolan never flew the busy skyways manually. But that's not what bothered him....Jack could tell. His friend still carried the same rigidness about him from when they first met at the Harbor.

"I knew it, man," Jack said, shaking his head regretfully. He stared out the side window at the other folks in their cars, oblivious to what nightmares sat in his trunk. "It was bound to happen....didn't I tell you?"

And that's when it happened.

A single shot from Nolan's Ion-blaster, point-blank, sending Jack straight through the side window, down through the skyway's misty light, to his death, 2,000 feet below.

The coward didn't even have the guts to look him in the face. Had he known how knee deep in this pile of alien-shit he was really in, he would've checked Nolan's neck before he showed him what was in that trunk. But whoever's that vigilant at such moments?

Phmph!!!

His own pal....

The odds were against him from the very beginning. He can only hope now, that whoever saved him, was on his side.

Jack must've been laying there for hours, before finally hearing the first noise a door. Then in comes his Whorganian client.

CHAPTER
EIGHT

NEVER, IN A single moment of Jack's life, was he happier to see an alien than he was right now.

He knew it was gutsy (kind of)the moment he met it. "It was you that snatched me?" But not this gutsy.

"I couldn't let you fall and die, Detective," the Whorganian said, coming up to his side. It spoke a long alien word that freed Jack's hands and feet of the mag-gurney's buckles.

Jack tried to sit up, but he couldn't. Something still held his body in place. He felt stiff, as if all his joints were frozen inside their sockets. "Why can't I move?"

The Whorganian ignored him. Its long fingers ran down the length of Jack's arm instead, squeezing a shoulder here, and poking his biceps there. The creatures small face came too close to his, examining each of his eyes. "Smile," the Whorganian said.

Without any conscious effort, Jack could feel himself grinning. He tried to stop, but he couldn't.

The Whorganian's finger slid across Jack's chin, and with sickle-shaped finger nails, began tapping on his teeth, one after the other; and pressing and prodding, pressing and prodding. When it finally felt satisfied that all Jack's teeth were intact, it stopped. "Open."

Again, without Jack having the chance to react, his mouth popped open on its own, and now, he was beginning to fear the worst. A horrible dawning seeped into his mind, causing him to mentally search every inch of his being for that essence; the very surge of life he'd become so familiar with and enjoyed since birth. The beating of his heart that rushed warm blood through his veins; the air that filled his lungs the bat of an eye; even the slight ringing in his ears that seemed to have been present for each second of his life---gone! All the indications that once assured him he was still alive....they were all gone! All, save the subtlest of things, a barely noticeable pain, like a scratch, on the side of his neck where a Symbiotic worm had more than likely latched on.

Unaware---and not caring---of Jack's distress, the Whorganian brought a gentle hand across his chest, but then hesitated when it felt the delicate wound, which Jack now regret hadn't killed him.

The Whorganian's small round head snapped up just then, looking across the room at the wall behind Jack, "You almost killed him. You fool. You were supposed to bring him here, unharmed."

"I had no other choice." It was Nolan---that coward---sitting there behind him, in silence, for all that time. "He was putting up a fierce resistance."

A coward, and a liar at that!

The Whorganian stood up and made a weird noise---which could've passed for a weary sigh at Nolan. "Close your mouth, and sit up," it said.

Jack could feel himself getting up as his jaws slammed down hard enough to clash the molars together in his mouth.

"Allow the host head-movement only," The Whorganian said.

At this command, the muscles in Jack's neck slackened, though the rest of his body remained as stiff as a pole. He turned to where Nolan was sitting, a rather, imprisoned in a cage, surrounded by deadly beams of criss-crossing lasers. He wasn't possessed (like Jack was) as far as he could tell, because he still had a head full of black hair, and his bare neck remained free of any tubes or parasites of any kind.

Judging from the band of pure light---that explained the room's unusual brightness---end the intricate alien carvings along the walls, Jack guessed they'd been snatched back onto the alien's ship. Nolan wore a transparent mask on his face, a bit similar to his own; which he no longer needed, because he wasn't using his lungs to breathe anymore. The Symbiot pumped oxygen directly into his bloodstream. "Earth'll blow your ships outta the sky for this!" Jack said, turning back to the Whorganian. "Then we'll hit your Mothership with so much nukes, not a single piece of her will land on our ground. This is a clear violation of our Galactic Treaty. War will be inevitable once our government finds---"

"War?" the Whorganian said, cutting off Jack's angry words. Sarcasm, ridicule, and disbelief, conquering its tone of voice. So much so, that Jack felt a bit embarrassed the word ever came out of his mouth. The truth is, we are helpless against these creatures, no matter how many nuclear weapons we possessed in our combined arsenals. They've proven so many times that they can turn any rocket or missile against its own user. Anything launched at any of their ships would only be sent back, destroying the Earth in the process. Jack's ramblings were nothing more than petty bluffs. They both knew it.

"Galactic Treaty?" the Whorganian went on. "You speak of such things, and yet, you haven't even managed to leave your own Solar System and return in the same decade. Galactic Treaty? What Treaty any Human can make that the rest of the galaxy would be bound to respect? Don't be silly! This man tried to kill you. If it wasn't for me, and my kin, you'd be dead."

By 'kin', Jack guessed, the Whorganian meant the parasite that had stolen his body. But whether parasite or not, the Whorganian did have a point. He turned back to his would-be killer. "How could you? After all these years?"

"To protect you," Nolan said. His voice sounded muffled through the mask.

"By killing me?"

"Yeah," Nolan replied. "Even if it meant killing you. I rather that, than seeing what you've become now. There's more going on here than you can ever imagine, Jack. There're things that have happened over the years, that certain men, like you, would never tolerate. You'd see the world blown to bits than have it taken from you---regardless of the circumstances."

"As all free men should live, Nolan," Jack said.

"And that's the whole thing, Jack. What you fail to realize, is that free man, such as yourself, are the minority in our world. The majority: the ones who'd rather live and be slaves, have sold us out a long time ago. Freedom is now an illusion, a great lie, that keep men like you from making us all pay for your insolent rebellions."

At the mention of the word "rebellions", Jack thought back to his theory of a Whorganian insurgency. He realized now, that Nolan might be right about one thing---he hadn't the faintest clue of what he'd gotten himself into. "Why aren't you guarding the Jhusrot?" he asked the Whorganian.

"The Jhusrot's been found," the Whorganian said. "And is now safely back at its rightful place."

"How so?"

"I don't know.

"I thought Whorganians are incapable of telling lies. Or is that a lie in itself?

"Nothing that I ever told you was a lie, Detective. The Jhusrot was indeed stolen. And now it has been returned---"

"I tried to keep you safe, Jack," Nolan said. There was a desperate haste in his words, as if he was running out of time. But why? "I tried to keep you away, why else do you think the Bureau discharged you with the highest honors? Even back then, our most powerful institutions were beginning to switch sides. They knew all along.

And then Jack saw it.

The cage...it was shrinking!

"---But that's not all, Jack. Any suspected rebels are reported immediately, then removed from the planet. I couldn't let them get to you. Even when you didn't know anything, you still felt something wasn't right. You still held on to your suspicions, whether or not it was a figment of your own imagination. But such thoughts are dangerous, Jack. So I got you out of the Bureau, then convinced you to go into private practice. Remember?

"For all those years, you went unnoticed, till today. You was doing fine, Jack. Until today. They set the whole thing up. They must've found out somehow. Probably something you said to one of their spies. And whatever that Jhusrot-thing is, it was used to lure you here on the ship. From there, they probably placed a tracker on you, while you chase after this phony thief. But then you wound up killing one of their Drones---so called free-men, such as yourself. You was on a direct path to ensuring the demise of us all. Our planet has become garrisoned by a war-like race called---"

The cage winked shut on him at that point. Nolan collapsed to the floor in a hundred pieces of cooked meat. Not a single drop of blood dripped from the cautered wounds. Just steam and smoke, wafting up into the air. Jack was glad he couldn't breathe, lest he got a whiff of the steaming remains of his friends.

"You Humans are quite clever," the Whorganian began, totally unphased by the chopped remains of Human flesh in the room. "Until today, the only thing that I did know about you, was that you were a well reputed Detective.

And when I discovered the Jhusrot had gone missing, I was told to seek your help. I'm guessing that it was one of the lesser life-forms, in which case happens to be a Human Drone, that tricked me into believing the Jhusrot was stolen. You yourself saw the device that was used to block the neuro-transmission between me and my host. That's a Human invention, I must say.

To date, no other species have ever thought to come up with such a clever device...that's very impressive. I can see why the General chose this particular life-form to serve in his army.

"When I returned to my post---after you left---the Jhusrot was already where it should be. They must've returned it when I went to retrieve the duplicate that you instructed me to replace it with. But I was kept in the dark of all these things, Detective. Us Whorganians are honest by nature. All deception are woven deeply into our own fabric of truth---the most effective form of deception, I think...So you see, you're no more of a pawn than I am, in the greater scheme of things. You were chosen to become a Drone. I don't know why. I'm simply the Keeper of Chambers."

"There were three of 'em," said Jack, not knowing why he felt like filling it in, after it killed Nolan. But what other choice did he have? He couldn't even wiggle his own toes. If it was up to him, he would've pulled this stinking worm from his neck and choked the pissy air out of this Whorganian.

"Three what?" The Whorganian asked.

"Three Drones. That's how they did it. One took the Jhusrot. The other replaced it when you weren't looking. The third one probably masterminded the whole thing. Child's play.... but anything'll work on you dumb aliens."

The Whorganian gave a derisive snort at the insult, and Jack relished under the fact that he'd pinched one of its nerves. As the moments went by in silence, it appeared to be thinking to itself as if trying to come up with something witty to say....

Jack waited....

"We're not aliens," the Whorganian finally managed to say. Jack wasn't impressed. "What?"

"Your friend was right, Detective. You still haven't fully realized what has become of your world. Even after all you've seen and heard, you still regard me as your inferior---which is so far from the truth. It is we, who have conquered you."

"You haven't conquered anything. The cities are still standing. Our nations are up and running---"

"Because you've surrendered them to us."

"I never surrendered anything to anyone."

"And that is what blinds you."

"What has?"

"You referred to men, such as yourself, as free men. And that is what blinds you---and others. It is your passion to remain unruled by another. A passion, that has left dreadful scars all throughout your history. All of your wars were fought in the name of freedom. Wars, fought by men, such as yourself. A most primitive notion, this freedom you regard so. It inhibits proper insight. It stifles the course of progress at its base.

"But what world you'd rather live in, Detective? A world, in which you free men wage a losing war against a superior race? Or the one in which you currently enjoy? Come now.... be truthful with your answer. Just think of what smoldering mess of world, free men would've left for: your kin."

"That's why we fight. For the freedom of our kin."

"But at what cost? So they can live freely amidst the rubble? So they can be free to suffer great tribulations? Come now Detective. I'd once thought you had more insight than what you're displaying to my right now. You call me alien, as if I came out of one of your halo-plays. You haven't the faintest idea of where we come from. There're stars a thousand times bigger and brighter than your own. Where massive planets---many times the size of your Jupiter--orbit, and giant beings, as big as your tallest buildings, call home.

You couldn't begin to imagine the size of their warships. This tiny planet is nothing but a grain of sand in their eyes. All of your oceans combined, wouldn't be enough to form the smallest pond on their worlds.

"Can you picture such things on that scale, Detective? It would frighten you out of your wits, if you really knew what creatures we share our galaxy with. How insignificant you are, compared to other life-forms, I couldn't begin to disclose. Your own pathetic planet is already dying as it is. And you're endangered of becoming extinct within the next 300 years, if you don't destroy yourselves first.

"We're a highly developed race, Detective. We've co-habited with dozens of other life-forms throughout our galaxy. Your world is the worst I've seen thus far. Many of our kin regretted even coming here. If it wasn't for our General, we'd be long gone by now. So you see, Detective. We....whether Symbiot, Whorganian, Llemaak, or Twaboon, are not the aliens on this ship. Nor are we alien to our own galaxy. All of our species---besides your own---are known amongst the countless other worlds in this galaxy. This Earth....this Human world is an unknown, diseased world, with polluted air and water.

Undesirable in the eyes of the lowest intelligent life-forms.

"So you see, Detective. It is not we who are the aliens, but you Humans."

Jack could've cared less what the Whorganian had to say as it rambled on and on1 about planets and what's in the galaxy. And he was glad when it finally left him, and what remained of Nolan, in the room by themselves.

As the Symbiot laid his defeated body back onto the mag-gurney, Jack couldn't help but think about what Nolan trying to say before he died. What was this "war-like" race that had garrisoned our planet? It sure as hell wasn't the Whorganians, but a race more cunning, more intelligent, and more dreadful. It was this race, to whom our leaders had secretly surrendered to. A race, for whatever reasons, chooses to remain hidden from the public.

EXPEDITION TWO

CHAPTER
NINE

SNATCH, IS A clever term used to describe the unexpected---and in most cases, unwanted---teleportation from one place to another. No matter a person's current location, or state of being, there's always the same sensation that accompanies the instantaneous transfer from this old place, to that new one. It's the feeling of being tugged, pulled, grabbed, or jerked backwards from where one made his sanctuary---right into his enemy's hands as his body materializes in a downpour of sparkling lights.

But the strongest and most common association with this demoralizing experience of teleportation, is the feeling of being snatched. Snatched...right out of your clothes...literally!

That was how Jack Dillon found himself: in a warm, bright room, somewhere on the alien's Mothership that orbited the Earth. Stark-naked, save for the thin transparent film that covered his bald head, and the glass tube that hugged his neck where an alien Symbiot laid comfortably in the clear fluid inside. A low rumbling sound, like a muffled chain-saw, could be heard. A heavy weight pressed down on his whole body that might've brought him to his hands and knees, had it not been for the defiant symbiot that kept him standing stiff at attention.

That was the natural gravity on the alien's ship. Much stronger than Earth's, now that they were out in space.

A small section of the floor hummed to life under his feet and jerked to a sudden lurch as it broke off in the shape of an octagon, pushing him up toward the ceiling. He feared for his head as he neared the top, hoping this wasn't the Whorganion's deranged method of execution: by crushing one's skull against the ceiling in one of their ships. But the ceiling did part (mere millimeters) to avoid the collision with his shiny head as the rest of his body ascended safely through the octagonal slot to the next floor. There, he learned the source of the low rumbling sounds he'd heard before. They were the cranky motors of awaiting droids that drifted quickly towards him on hovering soles.

Long mechanical arms (of shiny chrome) grabbed his wrists and ankles, hoisting him up in the air with ease. From there, he was tossed, twisted, and spun around by these nimble arms and pincers, juggling their maneuvers with eye-blinking speed. Bones cracked and muscles were stretched beyond their limit. Over a dozen needles entered his body. Thin probes intruded his mouth, ears, and nostrils. Spider-like things forced his eyes wide open, then shot beams of blue light into his retinas. A clear tube entered his rectum and sucked the intestines clean of shit and undigested food. An electric prod shocked him just below the ribs, and a pan was brought under his penis while he emptied his kidneys. A small incision was made behind his right ear where a tiny chip was implanted before another arm came to seal the wound with a gooey adhesive that welded the skin neatly back together. So fine and faint was the scar, it appeared as if no operation had been performed there at all.

No one would see it; no one would know it was there... not even Jack. In fact, with the communication between his brain and central nervous system temporarily shut down, he couldn't feel a thing.

His eyes spun about in their sockets as the droids eased him back down to the floor and retreated back to their stations as if the intrusive assault hadn't occurred at all. The octagonal patch---upon which he was still standing---cracked to life again with a soft hiss and lifted him up to the next floor.

Instead of droids, live beings awaited his ascension this time. Aliens....But unlike the Whorganions, Trofloons, and Llemaaks, he'd never seen this kind on Earth before. And what a species they were to behold! The most formidable (even more so than the dragon-like Trofloons) that he'd seen thus far.

There were five of them in the bright room, furnished with nothing but a levitating table (he prayed they wouldn't make him lay down on it). A single horn, ivory-white in color, curved out from the middle of their foreheads, all the way to the back of their bald scalps. Their faces, though boned and sharply angled, appeared strikingly feminine, with smooth purple skin that carried a faint sheen (as if glazed). Their eyes were black, pebble-sized beads, that showed conviction. Their ears were spiraled rims that whirled into a small dark hole like a maelstrom. Their nostrils looked surprisingly Human, and so did their mouths, where thin black lips pouted. And despite the devilish horns, there appeared something angelic about their faces, something with a graceful touch, something....beautiful even.

They had thick muscular necks (where their symbiots were wrapped in tubes of gray fluid). And long muscular arms and legs that defined the creatures that stood eight feet tall. They were all dressed in white, skin-grafting material that betrayed their shapely figures, which (in Jack's eye), were also surprisingly feminine. They had no breasts however (none that he could identify), which led him to guess that they might be the males of their species. But as he eyed the crotch of the one that stood before him, he found.... not a bulge, but one of the most distinctive camel-toes he'd ever seen on any Human woman. He was confused at this point (embarrassed, because he became horny as well).

The one that stood before him approached on big strapped boots that echoed on the smooth floor. The alien's wide hips swayed with each stride, and the legs muscles flexed visibly under the material it wore. A long purple tail whipped out from behind and wrapped itself playfully around its waist, fondling its abdomen with a blue, furry tip.

The creature stopped just a few inches from where Jack stood motionless. It hunched down a bit (this giant), meeting the Human face to face. "I should have it chopped off," she said, exposing short fangs as she spoke.

It didn't surprise him that she spoke English. All the other aliens did (they spoke all of Earth's languages); so why not this one? But what he hadn't expected, was to hear the creature speak in such a feminine way....a sexy way at that! It was the one thing the other life-forms on Earth couldn't, or were incapable of mimicking. They were more like the beasts on the land, for that matter, with no conscious sense of sexuality. And with the exception of the Whorganions, they were hardly interesting.

But these creatures standing before him, was of a different sort altogether. Despite their similar appearances, they still maintained an air of individuality. He could sense their charisma---especially in this one---filling every inch of the room. Even now, he could detect the creature's sense of humor, as she threatened to deaden his erection with a quick swipe of her laser-knife.

So out of sheer curiosity---and amusement---he decided to test the creature's true intelligence; her common sense. "If you do that," he said to her, with faint smile. "Then you have yet to discover what hidden gifts you possess....Be a shame to ignore it, over such trivial things as a rock hard man-cock."

Stifled sounds---from what could've only been alien laughter---came from behind her. The creature's back eyes narrowed, fixing Jack with a menacing glare. But perhaps, she wasn't staring at Jack at all. "If you cannot gain full control or your host," she began, placing one of her pretty purple hands on the glass tube around his neck. "I'll rip you right off of it!"

Jack felt his erection go down at that instant as the Symbiot redirected the flow of blood from his genitals. Then his jaws clenched themselves shut. The next words that came from his mouth wouldn't be his at all. "My apologies, your greatness," said the Symbiot, through Jack's own mouth. So inexperienced was the creature in its new body, it worked clumsily at Jack's vocal-cords, causing his words to sound slurred and hesitant. "A momentary lapse, is all. It won't happen again."

"As I trust that it won't," she said, standing tall again. "Could you imagine what might happen if we all have momentary lapses in control of our hosts?"

"Entire kingdoms can fall."

She didn't fuss anything further with the lesser life-form. She spun on her heels instead and strutted back to her group, who'd all reverted back to their initial seriousness.

"Step forward, Human," one of these horned creatures said.

Though he'd lost control of his own body, Jack could feel the heavy strain in his muscles and bones as the Symbiot struggled against the ship's stronger gravity. It felt like the equivalent of carrying 300 extra pounds on his back, with added weight tacked on with every step he took. Even his eyes began to ache in their sockets when he looked up at the much taller creatures, who appeared like gods before him, just standing there, light as feathers in their own natural environment while he could barely make three steps. It was only now that he saw his prior arrogance as folly. These beings were far more superior than any other life-form on the Whorganians' ships. And yet, he was only a man, not even fit to stand amongst them.

Coming to this harsh realization must've caused him to lose his will just then, because he collapsed---in fit of despair---to his hands and knees.

He could feel the Symbiot's attempts to force him back up, but it was no use. He couldn't go on. The ship's gravity was just too strong. His heart raced. Sweat covered his face, neck, and shoulders. He panted like a spent colt.

"Man-cock....?" The alien's mockery was like an extra ton being dropped on his back. She approached him...more slowly this time, as if to savor the moments of his suffering. But the instant she came within striking-distance, she whipped her tail out from behind her and yanked him by the ankles with it. She lifted his body in the air, dangled him by his feet like a naked rat, then hoisted him higher so that his upside-down face could meet hers.

The stern expression on the creature's face might've said it all, but Jack was more inclined to guess more malevolent thoughts laid behind her purple mask. She could squash him like a grape if she wanted to. Probably beat him to death with nothing but her tail.

"Do I arouse your man-cock now?" She asked, in a low, menacing voice. "You could hardly stand on your own two feet...Ha...! Puppy-cock!" Then she released him.

The fall would've broken all the bones in his body, had it not been for the table that suddenly shifted over to catch him. He immediately noticed the difference as he was now strong enough to sit up on his own. The tension in his strained muscles began to relax, his lungs labored less, and his heartrate slowed.

"The bed is adjusted to match Earth's gravity," the alien said. "Unlike ours, it won't crush you." She turned to one of her colleagues just then. "Check his vitals, and get his fittings."

Within seconds, he was surrounded by four equally graceful and beautiful creatures. They probed his entire body with nothing but their 3 fingers, checking his heart, lungs, and blood flow. It came as a surprise when they performed his physical manually, considering the rugged ordeal those machines just put him through. But then again, he thought, even on worlds light-years away, some things are still better off done by hand.

"Judging from physical strength," said one to her leader.

"---Height, weight, and overall health. A class-3 armored fitting is most suitable for Puppycock."

Again...stifled sounds like childish snickers, can be heard all around him. Only this time, it was at his own expense.

"Class-3 armor fitting?" The leader looked surprised. She turned to look down at the Earth-man's body, as if trying to assess what was so special about this one that he must get such high level of equipment. Most new arrivals are classified as class-1. Very few are qualified as class-2. But never a class-3. "Allow the host to speak freely," she commanded the Symbiot. "What did you do to become a Drone, Puppycock?"

"My name is Jack Dillon," he said. "Don't ever call me---"

Her tail sprang up from behind her and slapped him viciously across his face, drawing blood, as well cutting his words short. "I am the head engineer on this ship!!!" She bawled so loud into his face, his eardrums rung. "Chief Scientist of the 16th Stendaaran Fleet, in charge of all weaponry and armor---including the one you'll be wearing for the rest of your life! You'll do as I say, and let me know what I need to know, or I'll jettison you off of my ship---back down to your smelly little planet in a ball of flames. Now tell me...What did you do to become a Drone, Puppycock?"

What else could poor Jack have done? He was buck naked on an alien ship (Stendaaran, from the sounds of it), in the midst of beings twice as tall, and at least fifty times stronger. He had no weapons in his possession, and the only thing keeping him from being crushed under the ship's gravity, was a floating table. "I was a Detective," he said, defeatedly. He ignored the blood that dripped from his chin.

"A Detective?" The Stendaaran wasn't impressed. "So...? What did you do to earn the attention of our General?"

"I don't know. I was investigating a theft for a Whorganion, claiming that some ancient Symbiot relic was stolen. But it wasn't. It was a---"

"Relic?" She asked, becoming more interested. "Do you know the name of this relic?"

"They called it the Jhusrot."

There were gasps of shock and disbelief coming from all the Stendaarans in the room. "The Jhusrot's been stolen?"

"No," Jack said. "The Jhusrot wasn't stolen. It was a trick. They used the Jhusrot as bait, to capture me. But then I killed 3 of your General Drones---"

"No one cares about Drones," she snapped, cutting off his words. "What I want to know, is why did they go through so much pains to bring you here? Why not beam you through one of our portals?"

By portals, he guessed she was referring to one of their Teleportation Chambers. But as to actually why he was on board their ship, her answer was as good as his. However, he had a strong notion that she wouldn't understand. "I don't know." It was an honest answer. "I've been asking myself the same thing for the past two days."

"He's telling the truth," one of the other Stendaarans said, reading the data that was being transmitted by the chip implanted behind his ear. "He doesn't know."

"An abduction then," the leader said. "You solve crimes, Puppycock?" "No...." He hated that name. "Not anymore. I haven't worked for the Bureau in over 40 years. I was a private Detective before I came here. I specialize in finding things."

"You find things?"

"Yes. I'm the best private Detective in the city."

"So...." she said, rubbing at her chin thoughtfully. "The General needs you to find something for him?"

"I have no idea what the General wants."

"You will, Puppycock." She seemed satisfied to have solved this bit of mystery. Turing around to her comrades, she rattled off a string of Stendaaran words, in which they all gave curt nods in assent before tapping some commands on the flat device she held in her hand. Moments later, a twirling display of sparkling lights materialized before them from where a shiny suit of alien armor emerged. And what a wicked assemblage of shiny metals and fabric it was. "Dress him...and clean up his face."

Two Stendaarans dutifully tended to Jack's armor, fitting the boots that automatically adjusted to the size of his feet. Breast-plates an back-guards were strapped on, from where millions of nano-alloy descended down the length of his arms to form maneuverable sleeves. The same went for the ab-plates that eventually formed the leggings, all while a third Stendaaran patched the gash on his face with a strip of synth-skin.

"Your helmet is here," said the one who led them, swiping gently around the collar of Jack's armor.

The nano-alloys reacted instantly to the creature's touch, crawling up the back of his skull like an army of busy ants until his head and face were completely covered. The last to be formed were his eyes, where two air-tight slits were formed and two bluish lights sputtered to life.

The complete fitting was neither bulky nor discomforting, but grafted perfectly with every shape and contour of Jack's body, giving his skin a reptilian look. It even had a spiked tail, in which he could whip and swing about at his own command via the chip implanted behind his ear. Fully suited, the man appeared more alien than all the Stendaarans in the room. It was no wonder why their leader seemed so reluctant to believe that he had qualified for such weaponry. Just by the looks of it, bespoke of the great speed and power at the beck of his command.

"You can get off the bed now," the Stendaaran said.

He hopped off the table after a moment's hesitation, but wasn't surprised to find the ship's strong gravity no longer affected him. He felt light. He paced the full length of the room, elated that he was now moving with such ease....And he didn't mind having a spiky tail, either.

"I don't know what assignment the General has for you, Puppycock," the Stendaaran Said, while Jack was still admiring his own tail. "But one thing's for certain: you've joined our ranks. And there's no coming back from that."

Jack paused when he heard this, suddenly forgetting all about his tail.

"What do you mean by ranks?" "Control your host."

His mouth clamped shut just then. A hand came up to the armor's neck and swiped at the collar. The helmet retreated to expose his face once more, reminding him that he was still slave to the Symbiot attached to his neck.

Without another word between man and Stendaaran, the Symbiot walked Jack's body toward the other end of the room and stood on the octagonal patch. A second later, he was ascending to the next floor.

CHAPTER
TEN

JACK FOUND HIMSELF standing in an empty room this time.

No machines.

No Amazonian Stendaaran scientists.

Just four bare walls and a bright ceiling.

The symbiot moved him to the middle of the room, where a blue octagonal light glowed to life the instant he placed his feet there. At the subtle wave of a hand, a dozen alien symbols materialized out of thin air, They formed a circle, then hovered there like a crown gently placed on the head of an invisible king. They turned slowly at the symbiot's command as he selected five symbols at a finger's touch. One at a time the symbols rose from the floating circle, then vanished, only to reappear as solid shapes inside the room. The first one of these to appear was a levitating table (or what the Stendaarans referred to as a bed). Then a small six-legged droid materialized in the corner of the room. Alien art came next, magically furnishing the quarters with shaggy rugs, tapestries, and carvings. A chatter of alien speech would follow, blaring from a floating 40-inch holographic screen behind him. And lastly, an assortment of weapons, lining themselves along the wall in murderous fashion.

To say the least, the room looked no different from that of a young Human adult---a young symbiotic soldier from the looks of it. It puzzled Jack to learn that the Stendaaran's lifestyle was more similar to Humans than to the Whorganions. They even watched TV shows from Earth, with the words dubbed over in Stendaaran translations.

Upon first sight, he had readily assumed that all things alien, was indeed alien. That man had nothing to offer, in which the rest of the galaxy might be interested in. However (and not for the first time in his life), he saw that he could be wrong....

The table eased up behind him so the symbiot could plop his body down. Unlike the table on the previous floor, this one yielded perfectly to the shape of his body for extra comfort. The boot's nano-alloys retracted and exposed his bare feet to the warmth of the room---as did the armored gloves.

"The Stendaarans are seriously addicted to television."

The sound of the voice was so sudden, Jack might've jumped with a start if the symbiot didn't have such a hold on his body. The voice sounded soft, soothing, and distinctively male. But no other person, or alien, was in the room.... Maybe it came from some hidden speaker in the ceiling, he thought. Or maybe the TV itself could've spoken. "Who said that?" He felt silly as he swiveled his head awkwardly on his stiff body. "Where are you...?"

A light's sudden flash caught his eye just then, causing him to look down and see the little six-legged droid, gazing up at him with a dull expression on its triangular face. "And what might you be?" He asked. "Some kind of robotic dog?"

"It's a life-sized model of a Stendaaran Fleesch," said the droid, through its own little grill of a mouth. "Quite similar to your spiders on Earth." "And do Stendaaran Fleeks talk about themselves in the third person too?" "The actual droid isn't talking, Jack."

"Well...I'm looking right at yah....Looks like you're talking to me, about yourself, in the third person."

The droid appeared to give a sigh as the five blue lights that bedazzled its face began to dim. It floated off the floor, folding its legs into its chest as it eased down on the table next to Jack. The triangular head looked up at him again. "I'm your Symbiot, Jack," it said. "There's a chip implanted in your brain that allows me access to the ship's computers, as well as my droids, and a few other machines you'll soon become familiar with."

This bit of news left Jack speechless for the moment. It had never occurred to him that the Symbiots were, in fact, conscious beings, with personalities and tastes, with the need to decorate their rooms with art and vicious-looking guns. "So, this is how you parasites communicate, huh?" he asked, giving the droid a sly wink. "Through machines and computers."

'We... parasites...can communicate with your mind as well.'

"Whaa---" Jack's eyes popped wide open in shock and surprise as a voice, very different from that of the droid's, spoke directly into his mind. So loud and clear did it sound, it felt as if a megaphone had suddenly shrieked the words into his brain. It gave him a splitting headache.

"But until we learn to develop the correct bond with each other," the droid continued. "This mode of communication will have to do for now. I've already became quite familiar with our motor skills. But I'm yet to fully master our feet, hand, and eye coordination. Our speech will have to improve, but that requires a single harmonious link with our thoughts."

"Our thoughts?" said Jack, with much defiance, as he stared down at the droid. It was hard for him to see it as anything more than a machine, and a symbiot...a mere leech (with special powers) attached to his neck. He respected neither---not what they stood for, nor their way of life. "You mean...my thoughts. There's no way I'm letting you into my head. You wanna speak to me, feel free to use any one of those Stendaaran...Fleek-droids, to say what you have to say. And you better make sure you keep me tied up like this, because the first chance I get, I'm ripping you right off my---" His mouth snapped itself shut just then, leaving Jack with nothing more than a pair of glowering eyes to fuss at the droid with.

"You were dead, Jack," the droid said, turning its head to the TV. "Your friend, Nolan, did succeed in killing you. By the time you fell through the portal on the Whorganion's ship, most of your chest and heart had been vaporized by his Ion-blaster. But you see, the Whorganion's are a very resourceful species; the very best throughout the entire galaxy when it comes to bio-engineering and genetics. They're healers by nature. From the remains of your eaten heart, they constructed a whole new one, far more stronger and healthier than what you had before. Within an hour of your death, you were brought back to life again---a second birth. But none of it would've been possible, if it wasn't for me, Jack. Before that, you was just a corpse, hooked up to machines that pumped blood throughout your body, but nothing more. It was I, who touched your spine and transmitted my own energy into your cerebrum. You flapped like a fish out of water after that."

Jack felt his jaw slacken; he guessed the symbiot must've wanted him to talk. But he decided he wouldn't give it the satisfaction of knowing it had complete control---which it did---so he kept his eyes on the TV and remained silent instead.

"We're running out of time, Jack," the droid said, wearily. "Your life had already ended back on Earth. You weren't revived for your own interest, to live out your days on a Stendaaran ship. If the General sees that you're of no use to him, then he will kill you---and that'll be that."

Jack had heard the mentioning of this 'General' so many times that he'd become somewhat of an infamous figure in his mind. From the Whorganion's ship, to the Stendaaran she-things, and even Nolan, who in his last dying words had tried to warn him of a war-like race that had garrisoned the Earth. Well...he was here now...on their ship The General's ship. There was so much he still needed to learn. And in truth, he wasn't ready to die just yet....There was still something to live for. "Who's this General that I keep hearing about?"

"General Morlaak," the droid said. "Is the leader of the 16th Stendaaran Fleet. This ship, is one of the Stendaaran's many warships throughout the galaxy."

"So there's a war being waged somewhere in the galaxy?"

"For the past 500 years, there's been war between the Quadrants in the galaxy."

"Quadrants?"

"Yes, Jack....Our galaxy's been divided into four Quadrants since the great rebellion that led to the defeat of the Drofh Regality more than 800 years before. Stendaar, Whorgan, Tref, Earth, as well as millions of other worlds, all share and belong to the same Quadrant-the 4th Quadrant--- which you might know to be the outer spirals of our galaxy. The 2nd and 3rd Quadrants share the middle of our galactic disc, while the innermost---not to mention, the black hole- --is ruled by the 1st Quadrant: the oldest, and by far, the richest Quadrant in our galaxy. The 1st Quadrant, is where the Drofh Regality still reign, but they once ruled the entire galaxy for many millennia."

"Then what Regality rules this Quadrant?"

The droid turned to look up at him. "Just take a wild guess, Jack."

"The symbiots?" Jack said, a bit uncertain. "The symbiot Regality?" "That's correct, Jack. But we're not called 'The Symbiot Regality.' We belong to a small world, about 126 light years from here, called Meraachz. Home to the Meraachzion Regality of the 4th Quadrant."

Well I'll be damned, thought Jack. Earth is the property of an empire ran by symbiots...imagine that. But it wasn't too difficult of a thing to wrap his mind around once he considered how easily the leaders of the Earth surrendered the planet without a fight. The Whorganions and Trefloons might've surrendered theirs in a similar fashion. The mighty Stendaarans, on the other hand, had most likely put up some kind of resistance. Judging by their she-things, he knew a great dire burned inside them. They were fierce, passionate...rebels by nature.

A bit similar to some Humans. And so far, he liked them. They were his kind of aliens. "So," he began. "As far as empires are concerned. Do we share in the benefits and wealth of the Meraachzion Regality?"

"Of course. Hasn't life on Earth improved since our arrival?" "It hasn't gotten any worst."

"What kind of empire would it be if we left our worlds in turmoil?" "A real shitty one."

"And take my word for it, Jack. There's nothing shitty about the Meraachzion Regality."

"Okay.... So there're four Quadrants tied up in a galactic war. I doubt we're in a free-for-all to see who controls the whole galaxy; so what Quadrants are we allied with?"

"The 3rd Quadrant, which is ruled by the Dusphloea Regality."

"So our enemies are the 2nd and the 1st Quadrants?"

"No," the droid said. "Just the 1st Quadrant, who declared war against the 2nd Quadrant in order to seize control of the Seezhukan Regality more than 500 years ago. Since then, it's been fighting to take over the Dusphloeans. If that happens, our entire galaxy's lost."

"So it would make more sense to defeat the Drofhs in the 1st Quadrant, than to begin at the Dusphloean's front lines."

"Tactically, yes. Kill the Spaak, by severing its head. The Seezhukan Regality will instantly fall to its knees. At least that's been the plan for 500 years. It's more easier said than done. You couldn't begin to imagine what hellish, utterly powerful worlds exists within the 1st Quadrant."

Jack considered everything the droid had told him for a while and got a pretty good idea of what wonders stirred deep inside the Milky Way. But then something occurred to him that had absolutely nothing to do with wars, or Regalities, or Quadrants. It was a simple thing in itself, but something he craved to know, so he asked the droid. "What's a Spaak?"

"A vile, poisonous creature on Stendaar," the droid replied. "With no limbs on its long slender body. Quite similar to one of your snakes."

CHAPTER
ELEVEN

EKW, IS AN Earth-sized desert world in the 4th Quadrant, with two polar ice-caps that feed the planet' s rivers, lakes, and underground pools, due to the oblong orbit of its gigantic neighbor Tekw, whose strong gravitational pull caused the planet to tilt at a full 90° toward the sun each year to thaw its northern pole and replenish the parched world with seasonal floods.

This drastic change in Ekw' s climate caused life to evolve in unusual ways for billions of years as each organism competed for the scarce (but precious) life-giving water that filled the underground tables and wells.

Snouts, trunks, and long tongues are the preferred tools of all species of life that live there. The most dominant species have sharp teeth, short limbs, and long necks for reaching further into the shrinking water-holes at the season's passing.

On Ekw, there're only two main classifications of life-forms: those that dwell on the hot sands of the surface, and those live below it. By nature, the ones living on the surface are large, lumbering creatures that roam the hot sands for water-holes and shallow pools. Their wide bodies are ideal for storing and retaining excess fluid. They feed on shrubs and plants (which are scattered all over the landscape), whose far-reaching roots stretch deep down into the damp, spongy soil beneath.

The others, less adapted to the surface must scavenge in order to survive. The ones with sharp fangs and claws, and nocturnal vision for seeing in the dark caverns in search of, not water, but the blood of their prey for sustenance.

But only one species have evolved an Ekw, to adapt to both the harsh dryness of the surface, and the dark, wet terrain of the caverns underground. A creature with nocturnal vision. A creature...with a brain, that gave it the knowledge and intelligence to dig wells, and erect huge complex water systems to ensure its survival, no matter what time of the year.

Throughout the eons, this species developed and built great civilizations and kingdoms, where cities thrived in wealth and prosperity. But the Fruxsan beings (as the species are called), are a very tribal race whose long history had suffered its own share of wars. Due to the unnatural process of underground mining, the planet's annual supply of water could no longer sustain the growing population. Bloody wars were fought over resources, territory, and food, as the species became engaged in a deadly struggle for survival.... But then the Meraachzions came.

In exchange for suitable hosts (for that's all the Fruxsans could've offered), the Empire made mighty merchants of the Fruxsan race. Millions of gallons of water, from far away Aqua-worlds such as Taas, were imported daily on gargantuan ships, retrieving Ekw from the brink of destruction, to bring it wealth beyond measure. For centuries thereafter, the Fruxsans, more commonly known throughout the Quadrant as Ekwhaans, have lived in peace and harmony with each other. They now served and lived for the Empire, whose wars and conflicts would inheritably become their own.

One such Fruxsan, named Tytron, strode through the corridors of the Stendaaran ship that orbited the Earth. At just six feet, he wasn't that tall of a creature, but looked every bit as fierce. His whole body was covered in short brown fur, and a pair of tall fox-like ears stood on his head where a tuft of black bushy hair flowed in between like a Mohawk. He had bushy eye-lashes like a camel, that shielded his eyes from the windblown sand on his home world, and a long bushy beard that hung from the chin of his long snout.

He entered a room that resembled a tube where an octagon platform shot him through one of the many tunnels that snaked all throughout the ship. It came to a smooth stop some minutes later and opened up into a room where a Human stood----apparently expecting his arrival. However, it wouldn't seem strange, since the ship's computers had surely alerted the man of his visitor.

"May I enter your quarters, Cadet?" he asked, in a low, raspy voice.

"Please do, Instructor," said the six-legged droid standing beside the Human.

Tytron came into the room and immediately approached the man, giving him a slow once-over through his busy lashes. He noted the class-3 armor with mild indifference(for he himself was suited in a formidable class-6)then fixed his gaze down at the droid. "You are to report to training at once."

For a moment, the droid hesitated, but then its blue eyes dimmed. "The host needs time to fully recover from his injuries. He hasn't left Earth no more than six hours ago."

"Injuries?"

"It seems he got into some trouble with the other Drones. Took an Ion-blaster at point blank range. He was given a new heart, but the tissues need at least 3 days to fully strengthen."

"Damn reckless Drones," said the Fruxsan with a heavy snort. "We don't have 3 days. He has to go into training now. If his heart fails then we'll just give him a new one and try again..." he paused to pull up a transparent screen through his own implanted chip. He swiped through Jack's file, reading the data quickly. "Puppycock, you have class-3 clearance aboard this vessel. I trust that you are strong enough-"

"The name's Jack Dillon," said Jack, cutting off the Instructor. "And it was my own friend that killed me---not your idiot Drones." He held out a hand for the Fruxsan. "Name?"

The Fruxsan didn't care much for Earthly decorum. He ignored Jack and fixed an accusing gaze back down at the droid.

"It's like I said, Instructor," the droid began. "He's still recovering from his wounds, and I haven't yet---"

"Never mind that, Klidaan" the Instructor said. "We have strict orders to get him into training. Seems body functions and motor skills are where they should be. Just control his mouth until he learns that our way is the one, and only. If anything else, this Human's bound to learn that. And whether you like it or not, Puppycock...." The bushy lashes turned back toward Jack. "You're going in. You'll need your Symbiot more than ever....Now, follow me."

CHAPTER
TWELVE

CONSIDERING THE STENDAARAN she-things were elegant, beautiful creatures (despite having no breasts, and a horn jotting out from the middle of their foreheads), it came as a complete surprise to Jack when he saw the big ogres on the ship's hangar. They were purple-skinned hulks (some as tall as 9 feet), with hunched backs and four bulky arms that worked independently of each other. Unlike their female counterparts, they had no sexy tails. They had two horns, instead of one, curling up to the back of their heads like an Earthly ram. Three black beady eyes were tucked under their brimming brows, and a plum of a nose was mushed right into the middle of their faces that were angled off with perfectly squared jaws.

Since their bodies had naturally adapted to the ship's strong gravity, it seemed unnecessary that they were still heavily armored with suits that equipped them with wings, tails, and even shoulder-mounted cannons.

"This ship has a thousand more hangars like this one," the droid told Jack, as the two followed their Fruxsan Drone Instructor through the hangar filled with pod-shaped planes. "Each hangar's designed to house different ships.... The Gamlarrian starships, and the Lannsillion fighters for example, are housed on hangars #835, and #836 respectively.

This hangar, being a particularly small one, is located a bit more on the upper levels of the ship at hangar #059. It's only about 400 square yards, and houses nothing but these Drone fighter-pods you see here."

Jack had already taken note of the endless rows of the so-called fighter pods parked all throughout the hangar. But the crafts resembled nothing of what he understood to be an actual plane....No more than 20 feet long, these pods had no wings, nor tails, nor any thruster-jets---or anything that might propel it forward---of any kind. They only possessed the body of an Earthly plane, or the long tubular fraille of a small submarine perhaps, but nothing more. They were all very sleek, very black, and glossy...perhaps to reflect the stars and better mimic the utter blackness of space.

Many of the pods were being repaired by the Stendaaran mechanics, who had the inner parts and workings all laid out on the floor around them. This brought a bit of relief to Jack, to know that at least they had something inside them; that they weren't just empty coffins to be shot out-just like that---into space. However, his peace-of-mind would be short-lived as they came across some that weren't being worked on at all. They were beyond repair. Whole sections of these pods had been blasted off---he could tell from the molten metal---by an awesome fire-power...laser-cannon, most likely.

"How do these things fly?" Jack asked.

"They fly by thought, Jack," the droid replied.

Both man and droid paused as Tytron came to a sudden halt at a pair of Stendaarans who appeared to be standing guard for the two pods behind them....After a brief exchange of inaudible words and a few nods, the drone instructor turned around. "Step forward, Cadet."

It was the closest---thus far---that Jack had ever been to a male Stendaaran as he came up to the instructor's side. The two hulking creatures glowered down at him with grumpy looks, though he wasn't quite sure whether or not if their faces were naturally formed that way. Unlike the she-things, who had smooth purple skin, theirs looked rough and dull at first sight---leaning more on the border of dark blue. One held two stained rags in both of his hands, while the other two limbs dangled freely. His comrade was the first to speak. "So this is the one called Puppycock. The one that killed three of our Drones?" He didn't sound too impressed.

"The name's---" Jack began to say, but then his mouth failed him as the symbiot took control. "Cadet...Puppycock... chief engineer, Magn."

"You have class-3 clearance," the one named Magn, said. "So I'm guessing your two former hosts must've passed one."

"Not so, Magn," said the other, in a surprisingly high-pitched voice. "Gaan's been promoted to serve in the Gamlarrian squadron, so he's very much still alive. This one's been dropped lower. Isn't that so, Klidaan?"

"Only half-way so, Latrogh," said Jack's symbiot, through the droid's soft vocalizer. "Gaan's been promoted. But I wasn't dropped lower. I've been reassigned to this Human for reasons I'm yet to know. And he's been given class-3 clearance on his own behalf...not mine. On Earth, he was a private Detective; genetically made to find things."

"Find things?" Magn said, regarding the Earthling man with new-found respect. "Secret missions. High clearances. I guess you're worth three Drones.... Good luck, Puppycock.

Whatever your mission is, bring back my pod in one piece. And if you can't, then try not to get your sticky Human blood all over it."

"I'll try my best," Jack said, in a sarcastic tone that the Stendaaran either ignored, or simply failed to detect.

The creature gave an approving grunt then pulled up a holographic map that materialized before them at the blink of an eye. "You're to jump to the Oxloraan Sector in the 3rd Quadrant, where you'll receive your basic training and briefing."

"Thank you, Magn," Tytron said, as he made a quick mental note of the map. "It was nice seeing you both again."

"Likewise," said the two Stendaarans in unison.

At the approach of the Fruxsan, the glossy fighter-pod hummed to life (like a dog recognizing its owner) and floated effortlessly off the short propping-stilts on which it laid. Without a sound, it continued to rise before settling gently on its flat. base, towering above everything else in the hangar. As if by magic, a portion of the sleek metal dissolved into nothing, revealing---what appeared to Jack---a narrow cockpit inside, with barely enough room for the pilot to stand, or lay down flat (the cockpit wasn't designed for sitting).

"This will be your first lesson, cadet," Tytron said, standing before his pod. His armored anti-gravity boots increased in power to lift him off the ground with ease. Like writhing vines, two cables extended from the pod's cockpit to connect at the back of the armor's neck before gently pulling him back inside. "Through the chip implanted in your brain, you are mentally linked to your vessel's controls. All you have to do, is make it stand up." Without another word, he made a smooth sweeping gesture around the collar of his neck, causing a helmet to come slapping down in layers over his face, giving him the look of a fearsome robotic dragon with green eyes. From the tip of the pod, the sleekness returned, like wet paint, oozing down until the entire cockpit was glossed over to retain its solid blackness.

Jack took in the whole sequence of the feat in wonder, uncertain of whether he was capable of accomplishing the same stunt. Dubiously, he turned to look up at the two giant Stendaarans, who returned his gaze with expectant looks of their own, as if he should already know how to control the alien machine with nothing but his Human thoughts.

"It's very simple, Jack," the droid said beside him. "Follow exactly as Tytron did. Just use your will to make it stand up."

"Just like that, huh?" said Jack, shifting his gaze back over to the pod. Though it appeared like a dead metal thing, he still felt a sense that it beckoned him somehow. It was as if his subconscious mind was already in deep conversation with each nano.

"It's as simple as that, Jack," the droid replied.

Jack sighed, giving a resolute shrug. "Okay...." He collected his thoughts as best as he could, mentally commanding the pod to rise up in the air.

The pod rose at the subtlest beck of Jack's mental impulse, surprising him with the sheer suddenness of it all, and causing the thin streak of his thoughts to scatter and break the mental bond between man and machine. It rose no more than six inches before it came crashing back down on its own propping-stilts.

"I win!" came the high-pitched voice of an elated Latrogh from behind. "You owe me 12 slaag-sticks...! Pay up, Magh!"

A disgruntled Magh made a low grunt as he reluctantly reached to the side of his armor where 3 crystal sticks fell into his palm. He tossed them dismissively at Latrogh.

Three of Latrogh's arms reached out and caught the incoming sticks in mid-flight. "You owe 9 more. Where are they?"

"You'll get them later," Magn said, gruffly. He turned to walk away, but not before planting a playful smack at the back of Jack's head with one of his big beefy hands.

"You'll lose everytime, Latrogh said, as he left the Drones to catch up with his comrade. His words were already beginning to fade and trail off. "I told you...no one ever makes it on ttle first try. Maybe the second, or the third, but never on the...."

It now dawned on Jack, why the two Stendaarans were so silently poised behind him as if he was about to do something extraordinary. Turns out, it was just the anxiety of a friendly wager--not hopeful encouragement---that explained the weird tension behind him.

"Never mind them, Jack," said the droid, bringing Jack's thoughts back to the present. "You didn't do too bad. You have the mental strength, but try to stabilize your nerves this time....Now go on."

He didn't need the Symbiot's explanation to tell him what he already felt. He knew exactly what had happened and how to avoid it in the future. This time, he knew what to do. He only wished Latrogh and Magn were still there to see it.

He regrouped his thoughts and tried again. As before, the pod's ultra-sensitive controls reacted instantly at the first hint of his intentions (it was a marvel in technology) and lifted itself evenly off the propping-stilts. It then stood itself up on its flat base---a bit too fast for the Symbiot's liking---and wobbled like a grazed like a grazed bowling-pin before finally setting itself firmly on the floor.

"Now open it," the droid said.

Full of confidence from his last success, Jack thought it shouldn't be too hard to get inside the cockpit, but as he willed the pod to open, he reaped not the slightest response from the craft.

Standing tall on its flat base, the pod remained as dead as it was when they'd first arrived.

Jack shot a questioning frown down at the droid.

"What were you trying to do, Jack?"

"What do you mean?" Jack said, becoming annoyed. "I was trying to open the cockpit---just like you told me to."

"But how?"

"Just by---" He paused to think for a moment, but couldn't come up with any answers. "I don't know. By thinking...willing it to open."

"Then let this be your second lesson. To erect the pod was easy, because it was programmed to operate as a whole unit upon such a command. But this is not always the case when it comes to performing different operations, especially individual tasks such as opening certain components. For this, you'll need to understand what your craft is made of, and get to know its basic components. Pod-fighters are strictly drone vessels, used for spying and fitting into tight spaces when required; the only craft of its kind in all the Quadrants. It is not just a craft, but trillions upon trillions of tiny machines, all linked together at the atomic level, like your nano-bots on Earth, but far more advanced. As a collective whole, they'll move the pod wherever you want. But if you wish to enter, then a simple command for retraction anywhere above the cockpit will do."

"Like a zipper?"

"Like a what?"

"Never mind," Jack said, as he refocused his thoughts on the pod once more.

The pod immediately began to split right up the middle, like zipper opening a jacket from the bottom up (just as he'd pictured it in his mind) to expose the cockpit inside. It was very unlike Tytron's method, which presented a more mystifying, dissolving effect.

"Good," the droid said. It rose up from the floor and tucked in its legs as it floated over to the pod where it was welcomed by a cable that snaked out from the cockpit to plug itself into the droid's back as it found a comfortable place to fit inside. "Are you coming?"

Seeing all that he'd seen of the craft's capabilities, Jack doubted it could only be boarded by such common means. He was pretty sure that if he ran up to the pod while jumping into a fully tucked somersault toward the cockpit, those cables would still manage to shoot out and catch him in mid air. And tempted as he was to test the pod's true capabilities, he decided he already had his fill of dramatics for one day.

He was an astronaut now! A Space Drone...! Having never been in space before; on an alien's warship, with class-3 qualifications (whatever that means) within the ranks of the

16th Stendaaran Fleet, on the verge of boarding a fighter-pod that reacted to the faintest hint of his thoughts, on his way to the Oxloraan Sector of the 3rd Quadrant in the galaxy {probably hundreds of light years away) to be trained as a drone and fight in some galactic war for an alien General he'd never seen before in his life....

What a strange feeling it all was....

CHAPTER
THIRTEEN

HE FELT NAKED in space. Just drifting there in a black sea of nothing, yet surrounded by all that exists in the Universe. The Stendaaran warship loaned before him like an impassable mountain with no end in sight to its encroaching mass in every direction. From outside, he appeared like an ant, sizing up the herculean walls of a prison.

Turning ever-so-slightly, was the bluish orb of the Earth below. It looked comfortable there. Content. Snuggled in the dark womb of space. out here, was where it truly belonged, with its own paparazzi of satellites and chaperoning moon. It beckoned for attention, especially his, but he avoided looking down, lest he succumbed to its gravity and plunge the many miles to the ocean below.

Impossible as he knew it to be, he still couldn't shake the feeling that something was holding him up. God, perhaps. If released, he'll simply fall. Both he, and the colossal Stendaaran warship...down, down, down---

"Your fighter's drifting, Puppycock!" came the intrusive voice of Tytron through the pod's intercom. "Do you hear me?"

There it went again, thought Jack. The slightest break in his attention, and the pod shuts down. But how can one not notice the entire globe of his own planet---for the first time--without stopping to stare? "Yes...I hear you. earring to your position now."

Though it was nearly impossible to see the black glossy surface of the pod, he had a complete panoramic view of his surroundings through a transparent illusion inside the cockpit. It was this that had broke his attention from the craft's controls in the first place: the feeling of floating inside a glass tube.

The Drone Instructor's pod was displayed on a map in the window before him. With a single thought, he spun the craft around and followed it there. "I must take control of the pod now, Jack," said the droid beside him.

"We're preparing to make a jump."

He was more than happy to relieve the pod's controls to the droid. It was all too much for him at that point: the cramped quarters, his jittery armor, the feeling of floating around in space, and sharing information with the trillions of nano-machines that made up the pod. It was a real challenge to focus through all these things.

A jumbled display of stars materialized and filled the entire cockpit. "This is our current location," the droid said. From out the cluster of tiny stars, Earth's own yellow dwarf appeared, growing to the size of a lemon. "And here's our Quadrant." In zapping speed, the lemon-sized sun receded back into its position among the group of stars that were already being sucked into the brightness of a cluster, giving the illusion of being swallowed up by the entire galaxy that had so suddenly taken their place on the display inside the cockpit. "Not only is our Quadrant the largest in the galaxy," the droid said, highlighting the Milkyway's outer spirals. "It's also the most populated, teeming with billions of different intelligent life-forms....

The 3rd Quadrant is here; the second most populated.... And here's the Oxloraan Sector." The inner spiral of the 3rd Quadrant zoomed through the cockpit at the blink of an eye, causing a big greenish, orange planet----orbited by nine moons---to appear. "This where you'll begin your training for the next three days."

"Ready to link our coordinates," came Tytron's voice (from one of the planet's holographic moons, it seemed).

"Coordinates linked, Instructor," the droid replied. "Systems ready."

"Systems ready."

"Ignite jump to the Oxloraan Sector in 5,4, 3,2,1---"

Jack's fighter-pod couldn't have lurched forward more than 30 yards, before the planet Oxlor and its three visible moons, along with countless ships and an entirely different constellation of stars, suddenly appeared before him. So sudden, he thought it another illusion on the pod's window (like the map-display). But as his muddled senses slowly adjusted to the sudden change of worlds---and reality----he finally realized that they'd actually jumped (hyperspace, light-speed, or otherwise5)1,251 light-years, according to the calculations on the pod's display window, in a matter of seconds.

But what a surreal and awfully abrupt experience it all was! Like being pushed (unexpectedly) from a dark room, into a bright corridor. That's how Jack had felt. Gone, was the Earth, the sun, the moon, and the Stendaaran warship---replace so suddenly by the planet Oxlor: Military Sector of the 3rd Quadrant. And here, space buzzed with all kinds of activity.

The planet itself appeared three times larger than Earth. It was mostly covered with orange land, with few oddly shaped oceans and forests scattered all about like green, moldy fungus, growing on a rotting fruit. It was the scars of the planet's earlier civilizations: deforestation and pollution, which quite possibly led to climate-change and centurylong droughts that caused most of the lakes and rivers to dry up. The forests---telling from their battered appearance on the mega continents---were already beginning to replenish. But it'll be many millennia before it can return to its primitive glory---if ever at all.

As the Drones' fighter-pods maneuvered through the busy highways of Oxloraan space, Jack marveled at the many different ships and crafts that flew around. They were unlike any Whorganion or Stendaaran ship he'd ever seen. They appeared like automated machines all on their own, serving different functions other than flying and transporting passengers. Some flew up from different corners of the planet to join together, while others appeared from out of nowhere (from hyperspace jumps perhaps) to split apart and travel in opposite directions. Some zipped in and out of sight, while one just sat there like an old building in space.

The Drones, merged with traffic on such a road now, following a knife-shaped craft around the dark side of the world where the clustered lights of giant cities covered entire continents. The fighter-pods shot across the Oxloraan sky in brief streaks of light as they zipped past the cities in a matter of seconds. They crossed the black voids of oceans and deserts in a matter of minutes. Before Jack knew it, a complex grid of lights appeared below them. The fighter-pods dipped down through the night, and soon, the monstrous shapes of gargantuan buildings began to take form: a very small, but congested city.

Like the Oxloraan ships he saw in space, these buildings too appeared to be nothing more than tall machines (far larger than any structure on earth)that moved, changed shape, merged, and separated to suit their own purpose and needs. Looking down, he saw no roads, no land; just metal and lights, stretching down with no end or foundation upon which they were most certainly built.

A section of one of these buildings began to break off up ahead. The pods slowed down, prompting Jack that his 15 minute expedition across the galaxy was coming to an end. Like one-half of a draw-bridge, the front section of the building came down. The pods slid to a stop just then, waiting as a retracting door pulled itself up and washed their entire cockpits in a flood of bright lights.

Jack squeezed his eyes shut as the pod slowly began to move forward.

EXPEDITION THREE

CHAPTER
FOURTEEN

LANDROGH, BETTER KNOWN amongst the drones as 'Scrap City', was a manufacturing city stationed in the Oxloraan desert of Zan. It was here, where the mighty Oxloraan kingdom produced their wears of war. Every spare part needed for any starship within the Quadrant was made there; from warp engines, to plasma cannons, lasers, and force-field generators. Every kind of alien weaponry; from guns to explosives, to war-droids, and even the cherished nano-pelt armor (of all classes) were manufactured by the millions on a daily basis.

It was where the Oxloraan emperor held his dozens of ceremonies each year to celebrate the victories of the Quadrant forces against the Seezhukans; to commemorate past military achievements; and award any General whose outstanding command the Dusphloean Regality would be at a lost without. It was a mechanical city, where millions of machines produced a non-stop supply of military hardware for the 3rd Quadrant. A war-machine city, where the total area sprawls over an astonishing 100,000 square miles. A city of lights, metal, and fire...and nothing else....

Not waiting for the fighter-pod's cables to lower him down, Jack hopped out from the cockpit with the assurance that his armor's anti-gravity boots would ease him softly on the metal floor. There was a hissing sound as the droid disconnected itself from the pod and came floating down behind him.

Tytron, his Instructor, still stood in his own pod as if awaiting further commands.

The building's hangar---or garage---in which they landed was surprisingly small, and empty. It was just a metal box, barely big enough to house the two fighter-pods. And though they'd traveled thousands of light years across the Quadrant, no one was there to greet them. It was as if they weren't even being expected.

"What is this place?" Jack asked the droid.

"Here's where you'll get your training, Jack," the droid replied. "This is where all Drones cane to get their instructions before being shipped out."

"Okay...so...where is everybody?" Jack said. With his enhanced hearing, he listened for sounds of activity beyond the metal walls and ceiling, but only the faint drone of grinding gears and slamming doors could be heard. There was an eerie air of neglect and abandonment about the place.

"There is no everybody," came Tytron's echoing voice from the cockpit of his fighter-pod. His dragon shaped helmet had retreated back into its armor, so his tall fox-like ears and the thick fur on his goat-like chin was still pressed down. He allowed the pod's cables to ease him gently out of the cockpit. His armored boots made soft clanks on the metal as he approached them. "This entire city, and its buildings, is just one single machine that controls the functions of many smaller ones. But the building isn't unoccupied by any means, though. A few Oxloraans live here, mainly the mechanics and engineers, who oversee repairs and maintenance....Follow me."

The Instructor walked past them and headed to a wall at the other side of the room.

Upon their approach, the wall slid back to reveal a white corridor made completely of shiny chrome. "This is our hangar," Tytron said, pointing up at the alien characters written above the wall. "Number 19."

Further down the corridor, they walked past similar walls with different writings, before rounding a corner and nearly colliding with the first Oxloraan Jack would encounter.

It was a short, squat creature; a quadruped, no taller than five feet. It reminded Jack of the mythical Centaur, even though this creature took on more of the arachnid variation where its long upper torso sat atop its round furry bottom, from where four stumpy legs extended. It had one furry arm with a thin rat-like hand and fingers. The other arm appeared mechanical from the shoulder on down. Its head and face, to say the least, was surprisingly ape-like, with rough dark skin, two beady eyes, and thick black fur (like a beard) covering most of its face and chin. A creature, whose species were comfortably at the helm of the evolutionary race in its own world.

The Oxloraan spoke in a harsh alien dialect in which Jack could only guess that Tytron and the droid both understood. This was so, because the creature didn't have a Symbiot attached to its neck. Most likely because the Meraachzions didn't have any power in this Quadrant. And for that, Jack envied the creature.

Their conversation didn't last very long, and soon the Oxloraan snapped Tytron a stiff alien salute before trotting past Jack with a hard stare.

"Your quarter's right this way, Puppycock," Tytron said, leading them further down the corridor...They came to an oval-shaped panel in the wall.

"You have approximately 13 hours to get your rest before training begins. I advise you to use this time to fully integrate with your Symbiot. There're some places the droid won't be able to follow you."

"That's okay," said Jack. "But hey....My name's Jack---not Puppycock. I was born Jack Dillon. So from now on why don't you just call me Jack."

The Fruxsan glowered into Jack's unmoving eyes for what seemed a long while, but then relaxed with a reluctant sigh. "Name's are never important. Your file says that your name's Puppycock. There's no mention of a Jack Dillon, anywhere."

"That's because the Stendaarans played an awful trick on me."

"Why would they do that? The name Puppycock, don't seem to have any particular meaning."

"And that's exactly why I don't like it," Jack lied. "It has no meaning. But on Earth, Jack means warrior. So I'd rather you just call me Jack."

"Very well, Jack. I will call you by anything you so desire, as long as you get some rest and fully integrated with your Symbiot."

"Thank you."

The Fruxsan replied with a stiff nod before hurrying back around the corner in the direction of the Oxloraan.

"Okay," said Jack to the droid, feeling a little better. "I could use a bit of shut-eye. Let's go inside."

The panel slid open; however, instead of a nice comfortable room (like the Symbiot's on the Stendaaran ship), Jack walked into a noisy room, filled with dozens of alien Drones, all suited in class-3 armor. They acknowledged both man and droid with mild interest before carrying on with their alien card games and vid-chat holograms.

He followed the droid through the dorm while surveying the array of alien life-forms present. From the furry and fluffy, all the way down to the scaly and hairless; all were fashioned with the same Symbiotic tubes around their necks. All were citizens of the 4th Quadrant. The same levitating cots from the Stendaaran ship were seen all throughout the dorm, where some of the aliens sat and entertained each other with idle galactic gossip.

"This one's not occupied," the droid said, floating over to an empty cot near the end of the dorm. "We can rest here until we're called for drills in the morning."

Jack sat on the cot as he felt a sudden wave of fatigue surge through him. He stretched himself out, not even bothering to retract his armored boots. "When do we get to eat?" he asked, with a wide yawn. "I'm hungry.

I haven't---" He paused when he realized how long he'd gone without food.

"You'll no longer have need for food, Jack," the droid said. "I'll provide your body with all of its daily nutrients, which will be expelled through your pores as waste."

"Waste?"

"Just sweat, Jack. All of our nourishments are provided for us in this case, filled with life-sustaining serum. The supply's endless, as long as you remember to refill the case when necessary." The armor along Jack's forearm opened up just then, revealing a row of five small tubes of clear liquid. "You don't have to worry about eating or drinking, or breathing, anymore."

"That's a comforting thought," said Jack, in a weary voice. His eyes were becoming too heavy to keep open. "Why am I so sleepy all of a sudden? Is that you?"

"It is...Your body's in desperate need of rest. You'll feel much better when you wake up."

"Okay...but---" Was all Jack could've managed to say before drifting off to sleep.

When he awoke ten hours later, he felt refreshed: exactly how the droid said he would. But that wasn't just it. He felt more than energized. He felt stronger. His thoughts were clear, calm---and his mind moved faster. His sense of awareness heightened, but not too intense. His genetically enhanced sight, and hearing, though already beyond improvement, was somehow more sharp and keen than ever before.

By now, the dorm had quieted down. Most of the Drones had settled on their cots; some slept, while others just laid there, staring up at the shiny chrome walls in their own private thoughts. He spotted another Human just then:

A man, laying on his cot, some ways further up the dorm, staring over at Jack (for God knows how long) hoping to catch his eye.

The man didn't waste any time in getting up and walking down through the dorm's aisle to where Jack sat with his droid. He was a big man, about six and a half feet tall, muscular and well built beneath his armor. He wore the same thin clear plastic cap on his bald head. He had thick dark eyebrows above his steel-gray sunken-in eyes. His face, freshly shaved with a widebeamed laser.

"Well, well, well...look who's finally up."

Jack spun quickly around in the other direction (annoyed he hadn't sensed his intruder's approach) and found a short, chocolate skinned woman, standing right beside him. On a sudden whim, he looked down at her armored boots and felt satisfied upon seeing its anti-gravity field keeping her afloat three inches above the floor. So that's how she did it, he thought. She wouldn't have been able to sneak up on him otherwise.

"The name's Claire Ford," the woman said, not bothering to extend a hand for a friendly shake.

"You're American?" Jack didn't know why he felt surprised. But it was better than expressing his shock that she was a woman---which was how he truly felt. Though it'd been no more than two days since he'd discovered that the Meraachzions were using Humans as Drones the notion that women were also being abducted had never occurred to him.

"Born and raised," the woman replied. She was pretty, despite the plastic cap that made her bald head look shiny; and the vicious scar that curved up along the right side of her cheek. Like the Stendaaran she-things back on the warship, her long armored tail was wrapped loosely around her waist, no doubt for slicing and chocking the life out of rude alien men. "This here's Yuri Zubkov," she said, nodding over at the big man. She then leaned over a bit, skillfully maintaining her balance as her anti-grav boots began to make her body tilt. With a cocked brow, she said sarcastically: "He's Russian, by the way."

The big Russian gave Jack a subtle nod. "It's a pleasure to meet you, Mr. Puppycock. Another Human among us is always good."

"What?" Ford could hardly contain her amusement. "Puppycock?" She broke into laughter as she said the word. "Is that your real name? It can't be. No one's parents are that evil."

"No," said Jack, feeling foolish. "It's not my real name.... Let's just say I got a little...too cocky...with that Stendaaran female, when I first got here. She must've entered that 'Puppycock' thing in their database to get back at me. Everyone's been calling me that. But the name---my real name-is Jack Dillon. Just call me Jack."

"I gotta see this," she said, pulling up a blue holographic data-screen before her. It took only a second for her nimble fingers to spell out the ridiculous word, and sure enough, there it was in bold yellow letters above Jack's picture and profile. "Wow! That's zapped up"

"What is?" the big Russian asked. He was clearly at a lost of what they were talking about.

"Puppycock," Ford said, with a ticklish grin.

"His name?" The Russian was confused. "What's wrong with it?"

In English, it means he has a---" She, made a funny whistling sound as she brought a squirming pinky-finger near her crotch. "Ohhh!" Zubkov exclaimed, with a raised brow, finally catching on to the Stendaaran's cruel sense of humor. "Puppycock...! Ha, ha, ha...!" He was so loud, he disturbed the other Drones in the dorm. But he didn't care. "That's what it says in the database when I pulled his file.

So that means---"

"The entire galaxy knows this guy as Puppycock!" Ford said, joining the laughter. "But don't worry, Jack. These aliens won't have the slightest clue what that shit mean.... don't let it bother you."

"Yeah, Jack," Zubkov said, finally coming down from his ticklish high. "I wouldn't worry about it, either. The Stendaarans don't really care for names anyway. Like me, for example, I prefer to be called Zubkov. Sounds more strong and manly, you know. But all my file says, is Yori. Not that I hate being called Yori---but you get the point. These aliens... they don't care to understand Human customs."

"Yeah, Jack," Ford said. "Zubkov's right. I'm known throughout the Quadrant as Ford. You'd get the impression that I was a man, if you didn't know any better. But I don't mind. Claire...Ford....It don't make a bit a' difference to me. And in a strange way, I kind of prefer being called Ford. Makes me sound strong right Zooby?"

"Right," Zubkov said, though his dull tone indicated he didn't like being called that, either.

CHAPTER

FIFTEEN

YURI ZUBKOV, WAS a soldier in the Russian army for over 30 years before he was abducted to become a drone for the Stendaarans two years ago. Since then, he's been running spy missions, gathering intelligence from the enemy in the 2nd Quadrant. He told Jack grim tales of living machines that operated independently on their own as if they had souls. Not like those on Oxlor, tilat till needed programmers and engineers to perform certain functions.

The machines of the 2nd Quadrant was a robotic race that made up the Seezhukan Regality.

"Things live inside those machines," Zubkov said. "They crave wealth, and power, and things like that. Their war-droids number in the trillions; fearless things that fly through space to penetrate the hulls of starships and unleash their own hell inside. Only a fool of a Captain would near the rims of the 3rd Quadrant with his shields down."

"And what of the Drofhs?" Jack asked. "If these warrior AIs are so much trouble as you say, then what about the Drofhs? How'd they manage to defeat them so easily?"

Zubkov shrugged. "I don't know," he said. "I've never been that far into the galaxy. But I'll tell you what I do know about the Drofh. For one thing, they're same kind of telepathic race. And second, they're all immortal."

"They're more than that," said Ford, who'd managed to remain silent while Zubkov was busy recalling all of his missions.

"More than what?" the big Russian asked, skeptically. "What do you know about the Drofh? You're just a kid," he turned to Jack. "Eighteen years old. Can you believe that? They took this little girl from her good little school to throw her in the smog of space-war."

"You're wrong about 2 things, Zooby," Ford said, playfully slapping the Russian on his leg with her tail. "I'm not even 18 yet....I'm still 17 years old. I was snatched up at 14. And no, I never went to any good little girl school. I didn't go to any school. I'm World-smart."

Now that Jack could get a better look at Ford in this new light; behind the scar and the rugged alien armor, was nothing but a child. Like delicate flower seen for the first time under a lifting fog, so too did the stamp of fresh youth become apparent on Ford's face. She'd used her anti-grav boots to appear taller. But without them, she was barely 5 feet tall.

Her education, Jack knew, was entirely another matter. 'World-smart' kids are raised in the virtual world. They are the hackers, computer engineers, program and software developers, CEOs of trillion dollar cyber-tech companies, etc....Considering Ford's young age, she wouldn't have any need for school since most of her learning came through cyberspace.

The Stendaarans wouldn't snatch her up just like that if she wasn't useful in some way. And it shows, considering the fact she'd survived 3 years of intergalactic war. Judging from that nasty scar on her face, she'd seen some kind of combat, probably more so than Zubkov. And she was probably more wealthy than both of them combined.

"I'm assuming you've been to the 1st Quadrant then?" Zubkov asked, just for the fun of it.

"I have," she said. "And I'm the only one in this dorm that ever walked the surface on the Drofh's home world and return in time for my daily Balltrack practice," she smiled a sheepish grin.

"You're very skillful as a scout then," said Jack.

"Wait a minute," Zubkov remained a skeptic. He found it hard to believe that this little girl had been to the Drofh's planet, yet the mightiest of the empire's ships and fleets could barely make it through the Quadrant without being tangled up in decade-long battles. She had to be lying! "How can you be so sure that you're the only one in this room that's ever seen the 1st Quadrant? They're many drones---whole squadrons of them; fleets...that are assigned that far into the galaxy."

"And yet," Ford began. "No one in this room's ever served under, my command.

"Your command?" Zubkov laughed, though Ford's casual expression never changed. "You must know when to stop your joking, little girl. It's bad form.

"I'm not," Ford said. "And I'm guessing that I might be the only colonel in charge of communications here. You'll soon be under my command once we're briefed on our new mission."

"Our new mission?" Jack asked, before Zubkov had a chance to drill the Cadet any further. "So you guys have never met before?"

"None of us have," Zubkov said. "We're all strangers here. But this one grew on me like a vine," he looked up at Ford.

"Really?" said Ford. "So, the fact that we're the only two Humans---before Jack arrived---had nothing to do with it?"

"That had nothing to do with it at all," Zubkov said (they both knew he was just being stubborn). "I get along with all of my comrade drones. You just happened. to grow on me, that's all. Like a little sister. You're so small, I think you'll need my protection out there."

"Oh Zooby...." Ford said, leaning in closer on her grav-boots so that she could give the big Russian an affectionate stroke on the cheek. "It's sure nice to know that I'll have you to stand in front of me when the Drofh split you down the middle like a friggin' leaf with nothing but a wink of their oval eyes."

"They can do that?" Zubkov asked.

"Sure can," Ford replied. "Seen it down with my own eyes. Not to a Human, of course. To one of those Dusphloean cyborgs. Tore flesh from metal, or rather, cause flesh and metal to become undone."

"How'd they manage to do that?" Jack asked, sensing that Ford might be eager to share all she knew of the Drofh.

"Because they are the most evolved species in our galaxy, "Ford said. "Hundreds of billions of years ago, when our galaxy first formed, it began with the 1st Quadrant, then moved on to the 2nd, then the 3rd, and finally the 4th, which is where we are now. But all of this took billions and billions of years to happen. So by the time our planet had finally settled down to spawn life in her lakes and oceans, those living in the 3rd Quadrant were already building cities and traveling the stars----I'm talking about millions of years in advancement here. And while the 3rd Quadrant was still tinkering with their warp drives and force fields, those in the 2nd Quadrant had already become bored with such things, and integrated their living tissue with machines {it was a thing, to be a cyborg 2 million years ago). But the 1st Quadrant, the oldest by far, had already begun to successfully place their consciousness into their machines. These were the Drofhs; and they ruled the whole galaxy back then."

"So the Drofhs were the first AIs 2 million years ago," said Jack.

"Yes," Ford said. "And the Seezhukans were the cyborgs, and the Dusphloeans were still 100% beef; the way we are now. But it wouldn't take too long before we become cyborgs ourselves. The technology is already being fiddled with. Ahh...the process of galactic evolution...isn't it grand?"

"So, back to these Drofhs," said Jack. "What have they evolved into now?" "What else," said Ford. "Back to their original selves, the way they were 100 billion years ago. It's all about the survival of the species---remember? Darwin, anyone? But anyway...the ultimate goal of any species, is to continue on to the next generation, and so on. But this is only how we know it to be on Earth. It is why we tinker with our own bodies so much, with cybernetics and genetic-engineering. It is why my life-span's 230 years, instead of 40....But on a galactic level, or even on a Universal scale perhaps...the ultimate goal, is immortality. That, is the ultimate goal of any species that wish to evolve---and exist.-- in our galaxy. The Drofh, after billions of years, have attained this goal. They were the first Humans (so to speak).

The first cyborgs. The first artificial intelligence. And now, as of about 25 million years ago, the first immortal beings in our galaxy. They are at the pinnacle of natural evolution. They're the masters of their selves, their environment, and their world. They know no bounds; and time, to them is irrelevant. They're telepathic, telekinetic, and psychic---they know all that ever happened, and all that ever will. In a sense, they're like---"

"Gods!" Zubkov interjected; his voice filled with mild wonderment. "I was to say omnipresent. But yes, Zooby, you're right. They're like gods. The gods of our galaxy."

"That's it then?" asked Jack, fearing Ford had reached the limits of her knowledge of an enemy that seemed impossible to defeat. "You believe they're gods?"

"Yeah," said Ford, sensing Jack's dissatisfaction. "They're the gods of our galaxy, though very unlike the Human notion. They're just beings who've evolved as far as nature would allow. They can't create black holes, or teleport, or warp space with their thoughts. They can't even fly. They still need ships to travel, and warships to fight our warships with. If you shoot them, they still bleed. They can still be killed. But they are the true gods of our galaxy---the highest evolve. And it is widely believed that every galaxy has their own version of the Drofh....It is what it is."

"So," Jack began. "I'm guessing the race of artificially intelligent beings that rule the 2nd Quadrant---the Seezhukan Regality---is next in line to take this last step in the ultimate evolution."

"That's right, Jack." said Ford. "I see that you have a little bit of common sense after all."

"And the Drofhs seek to put an end to it," added Zubkov.

"That's right, Zooby. But that's not all. The Seezhukan Regality---"

A loud buzzer went off just then causing all the drones in the dorm to suddenly stop what they were doing. The door-panel slid open and in strode the Fruxsan drone instructor, Tytron.

CHAPTER

SIXTEEN

THE DRONES ALL snapped to attention as Tytron made his way to the middle of the dorm. "Okay Cadets," he said. "Gather around and listen up. As some of you may already know by now, a great discovery has been made near the Bhoolvyn Sector in the 3rd Quadrant. I'm not going into any details just yet, but I will say that it has something to do with the source of the Dark Void, stretching along the outer rims of this Quadrant."

At the mentioning of the dark anomaly, soft apprehensive murmurs could be heard all around.

Remembering Zubkov's tales of his missions in the 2nd Quadrant, Jack turned to the big Russian and nudged him lightly on the elbow. "Hey," he said, whispering softly. "What's the Dark Void?"

"Nothing?" Zubkov replied.

"Nothing?" Jack was confused. "Nothing...what? What do you mean?"

"I mean exactly what I said. The Dark Void, is nothing. It's not space. It's not a dimension. It's not a place where things exists. It's nothing. If you fly into the Dark Void, you'll fly yourself right into non-existance. It's AI technology. The Seezhukans must've figured out some kind of pre-big-bang thing---thee period before things came to be---and smeared it 10,000 light years across the outer reaches of the 3rd Quadrant. It's like an alien version of the Great Wall between the Quadrants. The Dusphloceans have no way of getting their ships across; and over the years they've lost countless fleets that jumped to hyperspace from the Bhyoolvyn Sector, never to return or be heard from again."

"So the Oxloraan Sector's the next Jump-point in the 3rd Quad rant, furthest away from the Dark Void," said Jack, adding his own piece to the puzzle.

Both Ford and Zubkov stared at him with strange looks on their faces. They seemed surprised that a new abductee should know that.

"Jack?" asked Ford, leaning in closer to him with a wry smirk on her face.

"Were you some kind of cop before you got here?"

"No," Jack said. "I was never a cop. I was a private Detective for 40 years. A federal agent before that."

"Ha!" Ford exclaimed, "Well, that explains it."

"It wasn't too hard of a thing to figure out." said Jack. "This planet, and all four of its moons, are clearly military outposts for the Dusphloean Regality. The rest is just common sense. The Oxloraan Sector must be located somewhere beyond the reaches of this Dark Void, so that the Quadrant's fleets can safely make their jumps."

"You're right, Jack," Zubkov said. "If you look at any map of the Quadrant, you'll see the Oxloraan Sector six light-years to the west from where the Dark Void ends. Our ships cross there, but at a heavy cost, since the Seezhukans can guess within 6 light-years where we'll come out of our jumps. It's a hitand-miss thing. Sometimes you'll jump right into an ambush. Other times you'll jump safely in empty space on the other side with no more than a minute to prepare for battle before the enemy homes in on your location. The Quadrants have been fighting between this Sector for centuries. On Earth, both sides would've called it a stalemate a long time ago, shake hands and forget all about it. But these aliens, man...with unlimited resources, galactic wars can last forever."

"Until now," said Ford, nodding up toward the instructor as he erected a blue holographic sphere out of thin air.

"For whatever reasons the General may have," Tytron said, with the blue sphere hovering near his face. "You've been selected for a special mission that can possibly turn the tide of this war. For years we've been searching for the source of the Dark Void, and now it appears that we're closer to finding its location than ever before. But getting there will not be as easy as it sounds....I say this, because it is suspected that this source lies at the heart of the 2nd Quadrant, on the other side of the Bhoolvyn Sector approximately 6,000 light years across the Dark Void."

"No one's ever been that far into the 2nd Quadrant," said one small furry drone.

"That's not exactly true," Tytron said. "How else can we know what we know, had we not ventured that far into the Quadrant? I didn't say it was impossible. I said it won't be easy."

"And what exactly is the source of the Dark Void?" asked another. "That is still classified information," Tytron said. "All I can say for now, is that the source of the Dark Void has not yet been located. But what leads to it, has." He turned to the floating sphere and moved his hand across the glowing surface. The sphere turned, causing the entire room to rotate along with it.

The instant the dorm lurched into movement, the drones floated effortlessly on their grav-boots---all, except Jack, who stumbled as he tried to retain his balance.

The dorm turned 180° before it began to rise up through the building like an elevator.

"All of your training and preparation will be done using Simulation Chambers," said Tytron, as the entire dorm continued to rise. "The training exercise will have two courses. One will be a 1,000 mile race, to determine the speed and reflex qualifications. And the other will be a combat course, to determine mental strength and endurance. Death-shock and paralytic-shock will be applied, so I need not remind you to treat the Simulation as the real thing."

The ascending dorm rose up in the middle of a wide floor, filled with dozens of erect fight-pods. They weren't as sleek, and compact, as the ones, Jack and Tytron flew in through the Oxloraan Sector, though. These appeared to be much older versions of the current pods; prototypes even.

They were twice as large, with dull metal plating slapped on to their pod-shaped frames. The cockpits were all exposed to show nothing but an empty shell of a pod, save for two thin wires that dangled inside. Thick cables reached down from the ceiling and connected to pods' nose, giving the illusion that they were all they were all that kept them from falling over.

Familiar with such drills, the Drones didn't waste any time in coming out of the dorm to find their pods. In fact, they seemed eager to get the whole thing done and over with.

"Come Jack," Zubkov said, wrapping an armored sleeve around Jack's shoulders. "Us Humans gotta stick together."

Jack began to leave, but then he remembered the droid; so he turned back around to see if it would follow.

It didn't.

It just sat there on the levitating cot, like an old dead box. No blue lights, no animated triangular head. No nothing.

"You comin'?" said Jack to the droid. An apprehensive tinge seeped through him as he began to fear it had malfunction somehow. Or perhaps, it had simply ran out of power. "Hey, you!"

'I'm here, Jack.'

The voice came so soft and gentle in Jack's mind, it could've been his very own thoughts. But it wasn't. "Are you in my head again?" he growled. He looked like he was talking to himself.

Both Ford and Zubkov became amused at his new discovery.

'You don't have a choice in this matter, Jack. I had to allow you to rest so that we may become fully integrated. Full integration is a---'

"I don't give a fuck about full integration!" Jack shouted out loud. He caught the attention of the drone instructor. "I told you to stay out of my head."

"What's going on here, Klidaan?" asked Tytron, leaping all the way across the dorm with his grav-boots. He stomped his feet as he landed, causing a loud BANG! to resound throughout the entire Simulation Chambers. "We don't have time for this. Control your host now and get it to training."

Though the Fruxsan glared deep into his eyes, Jack knew he wasn't staring at him, but the symbiot that mastered both his mind and body. He attempted to speak, but found his jaws clamped shut again.

"This will not be another one of those flyby-and-spy missions," Tytron went on, in a low, grim voice. "This will be the most dangerous expedition any Cadet has ever taken on; the possibility of combat is inevitable. I sense Jack don't cars much for his life," he paused to shoot two meaningful glares at Ford and Zubkov. "Nor for the lives of those who choose to be in his company."

"The Human has a sense that something of grave importance is at stake," the Symbiot said, through Jack's own mouth; its voice perfectly identical to that of its host. "He knows what we're involved in. He knows that his Earth, is as much involved in this war as any other world in our Quadrant."

"Then what's his problem?"

"That is his problem," the Symbiot replied. "He's frightened. It's a common Human trait: to fear the fear the unknown. But such fears are easily overcome with experience."

"I'm well familiar with the Humans' short-comings, Klidaan," Tytron said. "I've trained enough of them to know. But that don't excuse him of his defiance. Nor should a Human flaw have any bearing on any of our fates; but it do. Drones must operate as a unit. The slightest deviation can jeopardize the entire group. Make sure he knows that. Or this mission might very well be your last." Not caring to give the Symbiot a chance to reply, the Fruxsan returned to the Simulation Chambers with a single leap.

'You still haven't learnt to trust me, Jack,' Klidaan said, as he forced Jack to follow Ford and Zubkov out of the dorm.

'I don't care,' Jack thought back in reply.

'You feel as though your private thoughts are all that you have in your control, and I'm taking then away from you. But this in not true, Jack. Your private thoughts are your own. As two independent life-forms, it's impossible for our minds to merge in that way.'

'So how do you know that I'm scared shitless to go into some Bhoolvyn Sector, where a Dark Void is swallowing up ships?'

'Emotions aren't thoughts, Jack. Besides, your heart's been racing ever since the disclosure of our mission. It was only reasonable to surmise that it was the source of your distress.'

'So what am I thinking about right now?'

'I don't know, Jack.'

'Are you even trying?'

'Even if I tried for all eternity, I still wouldn't know what you're thinking.

'And how can I be so sure of that? How do I know you're not just trying trick me?'

'If it was possible, then you'd be able to read my thoughts as well....Can you?'

'Of course not!'

'Are you even trying?'

'Okay...I get your point. So what about this death-shock, thing? It don't sound too painless.'

'Death by mental trauma,' Klidaan said. 'The Simulation Chambers are designed to mimic real life through visual stimuli; and physical pain through special bio-nodes that will be connected to your brain's sensory cortex.

So in the event you get your arm shot off during training, the mental trauma caused by the shock will trick your brain into shutting off the link between the neuro-transmitters that send signals to your arm, rendering that entire limb useless. The same goes if you die during any one of the courses; your brain will shut itself down.'

Shut itself down... You mean...I can actually die in there?'

'Yes, Jack. We can die.'

'But is it permanent?'

'Of course not.'

Ford stole a backward glance and saw that Jack no longer held that deep frown on his face (she was familiar with the look someone gave when communicating with their symbiots). She fell back a bit and waited for him to catch up. "It gets better," she said, slapping his butt with her tail. "I know the feeling. That helpless, vulnerable feeling. But after a while, your symbiot becomes a part of you. Like an extra ear, or nose, or finger," she laughed: a childish giggle. "I'm Narla..."

"I'm Klidaan."

Both Jack and Ford stared at each other, bemused by the spontaneity of their symbiots. For Jack, it was a weird pause, due to the brief interruption. But Ford just smiled and gave him a knowing look.

"They'll do that from time to time she said. "After a while, it becomes natural. You'll learn to become one with Klidaan...."

The smooth floor of the dorm came to an end where the grated metal platform of the Simulation Chambers began. Most of the drones were already standing inside their pods, so they were the last few remaining to find themselves a machine. Jack watched as Ford and Zubkov made graceful leaps into their pods, leaning back in their cockpits as naturally as inverted bats in their caves. He hopped into the pod on Zubkov's right, half-expecting a clear sheet of metal to zip itself down over the cockpit.

It didn't.

'Just a reminder, Jack,' Klidaan said. 'The bio-nodes must be inserted through your nostrils to connect with your brain's sensory cortex. You will feel a slight discomfort during this procedure.'

'Could it be any worst than what those Stendaaran machines did to us?'

'No. Not even close.'

'Then I guess we're all set.'

"Remember Cadets," Tytron's voice blared from the tiny speakers built into the helmets of the Drones' armor. "Be aware of exactly why, and for what purpose these courses were designed....Good luck to you all."

'What does he mean by that?'

'It means that an actual void could be inserted into the program. But don't concern yourself with that too much. 'This will be the first time we'll be seeing action together, so allow me to lead. You just sit back and learn--do not interrupt.'

As Klidaan said this, the two bio-nodes uncurled themselves down like stringy vines across Jack's face, leaving thin trails of slime on his forehead. They felt their way to his nose---as if blind---then wormed up through both nostrils. He squirmed and wriggled his nose against the discomfort; sniffling, snorting, and sneezing as they tickled the mucous membrane inside. Globs of snot ran down his lips. His eyes welled and spilled two long streams of tears....A sudden jolt....A sharp pain in the back of his eyes as if they'd just been yanked....Then came relief. Pain and discomfort subsiding....It was over.

A thin, long device slid down the head of the cockpit where a pair of small metal prongs eased up to his face before reaching out and stretching his eyelids far apart to expose the big eyeballs. Two fine beams of light shot out from a cavity within the prongs, directly into Jack's pupils....His world snapped to complete darkness just then, causing him to fear he'd gone blind....He began to panic.

'Everything's still okay, Jack,' Klidaan said, sensing Jack's distress. 'It's all part of the Simulation. Soon we'll be in---'

The entire spectrum of deep space materialized before him in that exact moment. All of a sudden he was back in his fighter-pod---or what appeared to be. Directly on the cockpit's radar was the location of the other cadets nearby. And then--

BOOM!!!

A Stendaaran warship shot and blown to bits by enemy laser cannons; fiery debris spreading as far as the eye can see.

A sudden tug, then dive, as Klidaan moved the fighter-pod in the opposite direction of an oncoming ambush.

"Fighter 1, online!"

"Fighter 2, online."

"Fighter 3, here!"

And on and on, down the ranks as the cadets counted off. So far, out of thirty fighters five were already lost. Then six, immediately after.

Seemingly, from out of nowhere, green streaks of laser-fire were being shot at both their flanks, destroying one fighter after another. Jack scanned the space-battle while Klidaan flew the pod. He saw no enemy ships, save for the friendly's that were being destroyed. Holes as big as houses were blasted into their hulls from no apparent source. Or perhaps, the Seezhukan ships were cloaked.

'It's just a Stimulation, Jack. There are no ships.'

'Then where's the cannon-fire coming from?'

'Everywhere.'

"Fighter 6....You still with us? I'm surprised you ain't get yourself blown up by now."

"Is that you, Ford?" Jack didn't know he was "Fighter 6" till he recognized Ford's voice through the intercom. A flashing blip on his radar showed Ford's fighter 9 a few miles up ahead.

"Of course it's me, dummy."

"And what about Zubkov?" asked Jack.

"Fighter 13 still here," came the big Russian's voice in his ear. "Hey---no fair," joked Ford. "Jack's letting Klidaan do all the flying."

"And why shouldn't I?" said Jack. "This thing's too easy...." He lied. In truth, he was just beginning to make sense of the chaotic battle scene, which was nothing more than a gauntlet of laser-fire through which their pods raced. Klidaan zipped the pod through the ceaseless barrage with incredible skill and ease, like a fly avoiding the countless drops of rain. Had Jack been at the controls, their pod might've been one of the first to be blown to bits. There were too many things to pay attention to all at once. Instead, he focused on the patterns in which Klidaan swerved their pod in order to avoid being hit ....A left bank, followed by an upward pitch at 60°, then immediately darting to another left, dodging two green streaks that always zipped past his left flank, before finally veering right again to bring them back on course.

This sequence was followed by another, then another, each performing a different series of twists and turns; like a boxer's combination of counterpunches (and there were many), all one had to know, was when to bob and weave. There was nothing random about the enemy's fire. Two cannons were probably assigned to each fighter-pod where the Drones must quickly learn the first round of sequence in order to avoid being hit when the program resets---all this taking place within the first five seconds of the Simulation.

Firing at all the pods, all at once, merely gave the illusion of a hellish dog-fight, but nothing more. It all boiled down to simply learning the steps of the cosmic dance at extremely high speeds. This much he knew...

He memorized six sequences in all, one following immediately on the heels of another. He'd even prepare his own mental course, and memorized both Ford and Zubkov's sequences. Then he learned the sequences of the nineteen other Drones and noticed that all their courses contained only four. In fact, out of all the Drones, his course was the most complex, with the most number of sequences. He wondered if this was just a---

"Fighter 2, to Division," came the Division leader's voice. "Worm-hole up ahead at 300 miles....meet you all at the finish line."

Far up ahead, Jack could make out the beginnings of an electric storm as it churned into a fiery maelstrom. 'Are we supposed to fly into that thing?'

'That is where the course."

Two more pods disappeared from his radar.

"We just lost 11 and 20!"

Then three more after that. "Something's wrong...."

More pods were being shot down than ever before. Their numbers were dwindling---fast.

With his quick mind, Jack calculated the sequence of the nearest pod ahead of him, counting only four before it blew up in a ball of flames. The number of sequences had changed, but not altogether. It seems the Simulation was learning, adjusting to each pod's patterns---counter-punching the Drones' counter-punches. The only sequence that hadn't changed, was his. He knew this, because he hadn't been blown up yet.... "Fighters 13, 9, 7, 23, 29, and 2," he said, as he read off the radar's display of the remaining Drones.

"I'm sending you these new patterns."

"What is this, Fighter 6?" The Division leader asked.

"Your sequence patterns aren't complete," Jack replied. "That's why so many of us are getting hit. The Simulation's adjusted to your flight patterns, then added two more sequences. You have to learn these new patterns now, or you won't be able to finish the course."

"And how can you be so sure that these new patterns are correct?" the Division leader asked.

"There's no time to explain any of that now. You'll just have to trust me---you're going to fail the course if you don't adjust right away. The patterns you have are no good."

"Fighter 6, this is Fighter 9," came Ford's voice. "Adjusting to new sequence now."

"Fighter 13, adjusting to new sequence."

"Fighter 7, adjusting."

"Fighter 29, adjusting."

righter 23, adjusting."

"Fighter 2, has already adjusted."

Jack, and the six remaining Drones, flew with their new patterns through the course, each following an entirely new set of sequences, dancing their way in and out of the barrage of laser fire for the next 250 miles before plunging safely into the worm-hole's welcoming vortex.

CHAPTER
SEVENTEEN

IT WAS OUT of sheer will (or uncertainty perhaps) that prevented Jack from seizing control of the fighter-pod to steer it away from the moonsized whirlwind of lightning and fire. The enormity of what appeared to be the top view of a giant hurricane, crackling and spinning with terrifying force, did more than overwhelm his delicate senses. It did, in fact, paralyze him with intense fear. He did all but scream in fright as the pod shot through the black gaping eye at the center of the worm-hole, emerging in the calm, tranquil scene of space on the other side no more than a fraction of a second later.

Just like that, he found himself in a new world.

It did nothing for his rapid breathing and racing heart, though. The transition between the two Sectors was so instantaneous that the spectors of incoming laser-fire, sequences, and worm-holes, were still fresh in his mind. It was like awakening from a bad dream, suddenly jumping out of some nightmarish sleep, still wincing from the looming ghosts and demons that were long gone. His mind was still back in that world; it hadn't yet caught up with the present. It wasn't till some moments later that he realized the danger was gone. He was safe. They all were....But what a hellish trip it all had been.

"That was some good work back there, Jack," said Ford, still breathing heavy in his ear. "But how'd you know what my flight patterns were?"

"I didn't," said Jack. Though he knew they were all nearby, he still searched the starry space for what remained of the Division's fighter-pods. He couldn't see them. "I simply supplied you all with new patterns."

"Okay....but you'd still have to know the new set of correct sequences for all of our flight patterns. No one could think that fast in that situation Jack."

"Apparently, I can. It's simple, if you just---"

"No time for that now, Fighter 6," came the Division leader's voice in their intercoms. "I'm sending new coordinates for the jump to our next course. There's an infantry being pinned dawn by Seezhukan droids on a Gamlarrian planet, in the Llannsdun Sector. We're to report there at once."

"An infantry?" said Zubkov. "How're 7 Drones going to help an entire infantry, taking heavy fire from what must obviously be another enemy infantry?"

"We'll find out soon enough, 13....Prepare to link our coordinates in 3, 2, 1....Coordinates linked....Prepare to jump in 5, 4, 3, 2, 1---"

There was that push again. The passing of a billion streaks of distant stars. Then the sudden appearance of a ringed, gray, greenish world, facing the far-away light of a blue-white sun. It was about half the size of Saturn, with five colonized moons---two of which were visible from their pods. Over a dozen cargo and passenger vessels cruised inside its orbit. And with the exception of the glimmering sea of light that lit up the dark side of the planet, it appeared as calm and peaceful as a fetus in its womb.

"Picking up a distress signal on the southern pole," the Division leader said. "Set fighters to reflection-mode. Fall into parallel formations. Our friendliness might be too busy to notice our arrival, but the enemy won't...29, stay close to my tail."

"Already there, sir," the Drone known as Fighter 29 said. "Okay, let's go---fast and light."

The pods shot down toward the planet at a high velocity, forming two parallel lines before entering the atmosphere some 10,000 miles below the equator. They appeared like flaming meteors falling into the world. They plunged into the dark froth of thick, billowing clouds, where thunder bellowed violently above a swirling blizzard. For that brief moment only, they flew blind---passing through the gray mist whereforks and tridents of lightning flickered.

Because they flew at such incredible speeds, the white mountainous landscape was already rearing its icy crags as they skimmed the surface, kicking up rounds of fresh powder in their wake. The pods mimicked the white snow and sky, rendering them virtually invisible to the naked eye. In a matter of seconds, they would flit across an entire continent and an ocean that was frozen from shore to shore, before the first signs of smoke was spotted. The battlefield---covering the area of a small town---soon came into view. Scores of flying machines milled above, hurling deadly missile and laser-fire into the ranks of the allied infantry below. Blue orbs flashed around them each time their protective force-fields deflected a projectile.

"Enemy AI up ahead," the Division leader said. "About two AI forces of jet-fighter droids, a company of Demolition

Droids, and about two battalions of AI soldier droids....
About five AI Carriers in all."

"Enough to take on 2 infantries this size," said Ford.

"That's the whole point, Fighter 9," the Division leader
said. "The Simulation was designed to be almost impossible
to beat....We'll have to split up for now; start with the first 3
Carriers. Fighters 9 and 13, should pair together on the first.
Fighters 7 and 29, you have the next in line. And Fighters 6
and 2, are to stick with me on the third."

'Our friendly infantry has no fighters of their own,'
observed Jack, with some concern.

'It's the design of the Simulation,' Klidaan replied. 'But
in actual battle, there will be.'

'So we have to defeat those things on our own, with no
support?'

'We're just Drones, Jack. We don't actually do the
fighting. We only assist in intelligence gathering.'

'So what are we doing now? What intelligence do we
need on that thing?'

'You'll see.'

'What?'

'Just don't interrupt, and you might live through this....'

Their fight-pod fell in behind the Division leader's as
they approached an AI carrier that hurled a barrage of laser-
fire in their direction. Considering the previous course, no
sequence or patterns were needed to shake off the enemy's
attack. The challenge laid in boarding the enemy's ship,
which all the Drones---except Jack----are used to doing.

'Seems you have a good memory, Jack. You should take
a look at this.'

A blue, fuzzy hologram appeared in the cockpit's display just then. Jack forced himself to ignore the pod's sharp banks and rolls in order to study the diagram correctly.... Shaped like a bird's wing, the Carriers were giant warships about twice the size of the Whorganion cargo vessels on Earth. 'What am I supposed to look for?'

'An entry.'

'You mean, we're gonna be boarding that thing?'

Before Jack could get a response, he noticed both the Division leader and Fighter 2 slowing down to recircle around the Carrier. Both Drones then ejected themselves, free-falling harmlessly through the ship's force-field.

"You've got to be kidding me!" Jack said out loud. "How'd they do that without getting cooked on the force-field?"

'Hold on to your wits, Jack,' Klidaan replied, already causing the pod's cockpit to unzip itself. 'You'll get use to it in no time.'

Jack felt himself springing from the pod in a dramatic way, his body stiffening into a nose-dive. His armored helmet retracted, exposing his bald head. He can now see the entire surface of the Carrier in live color; scores of laser cannons firing on the allied infantry below.

'Hold on.'

The rest of his armor retracted just then, leaving him stark naked as he fell through the bitter cold sky---right through the barely visible blue tint of the Carrier's force-field. The ships black metallic surface was now 100 yards below, rushing up to crush him very quickly. His body tucked itself in a tight somersault as the armor's nano-alloys reconstructed themselves into the anti-grav boots on his feet once more. Then came the gloves, adding sharp claws at the end of each digit, before extending all the way up his arms and covering his chest as he landed atop the Carrier's hull with a loud clashing BANG!

He was already on the move before he knew it, making a great leap through the air as the rest of the armor's helmet covered his face....It was only then that he spotted the other two Drones, hunched behind the blindspot of a firing cannon; the force-field surrounding the Carrier like tinted glass.

"The ship's guards have been alerted," said a throaty voice through Jack's intercom.

'Why would they alert the guards?'

'It's the only way of boarding a ship of this class without engaging the system's defenses. Or would you prefer being blasted off the deck by one of those cannons?'

"Droids spotted at both the southern and eastern ends of the Carrier," said the division leader. "Hydraulic lifts are still visible....Looks like the standard patrol models---type AIPD-115."

Those were the ship's Patrol Droids, model type 115. Seeing that there were well over 300 different type of Patrol Droids, this particular model wasn't the Seezhukans' latest, by far. They were covered in smooth shiny chrome, which appeared to be armored plating. Their egg-shaped heads were split horizontally in half by a green band of swiveling light. Two long arms were affixed with hand-shields and laser-rifles. They walked with a steady pace on two pneumatic bows for legs as they stalked down the length of the ship toward the drones.

'Why do I feel cold all of a sudden?' Jack thought.

'Your armor's releasing a coolant to mask your heat signature against the droids' infrared sensors,' Klidaan said. 'Do you want me to put a temporary block on your sensory cortex?'

'Please do.'

At that instant, Jack went from shivering inside his armor, to not feeling anything at all. Though he knew his body temperature was still plummeting----in both the simulated and the real world---he didn't care, as long as he didn't have to put up with the uncomfortable chill.

"Switching to stealth," the division leader said. "Fighter 6, switching to stealth."

The billions of nano machines that made up Jack's armor buzzed to life like grains of vibrating sand. The rough, rugged surface of the plates became smooth, even the helmet, as it stretched itself to an oblong shape, splitting in half at the middle where a green band of light sputtered on. He gazed in wonderment through his new green vision, while his left hand transformed to a short rectangular shield, and the right morphed into a five-nozzled laser rifle. The chrome came last, seeping through, then spreading all over the armor as though it was nothing more than brittle cloth.

He stood up and headed toward the other drones who were equally clad in the clever disguise as they hunched low behind the cannon. By this time, more patrol droids were scouring the deck from the northern end of the ship, so the drones' sudden appearance didn't rouse any suspicion. 'What have you done to my legs?' he asked, when he noticed the drones' legs were curved backward in a crescent, then realized that his were shaped in the same way. They mad e soft hissing sounds with each step as the shiny pneumatic pumps stretched and compressed in order to support his weight. The armor had no bearing on their physical bodies, and yet, it appeared as if flesh had suddenly transformed to metal.

'It's just an illusion, Jack. For centuries, drones have been gathering mounds of intelligence on the Seezhukans. There isn't a droid, demolisher, fighter, star ship, or anything built within the 2nd Quadrant for that matter, that hasn't been spied upon, recorded, or stolen. The AIPD-115, is just one of the many droids whose scl1ematics have been filed in our database. With this information, we're able to make exact replicas of the original. But in certain cases, where physical anatomy won't allow to suit our purpose, then a 3-dimensional holographic rendering will serve in its place....In other words, your legs are fine.' 'And what about this shield and rifle? Are they 3-D holograms too?'

'No. Those are real.'

'That's good to know.'

Jack followed his fellow drones down the deck of the ship, the green bands of light on their helmets sweeping from right to left as they pretended to search for intruders. As he fell in beside them, two more hydraulic lifts appeared, and out poured another squad of droids onto the ship's deck.

"This is more than necessary," one of the drones said.

"The simulation's adapting to our tactics," the division leader said. "It's simply anticipating any one of our possible moves. It still doesn't know who we are."

"We're being approached."

"Just let me do the talking," the division leader said.

It came as a strange fascination to Jack how life-like the machines appeared. They walked with confident ease;

their shields and rifles hanging limp at their sides as if they already figured the alert to be a false alarm.

Their disposition were indifferent to the ship's rapid cannon fire, and the destruction they wreaked all around them....As they got within earshot of his enhanced hearing, he could hear them speak. One appeared to be shaking its head at a comment, as though weary. They seemed bored with the whole "Attacking-the-enemy's outpost" thing, as if they'd been doing the same attack for centuries; their-pride and enthusiasm long gone and forgotten, along with the purpose and meaning of the whole war. In Jack's eyes, they appeared all too Human.

The division leader babbled off a line of alien words when the droids neared.

To Jack's utter surprise, the enemy droid fell right in step beside them and joined their company on the stroll down the length of the ship's deck. One of them answered in reply, pointing up at the sky (with its shield-hand) at the droid fighter-jets zipping and darting by above them. He sensed a bit of sarcasm in the droid's tone---ridicule perhaps---to which its comrades seemed to be agreeing.

'What is it saying?' asked Jack.

'He's saying that they're wasting their time here. That this Sector holds no kind of strategic advantage. They should be defending the Dhalkyoon Sector, which was already conquered by our fleets 70 years ago.'

'Seventy years ago? If it's been that long, then why's it still-worried about a lost Sector?'

'Because, according to the program, the battle of Dhalkroon hasn't happened yet. This Simulation's one of the older ones.'

Jack found this strange. 'So we're being trained with outdated weapons and droids to execute one of the most important missions in the history of the Quadrant?'

'That appears to be the case, Jack. This Simulation's also no longer part of the Cadet training program.'

'Why?'

'I don't know. I can't remember ever seeing this particular battle in any one of our programs. I know most Dhalkroon battles...this one is not in the Simulation's files.'

'So there'll be no record of this training exercise?'

'No....'

Jack retreated to his own thoughts while both Drone and droid continued down the narrower length of the ship. He wasn't all that surprised when he heard Klidaan joining in on their conversations, speaking the alien language fluidly through his own lips. It felt so natural....like a group of friends out for a stroll. The AI patrol hadn't the slightest notion they could be among impostors. It was unbefitting. for one of the most powerful races in the galaxy.

'Tell me more about these droids, Klidaan. Why are they programmed to mimic real life-forms so well?'

'That's because they aren't programmed at all, Jack. There're actual living things inside those machines. They're conscious of all the same things as we are: sense of self, emotions, the past, the future. And from what I've learned, there's even a gender difference among them as well.'

'You mean...male and female droids?'

'Not just male and female droids...male and female everything. All intelligent life within the 2nd Quadrant have transferred their consciousness inside the circuits and networks of computers and machines....These droids, for example, were once creatures of flesh and blood, living on their own home worlds. But that was many millennia ago.'

'I wonder if they can still remember their old selves?'

'They do---'

Klidaan's words were abruptly cut short when the hydraulic lifts---all over the deck---suddenly appeared. A string of alien words ran across Jack's intercom.

All the droids hurried over toward the nearest lift, which lowered them back down into the ship.

'What's happening?'

'Another emergency alert. The intruders have now invaded the ship. All droids are to report back inside at once.'

The droids who accompanied them were already rushing over to lift that appeared close by. The Drones followed closely behind. Jack could feel himself breaking into a trot in order to remain at the Division leader's heels. He was the last to fall into the huddle inside the crowded lift, squeezing in with the rest of the company.

The gray horizon ascended and was replaced by the blackness of the ship's thick hull as they were lowered down. Sounds of grinding gears, and computerized chirps and beeps could already be heard thrumming up from the pits below. The interior soon came into view, revealing a jungle of twisted pipes and shiny metal covering the walls along the dozens of tiers where many different droids tended their assigned duties in the soft gentle light of an early day. Bots of all make and model dominated the air between the tiers like birds as they flew by on miniaturized jets and tiny propellers.

One of the patrol droids spoke, to which the drones' leader made his own reply by shaking his head. The droid gave a knowing nod.

'What's happening?'

'Patrol droids are assigned to the lover floors. They don't have any other obligations to work anywhere else on the ship: according to this one---'

Jack's eyes were averted to the droid standing near the lift's entrance.

'....They're going to loosen up somewhere until all this mess is over. They can't wait to get back out into outer space.'

All too Human, Jack thought.

The lift began to slow its descent, and soon the busy tiers were replaced by much larger floors filled with AI fighter-jets, demolition droids, and other giant machines moving across the floor. The droids gave a funny kind of salute---as the lift eased to a stop---by dragging their shield-hands across their chests before stepping on the busy floor, quickly blending into the bustle of the robotic throng.

"Not too bad of a bunch," the division leader said, without much admiration for the droids. "A damned shame they'll be going down with the ship." The lift began to ascend once more, moving back up through the tiers. He turned to face them, making a short wave of his hand, from where a green hologram of a multi-tiered cube materialized. "We had no other choice but to allow the patrol droids to take us off course," he said. He pointed to the bottom of the cube as it hovered before them. "We're somewhere above the ship's fighter-bay at the southern end. But we should've been here---" He flicked his wrist and the cube tumbled like tossed dice. When it settled, a different diagram appeared with rooms, compartments, and corridors, instead of tiers.

"----At the eastern hydraulic lift, where the ship's main engines and control rooms are."

Jack remembered the diagram. It was the same map he'd studied before being ejected from his fighter-pod. But this one was a complete diagram of the ship's main power station.

The drone leader's shield-hand swatted at the holographic cube, causing it to spin, then morph into a mini-sized model of the entire ship. It was oddly shaped, this ship, like the bent wing of a bird with the main thrusters and warp drives focused at the northern and eastern ends of it. They worked to counter balance the much longer and narrower southern end, which might otherwise drag the ship down like a broken tail. It was an ingenious design; one that ensure the ship stayed airborne, despite the gravity on any distant planet. It also betrayed the fact that its creators had a taste for aesthetics.

"We're inside an AIWS-1037," the drone leader said. "Artificial Intelligent Warship. It is also a Carrier---as you've seen for yourselves in the fighter bay. We're approximately 2,000 yards off course, and at some point, we're going to have to get off this lift--quite possibly very soon....Any ideas?"

"If we can get back on deck," Jack heard himself say. "Maybe we can hurry back to the eastern end."

"No, Puppycock," the Drone leader said. "The ship won't allow any lifts to break surface under high alert."

Too irritated at being called out of his name, Jack remained silent.

'You have to remember Jack, it's not his fault.'

"Anyone else?"

"What if we use those?" The other Drone (fighter 2) said, pointing outside the lift at a group of floating platforms moving slowly down the lane between tiers.

They'd already gone two tiers up before the Drone leader finally figured out how to stop the lift. After a few failed attempts, he managed to get it to reverse, and they shot back down, coming to a slow stop on the same tier as the platforms that resembled floating slabs of cinder block. They were unmanned, and appeared to be some kind of material transport, used for hauling heavy mechanical parts all throughout the ship.

With a quick scan from a device built inside his helmet, the Division leader was able to pull a complete holographic diagram of the floating platform before them. "An AIMC-76," he said, rotating the diagram slowly. "A Mag-cart, according to the archives. A materials transport; max-speed of 100 miles per hour. Very cranky personality. And---" He paused, and gave a regretful sigh. "They hate when other droids hop on their backs."

"That's discouraging," said Jack, picturing himself hopping onto the back of a wild horse. "A flying bed with a mean temper."

"It's the only way out of here," the Drone leader: said, swatting the diagram away. He turned to walk out of the lift, pausing just briefly to give one last command. "Wait for me here. I'll be right back." He then leaped all the way across the tier, landing on the back of an empty Mag-cart.

CHAPTER
EIGHTEEN

THERE WERE TWO things that Semhek (the Tekwhaan drone leader), wasn't quite sure, about when he made that long leap across the tier from the lift. The first, was whether or not the grumpy mag-cart would make a huge scene when he landed on its back. The second was whether or not it would take them where they needed to be at the opposite end of the ship. Both scenarios led to the possibility of a fight, in which the drones partook very little of. Though their class-3 armored suits were equipped to handle heavy combat situations, the success in their missions relied solely upon cunning and stealth. They were spies---intelligence gatherers for the Meraachzion Regality. The heavy fighting and battle missions were left to the mighty Stendaarans and Oxloraans, who manned gargantuan warships and heavily armed zippy jet-fighters of their own.

It was perhaps the most reckless thing he'd ever done. But he didn't care. It was just a Sim'.

He dropped like a rock on the platform, using his grav-boots' magnetic soles to clamp himself down firmly to the metal surface.

The Mag-cart was stunned out of its wits at first, as if jolted from a deep sleep. But then it began to shake violently in the air, blasting off a series of harsh, robotic oaths.

On the surrounding tiers, the serve-bots and other machines stopped whatever they were doing to see what the commotion was all about. But soon, their suspicions, turned to amusement upon seeing the bungling droid atop the furious Mag-cart as it bucked and veered about in the air.

"I'll have you thrown to the front lines for this, droid!" Exclaimed the disgruntled machine. It spat its words out with loathing distaste. "Get off of me and find the intruder, you fool! We're under high alert!"

"And that is exactly why I need your help, good friend," Semhek said, in a soft, robotic voice. "Intruders have been spotted at the northern corridor's main power station. My company and I found ourselves at the wrong end of the ship when the alarm was sounded. We only wish to get back to our posts. Do us this service, and I'll recommend you for a promotion. How does Service Inspector sound?"

The angry Mag-cart's violent shaking simmered down just enough to consider Semhek's suggestion. This might be its only chance to rid itself of the banged up, lugging body of a flying platform once and for all. The thought of living in a sleek, brand new frame on any of the serve-bots floating gracefully between the tiers, enticed it very much....No more long hours. No more heavy loads. And no more childish droids jumping on its back! "A promotion?" It asked, as if to ensure itself that it heard correctly.

"As soon as all this is over, and we leave this Sector, I'll have you back in the foundry to be fitted for the latest model. You can even choose your own metal."

"It's a deal then. Take me to the rest of your company, then give me the coordinates to your post. I know the ins and outs of this ship like I know this rusty bucket I have to live in. I'll get you there in no time."

Relieved that all the other bots and machines had long became bored with the petty confrontation and resumed to their different tasks, Semhek brought the Mag-cart slowly across the lane toward the lift where the two Drones waited. "Hop on," he told them, still speaking the AI's alien language. "He's going to take us."

Though reluctant to get on board the cranky platform, Jack could sense Klidaan's eagerness as they hurried onto the tier. Through the green vision of the helmet's lens, he could see the glowing red light running long the outer rims of the Mag cart. He wondered if it could see them from there---in those lights. Or was that where the machine's soul resided?

As he hopped on, he couldn't help but think he was standing on a living thing. That he was somehow violating a right-- invading the space of another. So much so, he might've apologized to the robotic creature, had it not been for Kidaan's control of his speech at the time.

The lanes between the tiers evoked memories of the busy skyways back on Earth. It had only been three days since he'd left his office for the last time; solved his last case, then watched his friend die. But those memories were already beginning to feel old---forgotten. Three days ago, most of his heart had been blown out of his chest. He was dead. A part of him was gone, he could feel it. It was lost the instant Nolan's IonBlaster tore through his vest. It remained in the cockpit of his sky-coupe while the rest of his body fell to its death, choosing never to return if he was ever resurrected, which (in his unfortunate case) he was. He wondered if that thing could've been his soul, or his conscience, and whether or not it was the same thing that lived in those machines.

The Mag-cart lurched forward and shot them down the lane. As it rounded the first corner, a whole new world opened up before Jack's eyes. Gone, were the rows of tiers with their hydraulic lifts, replaced by a sprawling construct of complex machinery, gleaming under the reflection of their own artificial light. A metal kingdom, it seemed, complete with wide roads, and pathways, and towers, and courtyards. Gone, were the Patrol Droids with their oval-shaped heads, and shields, and rifles. A different breed of AI machine milled about below them. These were graceful things of elegant shape; molded, then formed with artistic flare. They varied in size and contour, from the short to the tall, from round to flat, from the box-like down to the curvy, and so on...some had wheels to carry them across the metal surface. Some just floated within their own magnetic fields and drifted about as if enjoying an eternity of bliss, while others whizzed by heedlessly.

The sounds all around were nothing short of that in an ancient arcade, filled with a continuous stream of robotic clicks, beeps, and claps; all slightly above the din of the main engines' perpetual hum. In every direction, there were blinking lights that flashed, throbbed, and pulsated from the head, chests, limbs, eyes, and mouths of these living machines that communicated with each other in their own coded way.

These were the citizens of the Seezhukan Empire. The ones who'd traded their own living flesh for metal many eons ago; whose craving for immortality's so strong they seemed oblivious that the ship was on "high alert," and that hundreds of their own fighters were waging war on an enemy infantry below.

That thought sort of brought Jack back to the present, and the reality of the simulation. He'd become so immersed in the alien's world, he hadn't noticed the great source of heat through his infrared vision until he found himself swarmed on both sides by long reddish blurs as the mag-cart took them further up through the ship. These were the super-conducting tubes that fed the plasma generators, and they went on for nearly a mile down the entire stretch of the northern end.

The mag-cart climbed to a steady ascent after some ways, taking them just 20 feet from the ceiling before entering a narrow tunnel surrounded by throbbing green lights. He couldn't help the feeling they were being swallowed up---enveloped---on their way to being ingested within the bowels of the ship. Maybe the mag-cart had seen through their disguise, and were instead taking them to the ships incinerators. Or maybe they were to be gutted; their consciousness tossed into some lowly machine, perhaps like the very mag-cart they were riding on. Or maybe----

The tunnel came to an abrupt end, spitting them out into a world of dull brass and iron. The rows of tiers soon returned, and so did the patrol droids, serve-bots, and mag-carts, hauling heavy machine parts up and down the lanes. In the distance, bright sparks flared up in the air where metal was being welded together. The deafening sound of rapid hammering erupted suddenly from the laser cannons directly above, firing in short automatic bursts as they swiveled madly on their turrets to locate one target after another.

There was a greasy look, and feel, about the place. Far down below, the clean courtyards had given way to floors filled with huge engines, where the parts were all covered in grime as they pumped ceaselessly into their sockets like powerful pistons. It was the heart of the ship. The eastern end.... Their destination.

The Mag-cart slowed as it came to an intersection, allowing a fellow platform---weighed down with a pile of fused ball-bearings---to crawl by, before drifting over to the nearest tier.

The Drones hopped off with little ceremony, save for the customary alien salute (shield across chest), and the false premise of a promotion from Semhek.

The Mag-cart gave a long cranking sound sputtered its rim-lights in reply, as if to say it would find them if he didn't, then slid through the intersection and continued on down the lane.

They moved with haste through the throng of droids along the tiers. With the diagram of the ship's eastern end committed to memory, Semhek navigated the maze of elevated walkways before finally coming to the narrow passage-way he sought.

He dipped through there, glad to see that no other droids were in sight. Turning quickly to the others, he bade them all to gather around, then pulled up a blue holographic display---a map of the passage-way. "There're four corridors on this tier," he said, turning the map slowly to highlight the square from which the corridors had formed. "But only two of them leads to the main power station: the southern corridor, and the eastern corridor...here and here. The good news, we don't have to use neither of these corridors to bring this ship down. There's a serious flaw in the design of this particular Carrier. Each power source is connected to the main station. All we have to do, is find one and send an RPP through one of its ports. We're currently positioned near the western corridor, just around that next corner. There're several power sources locei.ted there---" He paused to spin the map, then highlighted three rooms. "Here, here, and here. Either one will get the job done. Then we'll finish off the other ships." He clapped the hologram shut, then led them down the passage-way.

An RPP, or Reversed Polarity Pulse, sends the electromagnetic waves of any electrical device in the opposite direction of its normal flow, destroying the source of power in the process. In small machines, such as fighter jets, or Mag-carts, it'll simply cause their computerized engines to shut down--killing them, in a less violent way. But when used on machines as immensely huge as a galactic warship, the blow-back caused by such a pulse would tear a hole right through its hull as easy as a bullet through foil.

The Drones entered the first room on the western corridor. Save for the smooth metal walls, and a long tubular device that stood on the grated floor, the room was empty. Semhek, the Drones' leader, didn't waste any time as he hurried over to the device, pulling a small disk from the folds in his armor. He lined it up to a matching key-port at the top surface of the device. But as he did so, that part of his arm was instantly sliced off at the elbow, falling to the floor like a chopped branch; bright yellow blood spewed from the wound. The stunned Tekwhaan howled in pain as the ruined armor abandoned its disguise to betray his true identity.

The assault had happened too quick for Jack's mind to fully register in time before Klidaan raised his rifle and sent two laser bolts into the device. Green flashes of an unseen force-field blinked twice as it repelled the bolts into the ceiling. The tube changed just then---or rather, what stood before it, began to uncloak itself.

Out of thin air, the meanest looking droid (that any of them had ever seen) appeared. Far more advanced than any of the Patrol Droids on the ship, this one had a large triangular head, covered in smooth black metal. Where its eyes should've been, a thin band of intense red light beamed. It wore a grimacing grill of a mouth. The neck was long and slender, which retracted quickly between its shoulders as it blasted a deadly ball of plasma through the chest of the armless Drone leader, sending his dead body to crash loudly against the metal wall.

The drones moved quickly, rifles blasting away at the super-droid, who deflected each bolt with eye-blinking swats of its own shield. Hot plasma shot from the gun in its hand, giving Jack no time---not even a split second's thought---before vaporizing his head from his shoulders.

EXPEDITION THREE

CHAPTER
NINETEEN

IT WAS THE loud ringing in his own ear that woke him up. A throbbing headache thumped inside his skull. He made a plaintiff groan under the discomforting pain. His eyes fluttered open, but he squeezed them shut against the sudden burn caused by the bright lights in the room. That thought quickly brought him back to when he'd found himself on the Whorganian's cargo ship a few days ago. The day his friend Nolan had blasted a hole inside of his chest.... The day he died!

At least he could still move his arms and legs, and it brought him comfort in knowing that he wasn't strapped down to anything. He tried to roll over on his side, but was suddenly held in place by a hand pressing down on his shoulder.

"Stay still, Puppycock!" A sandy voice (that belonged to the hand) said. It urged him to lay on his back once more. "Your sensory and motor skills are beginning to return. But you're not yet 100%."

The hand released him. He could hear many footsteps moving around where he laid. Two pairs of feet---by his count. They came to his left side. He could feel them looking down at him. He tried to open his eyes again, blinking the sting away this time, but his vision was too blurry to make out anything other than the white smudgy light all around.

"Can you see me'?"

"No." It was Klidaan that answered.

"Can you see anything at all?"

"Just white, and a few shades of gray."

"Temporary partial blindness. A common symptom of severe mental trauma due to Death-Shock."

"Death-Shock'?" Klidaan asked. Jack was equally surprised, even though it was the second time that he had died that week. However, he felt more defeated for having failed the Simulation, which meant they probably didn't qualify for the mission.

He wondered if Ford and Zubkov had managed to hold their own against the vicious droid that had wiped out his whole team in a matter of seconds. He imagined they might. They had more experience in the 2nd Quadrant, and had most likely dealt with the likes of that thing many times.

"Death-Shock, is how the data reads. And according to your Stimulation file, you lost your head----POOF! Just like that!"

"So that's what it feels like," Klidaan said.

"I wouldn't know, Puppycock. Never been killed before....Keep your eyes open...and hold still. I have to manually switch your vision back on. The Human brain is still a very primitive thing. Your occipital lobe still thinks you're dead."

He felt something---like a tiny bug---crawl into his left ear just then. His head jerked, and he reached up with a hand to tear at the irresistible itch, but paused midway as Klidaan seized control of his body. 'No Jack. You can permanently damage your brain.'

'What the hell is that thing?' Jack squirmed and writhed as the ticklish node wriggled further into his ear, burrowing deep like a worm through mud.

"Hold still, Puppycock....Eyes wide,"

His eyes popped open and a blurry figure came across his field of vision, A hazy light. like a dim bulb, came on. It moved from his right eye to his left.

"Can you see that?"

"Yes." he replied, in a weak, tremulous voice.

"Good."

He could feel the node beginning to retract, the ticklish discomfort subsiding. As it did so, his vision slowly returned, becoming clearer with each passing moment. The outline of an Oxloraan's rough leathery face began to take form. The distorted laser-light he held in his robotic hand shrunk down to a fine beam. A slab of bright light hung from the ceiling behind him. "Any better?" The Oxloraan asked. His beady, orange eyes, betraying a hint of amusement. He wore a brown, spongy fabric, wrapped tightly around his torso that dropped all the way down past his round body, partially hiding four legs beneath. It was what had fooled Jack into thinking there were more than one of them in the room.

"Yes," Jack said. He feared he might've been blind. However, the sight of the ugly Oxloraan, hunched over him, brought grateful sigh of relief. Even the slime that trickled down from his ear in the node's wake, was a welcoming feeling; a sign that his ordeal with Death-Shock was finally over.

"Are you seeing as you normally would?

"Yes. My vision's back to normal."

"Good. Now hold still while I run a couple more tests.... Release control of your host---" A thin probe stretched out from the Oxloraan's robotic finger. It dipped down, zapping Jack below the ribs with an electric volt, sending a quaky wave of tremors through his body.

"Ouch!"

"Can you feel that?"

"You just shocked me!" Jack protested, moving to hop off the levitating table when he noticed his bare legs and feet. He wasn't wearing any armor. He was naked. Jumping just five feet to the floor, under Oxlor's strong gravity, would break his legs. He turned to look back at the Oxloraan, who gave him a sympathizing, but foreboding stare.

"Hold still, means just that, Puppycock," the Oxloraan said, in a more serious tone. He gripped Jack firmly by the arm and eased him back down on the table. "Now just lay still while I finish my tests. We have to make sure that your brain is fully functional before sending you back out on any more missions. Or do you want your head to get blown off for real this time?"

Jack didn't answer. He just laid there---angrily---while the probe continued to zap him, giving curt grunts whenever the Oxloraan asked if he felt the painful shocks. All he could think of (as he laid there) was how unfair it all was. He was a victim in all this. It was the Stendaraans who'd sent the Whorganian to lure him onto their ship They chose him to be their slave. His friend Nolan, had killed him to avoid such a fate. But in the dark realms of death he could find no safe harbor. He was quickly extracted and brought back to life-to suffer an existence of fear, servitude, and pain. And this...was what he was made into: a Drone. He didn't ask for any of it. He was simply snatched up and thrown into deep space, in a tiny fighter-pod that flew him to a world where strange things crawled up his nose and ears to play tricks on his mind. He no longer felt alive. He felt used, violated. Helpless. At the complete mercy of an alien race....It wasn't fair at all.

"There," the Oxloraan said, stepping back; the same way an artist would to admire his own work. "We're all done. You haven't suffered any detectable brain damage. But if you begin to feel light-headed, or dizzy, within the next few hours, get back over here at once."

Jack sat up again and immediately began looking around the room for his armor. He wanted to leave...badly.

"Oh, that," the Oxloraan flipped up? a blue holographic display and tapped in a few commands before swatting it away up through the ceiling. A moment later, Jack's armor materialized in a flurry of glimmering lights. It dropped to the floor like a bag of coins.

'Hold on,' Klidaan said, as Jack moved to retrieve the Armor. 'You had never the opportunity to fully learn the capabilities of your implant. I think the time's suitable you get familiar with at least one trick.'

'What're you babbling about now?'

'Your implant's linked to the nano-machines in your armor--- the same as the fighter-pod. All you have to do, is think it, and they'll obey you.'

'You should've said so before.'

'We didn't have the time.'

Through the tiny chip implanted in his ear, Jack summoned his anti-grav boots off the floor. He marveled at the way they, reacted to the slightest shift in his thoughts as they rose up and latched on to his feet that dangled over the table. From his ankles, the armor began to spread all the way up to his legs end thighs.

He hopped off the table, landing gently on the floor as the rest of his armor slapped itself onto his chest and back, unraveling itself down the length of his arms like reptilian scales.

The Oxloraan seemed mildly impressed. He'd obviously seen much better. "It's funny," he said, moving to a nearby counter where a stack of clear, cloth-like fabric sat. He peeled one off and flapped it in the air, causing it to expand to the size of a towel. "You completed the first course with the highest score of any Cadet. But somehow, you managed to get yourself shot by a regular Patrol Droid....How come?"

"I think that's classified," Jack said. He figured if all the details of the Simulation were meant to be known, the Oxloraan would already know it. It became evident that new software had been uploaded into the Simulation's program then quickly deleted upon its completion.

Such a privilege of having this kind information was the perfect pill for boosting Jacks' confidence. However, it'd fed too much fuel to his inflating ego. He was refreshed, and fully armored---his strength regained. The Oxloraan was no longer his savior, but his subordinate. "All I can tell you," he said, in a new, authoritative voice. "...is that it wasn't a regular Patrol Droid. And by saying this. I'm afraid I might've told you too much already." He began to walk past the slightly offended Oxloraan.

"Where're you going, Puppycock?" the Oxloraan asked....When Jack turned back around, he tossed him the clear towel. "You should clean some of that mucus off your face before you leave."

Jack didn't care to feel embarrassed as he wiped at the node's slime that trailed from his ear. "I'm going to find my friends," he said, passing the towel along the side of his neck. "My name's Jack, by the way. Not Puppycock."

"Jack?" The Oxloraan looked puzzled. "But your file says---" "Forget what the file says....Just call me Jack."

CHAPTER
TWENTY

LUCKILY FOR JACK Dillon, the entire map of Scrap City was already uploaded into his implant. The blueprints of every last one of its countless buildings were ready to be viewed on display with a single thought. Had it not, he might've been forced to ask the Oxloraan surgeon for directions.

Following a direct route, chosen by the map's holographic display (and with Klidaan's help), he found his way back to the Cadet's dorm. But when he walked in through the door, he found the interior had gone through a drastic change. The dorm had somehow shrunk...literally. Down from the size of a football field, to no bigger than a classroom. The mag-cots that were lined up in so many rows were now reduced to just seven. Only six Cadets---from the last Simulation---were all that remained. They were all in bad shape too. Some looked more worst than he felt (with nothing more than a throbbing headache). Others hopped and limped around on paralyzed legs.

He found Ford and Zubkov on their cots. Ford was sitting down, hunched over, as if nursing a sore back. Zubkov was just laying there, propped up on an elbow. They both wore pained expressions on their faces.

"Well, look who it is," said Ford, as Jack came up to them. "The last of the Mo' Drones."

Jack plopped himself down on Ford's cot. He tapped her shoulder playfully with a gloved hand.

"Owww!" Ford gave him a push. "Watch it man! I got shot there."

"What's a Mo' Drone?" Jack asked, as if this question was apology enough.

"Something she probably made up," Zubkov said. "She'll say silly things like that from time to time."

"I didn't make up anything," said Ford, still rubbing her shoulder. "I just improvised on an old phrase. When you're World Smart, like me, you learn a lot of different things about our world and our history. The term's derived from an ancient Indian tribe of Old America, six centuries ago."

"Mo' Drone'?" Jack asked.

"No," said Ford. "Mohican."

"Don't forget, Jack," Zubkov began, with a wry grin. "She's World-smart. She didn't go to little boys school like the rest of us."

"That's right Zooby," said Ford. She eyed Jack with a bit of concern. "And what happened to you? Semhek said your whole team got scrapped in a power station."

"Got my head blown off," said Jack.

"Huh...." Zubkov grunted from his cot. "You're lucky."

"Lucky?" Jack shot the Russian with a defensive frown "I died, Zubkov.

I went through Death-Shock."

"So did I," said Zubkov.

"What?"

"We all did," added Ford. "None of us survived! the last droid. We all died in the Sim'. But what Zooby here's saying, is that at least you can still walk. Your nerves don't have to go through any of the crazy spasmic reactions like the rest of us."

"Even in Simulation," Zubkov said. "Getting shot in the head is still the best way to die."

"So," said Jack, looking over at Zubkov. "How did it get you?"

"Took one to the gut," Zubkov said. "Then it shot my whole leg off. But the gut-shot is what did me in, though."

Jack noticed how uncomfortable the big Russian looked as he laid on the cot with his left leg (the paralyzed one) thrown awkwardly across the right.

"It should all wear off in a couple more hours," said Zubkov. "But at least I didn't get sawed in half like Ms. World-Smart, here. Ooph! Not a pretty sight, Jack. Little girlie here, poured out in front of me like a cracked melon.... Blood and guts, all laid out on the ship's deck....Not a pretty sight at all."

"You ain't no pretty sight, either," Ford shot back at the Russian, who was now chuckling on his cot. "And you're still in one piece." "Ahhh...come now, my little bird. At least you know I'll die for you.

I took one in the gut, didn't I?"

A furry teddy bear of an alien came up to them just then. It was a small creature, no taller than four feet in height. Its entire body was covered in light-brown fur, save for its head and chin where thick tufts of white bushy hair plumed. Two big furry ears stuck out from the side of its small head where a stuffy round nose sat between two narrow, yellowish eyes.

It was a creature whose species had perfectly evolved for a life in the forest world, called Tekw. The Tekwhaan---as the species were called---shared the same solar system with its much larger neighbor, Ekw, which held an orbit closer to their sun.

"Ahh, Semhek," Zubkov called from his cot. "Judging by the way your arm's flapping around like that, I'd say it was blown off in the Simulation. But I dare not cast such lowly failings upon our fearless Drone leader."

Jack fixed an incredulous look at the little Tekwhaan now standing in their company. This couldn't be the same Drone leader that took us all the way through that warship, he thought. He remembered Semhek was much taller...Or was it just the Simulation's programming simply reacting to his mind's perceptions. He would never envision a leader that small. Or it could've simply been their armor's 3D rendering of the Patrol Droid's disguise, in which they were all made to appear the same size.

"I wouldn't call navigating the inside of an enemy ship, filled with hostile droids, a lowly failing," Semhek said, in a surprisingly deep voice. "I heard your team had barely enough time to get into your disguises, before succumbing to your deaths. In the face of such a defeat, I'd say that my end was a glorious victory by comparison."

"Yeah," said Zubkov, with a dismissive shrug. "Says you."

"No, Cadet Zubkov," Semhek said. "Not me. So say the file. But that isn't why I'm here. Tytron's to brief us on our performance---and whatever new secret weapon the Seezhukans had waiting for us. But for now...more mysterious matters need pressing---" He turned to Jack. The white tuft of hair covering his furry brow and most of his yellow eyes that peered intently into Jack's. "You. Puppycock," he said, exposing a row of sharp teeth. "How could you have possibly memorized all of our individual patterns in such a short space of time? Not even the pod's computers could've calculated that many patterns that quickly. You Humans make good pilots, but that's all you're good for.

So tell me...did Tytron plant you here? Is that why you two arrived in this Sector together? Did you have our patterns already uploaded to your implant?"

Jack gave Zubkov a questioning look, then shifted his gaze over to Ford, who seemed to have read his mind.

"The Tekwhaans are notoriously insensitive and obnoxious creatures," Ford said.

"What's obnoxious?" Semhek asked. It was his turn to be puzzled.

"He takes some getting used to."

"I was talking to Puppycock, Ford," Semhek said. "If he has any questions, he should ask me. I'm the Drone leader here."

"The name's Jack," Jack said.

"Your name's Jack?" Semhek asked. "What's a Jack?" He waved a furry paw and a green holographic display materialized before them. "Find Jack," the Tekwhaan commanded, to which the display didn't respond. "There's no Drone named Jack anywhere in the galaxy. I just checked...see? Your name's not Jack....Now watch this.... Find Puppycock."

The green display made a funny wink, but then Jack's picture appeared. "See?" said Semhek, pointing at Jack's file in the display. "Puppycock. Right there---the file don't lie. Now, where'd you get Jack from? Did the Death-Shock make you forget your name?"

"Just forget about it," said Jack. It was all he could say under his seething anger.

"Forget about what?"

"The whole name thing."

"Did you, or did you not forget your name, cadet?" Semhek's tone of voice became more stern.

"No...sir," Jack began to reply, feeling silly that he was being made to answer to a talking Koala. "I did not forget my name. It's just that you---"

"Then what's to forget?"

"Huh?"

"You told me to forget about it."

"No, no. That's not what I meant. That's just a phrase us Humans use whenever we want to change the subject of a conversation."

"I see...." Semhek said, nodding his head as if he understood. "You're more eager to talk about the Simulation's race course, because you did not forget your name after Death-Shock."

Jack gave a defeated sigh as he turn from the little furry Tekwhaan to Zubkov, who could barely contain his own laughter. "That's right," he said. "I did not forget my name."

"So your name isn't Jack?" Semhek asked once more, as if to make certain the confused Human hadn't forgot his own name.

Jack hesitated for a moment, but then thought, who the fuck cares anyway.

"No. My name's...Puppycock."

A soft snicker could be heard escaping through the big Russian's lips which was already tightly pursed.

Ford chuckled out loud, succumbing to her own ticklish fit.

Semhek spun around and stared dubiously at the two laughing Humans. He was obviously at a loss for what had transpired. "Is something the matter?"

"No sir," said Jack. "Everything's fine."

Both Ford and Zubkov burst out laughing; louder this time.

"Just ignore them," Jack said, warming up to the humor of the moment. He realized the Tekwhaan's childish ignorance was cause for amusement as well. "What did you want to know about the race?"

"Our sequence patterns," Semhek said. "How could you have known what they were? How could you have known the precise moment the program changed its own firing patterns? And more importantly, how could you have possibly known what our next patterns should be?"

"For each of us," the big Russian added. "I didn't," replied Jack.

"What?" Semhek found this hard to believe. "It's impossible not to know your sequence and still make it through the course, unless---" he paused when the sudden thought occurred to him. "Unless they were already uploaded to your fighter-pod's computers. That's the only way. I know your file, Puppycock. You don't even know your own Symbiot well enough to fly together. And you struggled to keep up with us on the ship....So tell me...." he rose slowly off the floor with his anti-grav boots until his furry head came close to Jack's face. He grimaced in what could've either been a smile, or a snare. "This was all Tytron's doing, wasn't it?"

"Tytron had nothing to do with it," said Jack, matching the creature's intense stare.

"So how'd you do it?"

"I learned the course."

The little Tekwhaan gave a throaty kind of snort while his paralyzed arm dangled freely at his side. "Lies!"

"It's a very simple thing," Jack spoke quickly, cutting off the Drone leader. "It's an old trick I learned back on Earth, while navigating through our skyways. Most people pay attention to what's in front and behind them. There're many different lanes and traffic signs, programmed to dictate their movements, sort of like your Simulations and your pre-programmed sequences to help you navigate through the course. These sequences, just like Earth's skyways, lanes, and traffic signs, are your safety-net. Take them away, or simply change them, and chaos will soon follow.

"But on the other hand, if you could imagine a sky-way without such safetynets, where the traffic flows freely, you'll see each pilot reacting to the overall flow of the traffic, and not what's ahead, or behind them. The flow of traffic becomes much faster, since there aren't any signs to say when to stop or slow down. Turns become more spontaneous as obstacles and collisions are anticipated much further up ahead; each pilot reacting to the other until the very flow of traffic becomes a naturally flowing thing, like a stream, and the roads and signs are no longer necessary. In the absence of these programmed routes to guide and dictate the flow of traffic, all vehicles in the air may resemble a flock of birds, or better yet, a swarm of bees, where the collective mass functions as a single unit no matter what stands in their way....This is how I'm able to manually navigate our skyways."

"By breaking your city's traffic laws?" Zubkov asked, attempting to tease his Human comrade.

"That all sounds feasible on Earth, Puppycock," Semhek said. "Humans do make good pilots. I said so myself. But harmlessly navigating through a road, and dodging your enemy's rapid bursts of laser fire, are two different things."

"It is," Jack admitted. "Call it a trained eye if you must; but my mind's still able to recognize the gaps in your flight patterns in the midst of enemy fire as naturally---and instantly---as you would recognize a table upon first entering a crowded room. Each sequence of fire was programmed to anticipate where your fighter-pod should be. I simply gave you a sequence that follows a path where the enemy's fire would not."

"And you recognized this the instant we first entered the course?" Semhek asked.

"No," said Jack. "Only when the program began to readjust, and a visible change in your flight patterns became noticeable. It was easy to send each of you a new set of coordinates from there."

"Like a swarm of bees," Zubkov said. "Parting to avoid a flying fist."

"All while not crashing into each other," Ford added.

"Now you're getting it," said Jack. "Birds and insects that fly naturally, don't follow any traffic signs and patterns. They use their instincts."

"We have birds and such things on our world too, Puppycock," Semhek said. "Are you saying, that by sheer instincts alone, you led us through that course?"

"Yes," said Jack. "I didn't follow any patterns or sequences (which the Simulation expected I would), I simply used them, by creating my own to get us through."

"You'll be very useful to us then," Semhek said, finally feeling satisfied that Jack's claims were authentic enough. He extended a good arm until his furry paw pressed gently on Jack's armored chest---a Tekwhaan gesture of respect. "I welcome you to the rest of our squadron. There's 7 of us in all...You've already met your Human friends---the best Drone pilots in the galaxy. Now it's time you meet the others." The little Tekwhaan turned, then floated right over Zubkov---still laying on his cot while the big Russian followed him with his eyes as he made a gentle landing across the room where the other Drones were.

"This shit is for real...right?" Jack asked, in a low voice, once the Drone leader was out of ear shot.

Both Ford and Zubkov shared his dilemma with subtle nods of their own. Their grave expressions assured him it was neither dream nor Simulation, but as real as whatever life he lived back on Earth.

"We're not on Earth anymore, Jack," Zubkov said. "Human rules don't apply here. Size don't matter. And the only thing keeping us in one piece, is our armor....You were just now talking about bees, and natural instincts. Well, I advise you to start converting some of those natural instincts to your everyday life, right away. You'll need it, if you wish to continue living."

"Yeah," said Jack, in a dreary tone. He saw that Semhek had spoken to the other Drones, and they were all now looking at him from across the room. One had four unblinking eyes and huge bat-like ears sticking out from the sides of its head. "Thanks for the advice," he said, rising up from the cot. "I have to go meet the rest of the squadron. Be back in a jiffy."

At 7 1/2 feet tall, the four-eyed, bat-eared Drone, was much taller up close. It's rough, dark skin, appeared gray under the dorm's bright lights. It had a bald head and a low-brimming brow, where four dark eyes sat beneath. Two almond-shaped holes served as its nostrils, and a horse-shoe of a frown formed its lipless mouth.

The other Drone was closer to Jack's height, and less strange in appearance. It had a long pear-shaped head, completely covered in black closecropped fur. Between its two big red eyes, a long flat stem of a nose stretched down, broadening at the base just above a wide mouth, hidden under its own fur. If it had any ears, they were hidden from sight as well.

"Meet Ghan," Semhek said, coming between Jack and the tall Drone. "He's a Lannsillion, from one of the dark worlds, in the 4th Quadrant's Ghoric Sector, called Lann. He flew as fighter 2, and he also accompanied us on the ship during the Sim'."

"You served us well, Puppycock," said Ghan, in a deep, throaty voice. He shot a long arm out that touched Jack's chest with spindly fingers. "It's a comfort in knowing you'll be flying with us from now on."

"Thank you," Jack replied. He reached out hesitantly and palmed the Lannsillion's chest, uncertain of whether he was performing the correct gesture in return. "It's good to finally be amongst friends."

The Lannsillion looked down at him with its four eyes (two of them blinking independently) then gave a solemn nod. One of his big ears twitched, as if hearing a distant noise.

"And this here's Meerk," Semhek said, turning to the black furry Drone. "He's a Gamlarrian, from one of the better known worlds throughout our quadrant, called Gamlarr home of the exotic, and enchanting, Shaapkrot." He said these last words with reverent flare, as if describing a fruit, in which the very thought of its sweetness evoked the warmest emotions.

The husky Gamlarrian hopped just a few steps---dragging his paralyzed leg along---to meet Jack's chest with a chubby hand. "Nice flying, Puppycock," he said, exposing a pink tongue, and a neat row of brown teeth. "We wouldn't have made it to the worm-hole without you."

"Thank you, Meerk," Jack said, touching the Gamlarrian's armored chest. He couldn't help but notice how much the Drone resembled one of Earth's gorillas. Though they stood about the same height, Meerk's body was broad and wide, which bespoke of the creature's great strength outside of its own armor.

"Semhek says that you can fly through just about anything," said Ghan. "That's right," said Meerk. "And that you're invincible in the face of enemy fire."

"Uhh...." Jack didn't know how to respond. He stole a glance toward the little Tekwhaan, who looked as sure of his assertions as he was sure of his own age.

"They say that you fly like it's your second nature," Meerk went on, with mounting excitement. Out of the three Drones, he showed the most enthusiasm. "They say you can fly right up to the bridge of any warship and shoot the AI right in its face."

"Uhh...not exactly," Jack began to say, but the animated Gamlarrian wasn't having any of it.

"Your modesty's not welcomed here," Meerk said. He gave a vigorous shake of his long head. "That's why Tytron brought you here, all the way from Earth; you're the answer to the Seezhukan's secret weapon."

"Getting your head blown off is hardly an answer to anything," came the sudden, raspy voice, from a drone walking up behind them. It had a fat round face, and scaly dark-blue skin. A crested fin arched all the way to the back of its head from where straggly brown fur fell like long hair. It had two black beady eyes in the middle of its face, just slightly above a thin line of a nose that slid sideways; and when it spoke, its mouth opened laterally to expose sharp piranha-like teeth. It appeared to Jack as a cross between a walrus and shark.

"Braak!" The drone leader was pleased to see the creature was up on its feet again. Braak was the first to recover from death-shock, though both of his legs had suffered from paralytic shock as well. For the past few hours, he'd laid silently on his cot. But now, it seems he was also the first to recover from his paralysis. "The pessimistic Taaschlon, from the watery world of the 4th 'Quadrant's Haleon Sector, known as Taas. It seems you've already read up on Puppycock's file."

"I have," Braak said, pushing his webbed hand on Jack's chest. "His symbiot did all the work."

"As did all of our symbiots when we first became drones," Semhek replied. "So he didn't do anything," Break shot back. "He wasn't under any kind of combative stress. He had all the time in the universe to play around with patterns and sequences in his mind."

This new bit of information seemed to dampen Meerk's excitement, as well as dissolve some of Ghaan's admiration. However, it did nothing to change Semhek's initial assessments of the new Cadet. "You've once again failed to see the potential of a situation, Braak," he said, in a calm, but lecturing tone. "It's the most common short-coming among your race: depth, perception, insight. Without these, you'll never realize that the Human did this on his own---without Klidaan's help. And had he flown with him, he might've achieved more, for it is the Symbiot that enhances the abilities of his host. Had you kept this in mind, you would've realized that what Jack displayed was only a fraction of, his talents."

It was obvious "the obstinate Braak had received similar chastisements from the Drone leader in the past. But it was equally obvious that he often dismissed Semhek's lecturing as Tewhaan rubbish. He did so now, brushing Semhek's comments aside. "What good is all that fancy flying against those new droids that killed us all? Even you, Semhek, with all your skill, was the first die."

None could respond with a suitable answer to Braak's question.

Even Semhek was forced to admit that the cynical Tasschlon did indeed have a point, for he himself struggled with this problem in his own private thoughts.

The floor under their feet jerked to a sudden lurch, and the walls began to sink as the entire dorm began to rise up to the ceiling. And as the ceiling split apart to reveal a patient Tytron, staring down at them below, they all got the notion that the solution to their new problem would soon come.

CHAPTER
TWENTY-ONE

THE ENTIRE DORM rose up into a much larger (but less bright) room. The drones found themselves surrounded by an assortment of weapons ranging from pistols, rifles, cannons, mech-suits, and armored plates of various classes, sitting on long rows of racks and shelves. The faint 'twang' of laser-fire could be heard somewhere in the distance, perhaps in an adjoining room where a firing range or training grounds were kept.

A composed Tytron now stood before them; quite different from the stern drone instructor who had briefed them in the Simulation Chambers. With his arms folded, he kept a rigid posture that warned that strict silence must be observed. He swept a resolute stare across their scant, beaten numbers, indifferent to the brutal defeat they suffered. He ignored the anxious, expectant looks they all gave in return, because now, while laying paralyzed on their cots, they appeared more helpless than ever. He would allow them to wallow in their defeat for as long as they could. He wanted that helpless feeling to sink deep down into the marrow of their bones (or cartilage) until they believed their entire way of life, their planets, the Quadrant, or even the whole galaxy for that matter, was lost.

For as long as these short moments would allow, Tytron would give them nothing. Let the seconds tick by with the uncertainty of their futures dangling from the brittle stern of their thoughts. The reality of the encroaching peril must build and grow with each passing moment. It must consume the entire room; shroud the most advanced weapons in their possession in a blinding fog of futility and despair. He wanted it to grow and become more frightening than the enemy.

Such a developed and ripe moment was all the motivation they would ever need. It would fuel their drives to win at any cost.

In the next few seconds, it will combine their convictions and purpose into one single cause. In another moment, their fears will evaporate. The fog of uncertainty dispersed by the winds of determination. And only when such a moment had passed, did Tytron decide to speak.

"Over the last century," the Drone Instructor began. His amplified voice filled the entire room. "There've been a series of events taking place in a tiny Sector along the outer reaches of the 2nd Quadrant. This Sector, is called the Plogg Sector. And with the exception of a few Stendaaran and Fruxsan generals, it is virtually unknown by anyone else outside of this room."

From the palm of Tytron's leathery hand, a green holographic orb appeared, blowing up to the size of a beach bell. Within it, floated bright yellow spheres, like glowing lemons, surrounded by dozens of pebble-sized planets drifting slowly around to the beat of their own cosmic waltz. "This is the Plogg Sector," he said, standing beside the floating hologram. The bright display reflected off his face with a greenish sheen. "It is found near the rim of the Balghun Cluster; and as you can see, it consists of 515 yellow stars, and spans 8 light-years in diameter. This Sector, had been a province of the Seezhukan Regality for many millennia, but was highly ignored due to its remoteness and lack of resources.

"Because of the Balghun Cluster's high levels of radiation, the barren worlds were ideal for the early AI pioneers who settled there. Within just a few centuries, the worlds grew and flourished while drawing little attention to the Regality. Thus, developing their own sense of sovereignty beneath the sovereign wings that were already spanning over the entire Quadrant. For many millennia, this tiny Sector functioned as an empire, enjoying the freedoms under its own self governance.

"That is...until the great war between the 1st and 2nd Quadrants began....Without adequate protection from the Regality, the Plogg Sector was one of the first Sectors to fall under the mighty power of the Drofh. For centuries, the worlds of the Sector suffered under the foreign rule and occupation.

"It wasn't until 500 years ago that our Quadrant entered the war, fearing the Drofh would seek to conquer the entire galaxy once more....In an effort to consolidate their forces, the Drofh began abandoning their garrisons within the 2nd Quadrant's Clusters and Sectors, for they served no, strategically advantage. The Plogg Sector was one of these Sectors, filled with worlds whose citizens longed for the days of freedoms they once enjoyed.

"With so little Drofh forces remaining to oversee, and sufficiently rule the worlds, small pockets of resistance and rebellions were left to grow unchecked. Soon, entire syndicates and rebel armies were being formed, and before the Drofh knew what hit them, it was already too late. One by one, these garrisoned realms fell as the citizens began to reclaim their worlds until more than half of the entire Sector was liberated....Though the Drofh did manage to regain some of their lost possessions, they were never able to re-conquer the other half of the militarized Sector without engaging in a full-scale war, which...in the eyes of the Drofh....would be a fruitless waste of resources, since (other than being base trophies) their worlds had never served any real purpose to them in the first place.

"So, this is where we are today---in respects to the Plogg Sector. And according to reports from our latest intelligence, something else of great importance is beginning to brew within this tiny empire of a Sector. Some of the newly liberated worlds, now controlled and governed by the powerful syndicates that rose to power during the past century's rebellions are beginning to secede from the Seezhukan Regality altogether."

Using his own implant, Tytron caused one of the hologram's stars to inflate to the size of a melon. A brown planet, orbited by three obedient moons, made its way slowly around the tranquil sun.

"This is Strong," 'Tytron said, pointing up to the drifting planet. "It's one of the six worlds orbiting this star---the wealthiest in its solar system. It's also the most powerful world in the whole Sector, and one of the first to secede from the Regality....Strong is home to the Sector's most dominant syndicate, called the Kraaglor Front----named after the famous battle within the Kraaglor asteroid field, where the syndicate's called defeated the Drofh near the cuter rims of their solar system.

"The Technician, is a code-name we've attached to a genius serve-bot who designs all of the Regality's warships and battle droids. But over the past two decades, production the Regality has slowed considerably, compared to that of decades and centuries past....Around the same time, the Void appeared in the Bhoolvyn Sector, and it is suspected that the Technician knows why.

"According past intelligence, the Technician had been fervently working on a secret weapon that can literally stop time and destroy the fabric of space....Little else is known of the Technician, but he's our primary source of locating this weapon. It was also suspected that this weapon is what created the Dark Void.

"For many decades, it's been known that the Technician---for his own reasons---withdrew his pledge from the Regality and took up the cause of defending this Sector. It was most likely his innovative design of weapons and droids that aided in so many of the Sector's victories over the Drofh. It is now believed that he's made Strong his new home; and there's no doubt that he's under the protection of the Kraaglor Front. Your mission, is to find this Technician, and bring him back to the Epsilon Eridani Sector to a garrisoned world called Earth."

From where he stood (near the three alien drones) Jack turned to stare across the room where both Ford and Zubkov returned his gaze with surprised expressions of their own. However, he had a strong sense that their thoughts weren't running along the same lines as his. They most likely shared the same concerns that their lowly planet was chosen to harbor the most wanted fugitive in the galaxy. But his mind were skipping across the stream of much simpler thoughts. The fact that his planet, Earth, belonged to a Sector, had never occurred to him. It sent shivers down his spine to know this now; goose bumps reared up and down his arms. The very thought brought a new sense of worth to his own solar system, where only one planet supported life.

The Epsilon Eridani Sector, he thought with pride. He figured if the Epsilon Eridani star was 11 light years from Earth's own sun, then the entire diameter of the Sector--which consisted of ten stars---must stretch across 22 light years; nearly three times larger than the Plogg Sector!

"So that's it then?" Semhek was the first to speak. He sounded disappointed. "We are to enter a star-cluster deep inside the 2nd Quadrant. Then land on a dead planet controlled by AI rouges; kidnap the architect responsible for transforming light years of space-fabric into nothing, where the brightest of the Bhoolvyn Sector's stars vanished. Then bring him back to Earth, before we all die of star-dust radiation, which could be....the instant we leave our fighter-pods....It's one of the best plans I've heard of since becoming a drone for this weaseling of a Quadrant....Yeah....I'm all in, sign me right up."

Jack was taken aback by the Tekwhaan's sarcasm; even the criticism of his own symbiot, and his sentiments, to which all the other drones appeared to be in agreement. He pondered on the word "weaseling", and wondered if it could be some kind of parasitic leech found on the Tekwhaan's home world. He thought he was the only one who rejected the symbiot's invasion. But now, he realized, they all somehow objected to their own symbiot masters in their own way. It was probably why they were chosen to become drones. The Whorganion had once called him a free-man....said he would rather see his own garrisoned Earth destroyed than to live knowing they were slaves. He remembered Nolan saying that men such as himself were snatched off the planet, never to be seen nor heard from again. He now wondered if Semhek, and the other drones, were like him: free men---or aliens. Men and women who'd been snatched off their own home worlds. He wondered if that---the spirit of rebellion----are what all drones were made of.

"We haven't come to the end of our briefing as yet, Cadet," Tytron told Semhek, showing contempt for the Tekwhaan's reckless outburst. "So until you've received all that I have to provide, I advise you to suppress any opinion you feel eager to share."

The Tekwhaan bristled under the command, but he said nothing further.

"Very well then," Tytron said, as he prepared to continue. "As incredibly daunting as this mission might sound, it is a very possible one to carry out. I've carefully studied all of your files, so I know this isn't the most difficult mission that you have taken on for our Regality. Even you, Jack, have solved more difficult cases back on Earth. You were specifically chosen for this mission. Detectives find things, do they not?"

"We do," said Jack.

"Then I have much faith in you, finding the Technician."

"Jack?" Semhek looked up at him with a questioning frown. "So your name is Jack? Was that your name before death-shock? Or is this un alternative from the one in your file? I sense you don't particularly like Puppycock, which is your true name. Is that so?"

Jack gave a grievous sigh at the creature's simpleness. "Yes," he replied, nodding in feigned embarrassment. "I prefer to be called by my alternative name, which is Jack."

"Jack it is then, Semhek said, all too happy to oblige. "And that goes for the rest of our squadron as wall."

"Are you done?" Tytron interrupted.

"Oh. yes sir," the Tekwhaan replied, turning back around to face the instructor. Please, continue."

"As mentioned earlier," Tytron went on. "The Plogg Sector had always maintained their own sovereignty from the rest of the Seezhukan Regality; long before the wars between the Quadrants had even begun. It is governed very differently from the other well known Sectors in the Quadrant who rely more heavily upon the Seezhukan's influence and power. It's the only sector in the Quadrant that hasn't partaken in the war, other than the war to secure their own liberation from the Drofh.

"The worlds that exists in the Plogg Sector haven't been worn down and transformed by war. There aren't any governments wary of visitors entering the Sector's space. These worlds are wholly self sufficient and self governed. You won't have to sneak your way through any check-points and inspections in the Plogg Sector. You can enter Strong as freely as you've entered this planet. No one's going to question your purpose for being on their world, unless, of course, you are of the Drofh....

"The only difficulty in the mission, is locating---then extracting---the Technician. It is only suspected that he's on the planet Strong. However, he could be on any one of the worlds at any given time. But there's a strong possibility we have the right planet, so you'll start on this world, then move on to another if necessary.

"There're many dangers on these lawless worlds. But none more so than this---" Where the holographic display of the yellow star, and planet, shrunk down to the size of a dime, the life-size image of a Guard Droid appeared. The same droid that had killed them all in the Simulation.

To Jack, the droid looked less menacing in the hologram, turning ever so slowly in place. Less so than before, considering the fact that he now had the chance to get a better look at it.

Other than having a wide barrel of a torso, and a praying-mantis's head, the droid's long neck and slender limbs were bone-thin, giving it a more insectoid appearance than anything else.

"What you're looking at," Tytron went on. "Is an AIGD-2381. The latest model of the Technician's guards. It has the most high-tech system of x-ray vision than any of the earlier models, which was why it was still able to see through your disguise. But what makes this droid so different, and more dangerous than the others, is right here---" The droid's midsection was suddenly highlighted, and a red liquidly sphere (like molten lava), floating inside a translucent cube, came into view. "It's a Plasma Generator," he said. "Producing enough plasma to ensure that it stays alive forever. This is what powers its force-field: a photo chromatic window, capable of deflecting virtually anything that's shot in its direction---especially lasers. Regular projectiles, such as bullets, missiles, or rockets, will be incinerated the instant they collide into this kind of shield.

"But as luck would have it, the only element durable enough and capable of penetrating the droid's defenses, is the most plentiful metallic element on our world, Meraach."

"Jhusrot Stone," said Ghan. "The only metallic element that exists nowhere else in the entire galaxy."

"That is correct," Tytron said. "Specially modified rifles, armed with Jhusrot stone, would penetrate any---"

"Wait a second," said Jack. "I have a question." "What is it?" Tytron asked.

"Are those the same metals that make up your precious Jhusrot cube?" "It is." Tytron replied.

"There's one mystery I'd like to know then," Jack said. "Back when I was on Earth, I was tricked into investigating a phony case of a missing Jhusrot that was in the shape of a cube. It was kept in the Whorganions' ship as the most prized possession in the whole galaxy."

"It is," Tytron said.

"So I was told," said Jack. "I was also told that it was the most valuable piece of art ever created."

"It is."

"But how could this be?" Jack asked. "It's just a simple cube. Anyone could take something and form a cube out of it. Even a perfect cube. It don't take an artist (of any kind) to make a simple shape. So what's so special about this cube that stands out from all the other beautiful carvings and sculptures in the galaxy?"

"This is so, Jack," Tytron began. "Because the Jhusrot stones are indestructible. It cannot be formed, molded, or shaped into anything. You could shoot it into the heart of the brightest star, and it would simply come out on the other side as cold and jagged as it always is, and ever will be....Because of its indestructibility, the metal is completely worthless sort of like the rocks and pebbles that cover your Earth....So, how can something that can't even be molten by the heat of the very sun, be shaped into a cure?" Jack was forced to admit he had no answers to that, either.

"This is why the Jhusrot, is the greatest mystery in the Quadrant, as well as a work of art. No force in nature can create such a shape where the dimensions are so precise. Someone had to have created it. And whoever this creator is, must possess enormous power....This is why we cherish it so.

It is just a simple cube, but it also reminds us that a far greater power exists somewhere in our galaxy....Have I answered your question?"

"I think so," Jack said.

"Good," said Tytron. "If you wish to learn more of our galaxy's precious metals and gems, you must consult the archival data of your implant....As I was saying---only a projectile made of Jhusrot can penetrate the 2381-droid's plasma shield. The obvious weak spots of this particular model, are here---" The display of the plasma generator shrunk back into the droid's abdomen as a complete diagram of its anatomy appeared. A thin bony arm was highlighted where a wickedly assembled rifle was joined at the wrist. "This plasma gun is also a part of the droid's arm, so a severance anywhere along the limb would render it partially defenseless, especially here...at the wrist, where an automated valve that controls the flow of plasma is located.

"Another vulnerable spot would be here...directly at the droid's mid-section where the plasma generator is located. With the loss of its main source of power, the droid dies in a matter of seconds."

There seemed to be a collectively inaudible, yet strongly felt sigh of relief among the Cadets upon learning that this formidable droid would be defenseless to the Jhusrot, which would obviously be their only weapon against it.

"These droids were designed by the Technician to be his personal guards," Tytron went on. "They're assigned to protect him, and him only. Wherever he goes, they go. And wherever you happen to see one of these droids, the Technician's certainly nearby. And such droids were reported to have boarded a vessel bound for the Plogg Sector, destined for the planet, Strong."

The hologram of the droid faded away.

A metallic box, the shape and size of a small black book, appeared on Tytron's holographic display. There were no fancy lights, weapons, or gadgets attached to it. It was just a plain, dull-looking thing, more fit to be a paperweight than anything else. So insignificant did it appear, Jack thought it to be a second piece of Jhusrot art.

"This is the Technician," Tytron said, pointing at the hologram.

Loud snorts and grunts of disbelief came from all the Cadets in the room.

A few of them even laughed.

"I advise you not to be fooled by its simple appearance," Tytron said. "The Technician is one of the most clever and powerful machines in the 2nd Quadrant. It is the mind behind the designs of countless warships, droids, destroyers, and not to mention...the Dark Void. It even designed itself, preferring to be nothing more than this solid metal block."

CHAPTER
TWENTY-TWO

FROM THE SNUG cockpit in Jack's fighter-pod, Adellon (Oxlor's smallest moon) appeared like a giant snowball just floating around in space.

This was due to the moon's powdery surface being made up of mostly a white crystalline compound, like calcium carbonate, or chalk. Even the icy caps of its poles were indistinguishable from the fine dust that covered this bleached skull of a moon as it reflected the sun's light with a pearly glow.

As if not wanting to deface the natural beauty of their own lunar satellite, the Oxloraans had constructed just one space-port colony, where everything was made entirely of glass.

Molten from Adellon's own white sand, and reinforced with many layers that formed huge slabs and blocks of windows---some 3 feet in thickness---buildings and structures were made. From space, Adellon's only colony basked in the pretense of remaining untouched out of all of Oxlor's nine moons.

Only upon approaching an atmospheric distance from Adellon's surface do this crystal city of a colony, called Loovenor, suddenly appear with the fleeting glint of a diamond. Its massive dome bubbled protectively around it, yet so clear it appeared weak, fragile...very likely to POP! to a billion shards at the slightest touch.

Only then can the grimy engines that power the mechanical buildings be seen, like bits of rock, frozen in blocks of laboring ice. Citizens---of both the 3rd and 4th Quadrants---filled the see-through floors, oblivious to the stealthy pods that zipped by just moments ago.

In blurs of smudgy yellows and greens, acres of farmland slid under the dome like moss in a hidden creek. But the Jack's pod swooped upward, yanking his view from the crystallized colony below---briefly pushing him back out into space, before dipping down again in a steep dive.

Adellon's white surface came up fast, where a yawning mouth of a hole began to part. It gobbled them up in a single gulp before reclosing itself shut.

Strobes of light stretched for miles to aid them through the complex maze of tunnels that formed the veins, guts, and arteries deep within the dark soil of this white moon. Where Loovenor appeared like the sole bubble of air left remaining on the calm surface in a bowl of milk---these tunnels, with their winding paths and forked passages, appeared to Jack all too much like the subways, sewers, and aqueducts that ran under so many of Earth's cities. However, these systems of tunnels were built on a much larger scale. Whole starships and cargo vessels lumbered lazily through them.

These tunnels were much too wide for their walls, ceilings, and floors to be seen. Whole systems of coded lights were used in order to monitor this beastly flow of traffic, where their fighter-pods appeared like tiny flies drifting amongst lumbering herds of cattle.

He'd once found it strange upon first seeing the so-called spaceport that was nothing but a barren moon where only one colony existed. But now, it all began to make sense to him. The Oxloraans, with all their mechanical genius, had managed to build an entire galactic spaceport, right below the surface of one of their own moons.

They would fly through these tunnels for another 10,000 miles before easing into the shuttle bay of a black beetle-shaped starship, docked at a busy port. Their pods made smooth upright landings---one after the other---at the eastern end of the bay, like a row of lacquered rockets.

As his fighter-pod's cockpit unzipped itself, he thought twice about hopping out on the floor (which he enjoyed doing very much), and allowed the pod's cables to ease him down instead. He suspected his leg still suffered the paralytic shock from their last combat simulation where they battled several AIGD-2381 droids in an open arena. His leg fell limp as he took his first step, but he was still pleased with himself that he hadn't gotten his head blown off this time.

The other drones didn't fare too well, either.

With both of her legs in paralytic shock, Ford resembled the floating ghost of a dead cat as she went adrift (lopsidedly) on her grav-boots while using her armored tail to keep the rest of her body balanced in the air.

One of Zubkov's paralyzed arms fell limp at his side. Braak had taken a blast in his stomach.

Meerk was still nursing his side where a plasma beam had eaten away at most of his ribs.

Only Semhek and Ghaan remained without injury.

Though none of the drones had actually died in the last simulation, it was still frightening to think that he could lose a leg, or an arm, on the mission. The Technician's guards were incredibly swift and agile. They had precise aim, and they dodged incoming fire with primal ease, Only from paired and timed shooting did they fall, attempting to parry one blast while getting shot down by another.

But even though they were no longer invincible, the droids weren't exactly sitting ducks, either. They were still specially trained in armed combat, and they fought, and died, as if they had nothing to lose.

A hovering, driverless vehicle (like a small bus) came down the length of the bay and slowed to a silent stop in front of the Drones. The chrome plating that covered its frame mirrored their haggard faces to near perfection. It made a rapid, honking noise, as it slid open a door to allow them in. At the base of its long body, a curved tube of bluish light flicked and caught Jack's attention.

"I think this is our ride," Semhek said, before entering the floating bus.

One by one, the others filed in, finding their own seats in the semi-lit interior, grateful that at least something had came along to show them out of the bay.

They sat quietly as the bus lurched forward, making, into a sharp u-turn to take them back in the opposite direction.

Out of sheer boredom, Jack looked out the narrow window that ran around the top half of the bus like a dividing strip. With the exception of only a few cyborg aliens he couldn't yet identify, he noticed that most of the life-forms working in the shuttle-bay was mainly made up of Oxloraan and AI machinery.

"Some place, huh?" said Zubkov, from the seat across from him.

In the dark cabin, Jack could see the big Russian smiling. "Yeah," he said. "Never seen anything like it."

"They call it: The Egg," said Ford, sitting next to Zubkov. "A plain ole' looking moon on the outside, that breeds all kinds of mischief and mayhem right under its shell....The Oxloraans figured that if the Seezhukans ever happen to invade this Sector, they might destroy their planet and all of its moons, but they'll simply ignore this one."

Using his implant, Jack pulled up a small holographic diagram of the bus that drove them out of the shuttle bay. Reading the short file, he learned it was an AIPT-856: an Artificially Intelligent Personnel Transport. It was a very old model, the 856th version of its kind....Scrolling down through the voluminous data, he saw that an AIPT-3453, was the Regality's latest model that transported combat droids all throughout the 2nd Quadrant. Next, he switched the diagram to that of the starship they were now in: an AICS-261...a cargo ship, also very old, being a more sleeker AICS-516 was now what's fashionable in the 2nd Quadrant. "These are all defectors of the Seezhukan Regality," Jack said, reading from the data in the hologram.

"You'll soon learn that not all machines are evil," Semhek said, from somewhere in the dark cabin. "Up until 500 years ago, we were at peace with the Seezhukan Regality. This particular ship has been trading with this Sector for well over 1,000 years before the war began. There're many AI who never agreed with the Seezhukan's ways in the first place. And when war between the 1st and 2nd Quadrant broke out, a lot of them fled to different worlds. A lot of them are right here, in the Egg."

"So that's how you manage to enter the 2nd Quadrant to spy on the empire unnoticed," said Jack, with a tint of enlightenment. "You use these kinds of ships to sneak into the Quadrant. An AI would never suspect its own."

"It's not that simple," Semhek said. "A few modifications and updates are always necessary. To thwart the enemy; The Seezhukan's are in a constant mode of change. Upgrades and new modifications are happening all the time.

A cargo ship, such as this one, has long been discontinued and scheduled for demolition. It would never stand up against the scrutiny of a scaninspection.... As drones, it's our sole responsibility to gather the latest updated intelligence on all droids, ships, and fighters. A task we sometimes struggle to keep up with. There're incidents where a team might sneak into the Quadrant in a ship that's three or four models behind, and it gets blown to bits before anyone has time to react."

"So the Egg is the safest place for our friendly AI?" Jack asked.

"They built the place," said Ford. "And without their help, and intelligence, it would've been a very different war. That's why the Oxloraan Sector's the most important Sector in this Quadrant. It's disguised as a major jump-point and trading hub, but this Egg...is the real star of the show. All Drone missions begin somewhere inside here. And without us Drones, the war's lost."

This was the first time that Jack had actually 1oot an AI Machine in real life. The last few Simulations had felt so real, there was hardly any difference between that imaginary world and the one in which he was presently in. "There's something about these machines that are so life-like," he said. "It's as if there're real people living inside them."

"That's because there are," said Ford. "Well...not actual people. Their consciousness. In the everlasting quest to achieve immortality, certain lifeforms in the galaxy have begun to abandon their physical bodies for more durable, mechanical ones. Certain metals can last virtually forever. And if one gets tired living as a droid, he can always transfer his consciousness into a civilian robot. A person can live this way for thousands and thousands of years....perhaps forever."

"Unless they die from an Ion-blast," Zubkov said. "Then they're gone forever. Like the rest of us normal, living things."

"Yeah," said Ford. "They aren't all that immortal. But that's what makes the Seezhukan's so different from the normal AI. Despite their metal bodies and robotic appearance, the Seezhukans still fear death. They're still emotional creatures with wants, and desires, and habits. They still partake in the things they enjoy and find so much pleasure. This is why we still have allies among them---those who don't want war. In a sense, they're still living things, like us."

"They still need our help to maintain them," Zubkov said. "The Oxloraans can keep a bucket a' bolts, like this 1,000 year ship, running for another millennia if they need to. So they have something to gain from our victory as well."

"Stars will explode, and new ones will form before this war's over," said a cynical Ghan. "I hate saying that we might not be here to see such a day."

No one could find argument for the grim truth in the Lansillian's words.

A speechless moment went by as they all fell into their own apprehensive thoughts.

At a leisurely pace (no faster than a bicycle) a mag-bus took them all through the ship's broad passageways. Jack gazed through the window, studying all the different droids and serve-bots that went by. They were old, worn out things, a thousand years older than the old droids in the Simulation's AI warship. Some were in desperate need of repair. Some limped on malfunctioning legs where a pressurized valve, motor, or gear, had long since rotted away. The smaller bots flew by in shaky, sputtering flight-patterns.

The inner hull looked badly rusted in some parts where whole sections had to be removed and newer material were welded on. The entire wall along the corridors were riddled with this kind of patchwork; a thousand years of constant repair and remodeling.

Jack couldn't help but feel he was trapped in the belly of an ancient oil-tanker, broken and washed up on some abandoned beach. Rust and grime had caked up in the corners where the wall met the floor. Some of the wall panels looked warped from age, and bent inward where the welds were the weakest, to expose the narrow gaps in the inner hull.

When the mag-bus finally slowed to a careful stop, it drifted across the passageway to fit snugly into an awaiting compartment, obscuring Jack's view. He could feel the mag-bus being lifted as the floor fell below them. As they rose past each floor, a different scene came into view ever-so-briefly: a cargo bay here, a dark scrap-yard there, a fancy (albeit ancient) robotic plaza that just went by.

The mag-bus settled on the next floor and the door slid open. The drones filed out onto a narrow corridor where a tall, shiny droid stood.

"Welcome, Cadets," the droid said, in a soft melodic voice. It had a box-shaped head that shone like copper under the light. "My name is Kronlore. And I welcome you to our noble ship."

"Greetings, Kronlore," Semhek said, stepping to the front. "It is a pleasure meeting you, and I look forward to us working together on this most vital mission. Unfortunately... the rest of my team have suffered some temporary injuries and they'll need rest to recuperate. If you'll show us to our quarters, we'll Lie most grateful."

"We're very much aware of you paralytic states, Commander," the droid said. "It is why I'm here instead of Commander Draxx. If you'll follow me, we shall take care of those injuries right away." The droid turned just then and headed down the corridor---not bothering to look back to see if they were following close behind.

It led them through the winding halls that made up the higher floors of the ship. It rounded a corner that gave way to a hanging tier, overlooking a long drop to the dark bottom below. About 30 yards up ahead, was a dead-end, where an arched door slid up to allow them into a bright room. It appeared larger than their dorm, though not by much. Along the walls were mechanical boards and instruments where several serve-bots hovered and busied themselves.

From the ceiling, great tubes fell like columns where narrow compartments had been carved out; quite similar to the cockpits of their fighter-pods.

"These are some of our Transplantation Cells," the droid said. "They're used by our serve-bots to switch models once their current machinery are no longer fit for use. The Simulation Chambers on Oxloor were built based on their design. It is how they can upload your consciousness into any file, the same way I can upload mine into any droid. All the components necessary to make your Simulation Chambers function, were designed after everything in our Transplantation Cells---all, except one: a Revival Key. It's used to reboot the machinery once the transplantation's completed, to ensure the consciousness and circuitry are fully harmonized. The transition wouldn't be possible without it. But in the case of your Simulation Chambers, the Oxloraans saw fit to leave this component out."

"They prefer to reboot us back to life, manually," said Ford, still using her mag-boots to keep her paralyzed legs off the floor. "So that way, we can still suffer the effects of trauma without actually dying."

"That's correct," Kronlore said. "For all training purposes, the Oxloraans wanted their Cadets to experience the full aspect of war; the shock of losing a limb, and the pain of dying....Nothing that I, myself, would prescribe---but it's their Sector." His metal shoulders jerked to a kind of shrug, as if to say that things might've been different, had he been in charge. He clicked a stream of robotic commands at the serve-bots who immediately flew into action of preparing the cells.

Before the Drones had a chance to realize what was happening, one of the cells hurried to life, followed closely by all the others to the sound of a throaty, single-toned mantra. Their enclosed compartments awoke with a soft saffron glow.

Through the metal floor, the Cadets could feel the subtle vibration of the cell's power.

Kronlore turned to the drones. "Any one of these would do," he said, left arm bending unnaturally at the elbow to point toward the Cells. "All you have to do is step inside. The Cell's electro-nodes will do the rest."

An inward shiver coursed through Jack's body at the mention of the word 'node'. He'd grown to dislike the feeling---the very thought, even---of anything squirming up through his nose and ears.

But what other choice did he have?

The others were already making their way toward the Cells.

CHAPTER
TWENTY-THREE

IT HAD TAKEN a full week to fully load the cargo ship with precious goods, sent from dozens of Sectors across the two Quadrants.

As it turned out, this particular ship had the only route into the Plogg Sector, and has been making the same runs for the past 800 years.

Still maintaining an expensive taste for the galaxy's finest art and merchandise, the free worlds of the Plogg Sector conducted the most lucrative trade in the whole Quadrant. Precious metals, from the cold dark worlds of Lann and Glibdhar, were still in high demand there. So too, are the rubbery Stendaaran cloths, and the fluffy Ollsannian fabrics. An entire uninhabited forest-world, known as Thrann, in the 4th Quadrant, had once been chopped clean of its durable rockwood, to supply the millions of carvers and sculptors throughout the entire Plogg Sector.

But none of these were in higher demand than robotic body parts.

Lacking the artistic vision and creativity of a being with a normal, fleshy brain, the AI have to rely on the speed and power of their processors and circuitry to mimic the beauty of the natural world around them. As a disappointing result, their paintings and innovations are mediocre at best.

Upgrades and modifications of their robotic form and figure differed ever so-slightly.

Thus, if a bot desired a multi-purpose arm, or leg, to match the design of its original body, it would have to seek out the mechanical genius of an Oxloraan engineer, or a Rhackloon technician, and not some Seezhukan golem who hadn't sparked an original thought in 10,000 years.

Huge house-sized crates were packed so tight in the ship's cargo-my, a man could barely fit between the narrow aisles. Each crate contained a different shipment of fancy robotic part---wings even. But none more so than the exotically designed robotic heads; the most popular feature on any body (flesh or metal), that were in such high demand. Such crates, or "Headcrates"---as they were called---made up the most of any shipment destined for the Plogg Sector. From the one-band Cyclops, to the six-eyed arachnoids.

Those with oval-shaped, squared, or triangular heads. From automated mouths, to the those with long bands of blinking lights. Jaws, chins, cheeks, and foreheads of all shapes and sizes. Big ears, small ears, to none at all. Metal, plastic, or silicon, to give the appearance of living tissue. They were all mixed in infinite numbers of combinations to mimic the look of the most beautiful creatures in the galaxy.

The cargo-ship wobbled slowly as the latch-mechanism released its hold from the docking port. Like a dead whale, it drifted away, using the momentum of its own weight to clear the wall of the great tunnel before turning around and heading in the opposite direction. At 200 mph, it cruised the lanes, navigating the complex maze inside the Egg. It rushed through the straighter, wider lanes, that reached down to the moon's mantel, rounding its outer core before shooting back up toward the surface.

There are no crystal colonies on the dark side of this white moon. Just the faintest light that would occasionally flash at the base of a shrouded canyon. Every once in a while, great doors may part open there---deep down in that gorge---causing a mile-wide beam of light to shoot up through the darkness, briefly illuminating the canyon's magnificent cliffs and edges as if the mouth of a sleeping god had suddenly yawned.

But alas! The void, soundless space...!

View in silence...the bow of this gargantuan ship, leaping from the gullet of the canyon with lightning speed! A blinding flash! The thrust of its powerful engines, violently spewing flames and massive plumes of moon-dust in all directions. All without the slightest sound! And long before the great gates close and the lights that revealed the canyon are covered, the ship would already be in deep space. Long before the stirred clouds of moon-dust settles. Long before that, it'll make the jump---emerging some minutes later in the Plogg Sector.

In a star-cluster, where several nebulae twirl together in a colorful spectrum of interstellar dust, space...is no longer dark.

In every direction all around, bright radioactive gas form a stunning display of merging blues, pinks, purples, reds, yellows, and greens. It provided the illusion of having a solid background, a colorful wall within a sphere. A breathable atmosphere even. It brought the illusory feeling of terrestrial gravity that whole starships may fall, forever, if they ever ran out of fuel.

Great explosions, powerful enough to destroy entire worlds, happen frequently beyond a fog of pink and green stardust. It was an awesome site, both frightening and strange; nauseating even...but...it was still space.

Jack was laying in his own quarters when the ship came out of its jump and the sudden brightness shone through his window. He never saw anything like it.

He stood at the porthole for a long time, trying to make sense of what he was actually seeing. His mind was too used to the blackness of space---he understood that---but this... this was something else. It overwhelmed his senses. The world, that wasn't even his world, had became too strange.

His stomach turned.

He felt dizzy.

He left the window....

'The Plogg Sector's inhospitable to all organic life-forms,' Klidaan said. 'If you're trying to make me feel better,' Jack said to the Symbiot.

'You're not.'

'I wasn't trying to make you feel better. You're body's reacting to an unknown environment. I was simply explaining why. But if you want me to make you feel better, I can always do this---'

Jack gasped as the sudden rush of endorphins entered his brain, giving him the pleasurable feeling of bliss. He relished in the tender euphoria it brought. 'Thank you,' he said. 'Now that feels better.'

Anything else you would like to know about the Plogg Sector?'

'Other than the radiation and what I'm seeing out there...? No....Just lemmie' sit here and relax a while.'

'I don't think you have much time for that, either.'

'What? What are you talking about?'

A translucent, holographic display suddenly appeared before him. The highlighted message reminded him that it was the last day of training.

'Wasn't that yesterday?'

'Today is yesterday.'

'But how---' He paused, then shook his head in frustration. He still hadn't fully learned the paradox of time in space travel. It would take an ordinary Earth-ship (with no warp-drive) thousands of years to reach the Oxloraan Sector. A million years might've flown by before it entered the Plogg Sector. By that time, the war would be over, and the Seezhukans would be ruling the galaxy.

But (luckily) other life-forms in our Quadrant had long overcame this problem, traveling so fast through space and time, they occasionally jumped back a few days in the past. It was the closest, and safest, calculations that ensured one wasn't too late for anything when jumping back into the older Quadrants.

'Never mind,' he thought. 'Just get that stuff outta my head....I can't think straight.'

'Okay---'

The flow of endorphins stopped. Jack's high slowly began coming down....

The other Drones already assembled in the Training Hall by the time Jack showed up. Draxx, their AI-Commanding Officer, was also the Chief Intelligence Officer of the Plogg Sector mission---a very charismatic droid. Over the last few days, it was he who trained and prepared them for life on the planet, Strong. He briefed them on the planet's customs and traditions. Detailed information on all the planet's syndicates were uploaded into their implants. So were scores of detailed maps of all the Sector's free worlds.

Jack fell in at the end of the line---next to Meerk---where the rest of the Drones had assembled. There seemed to have been an important speech in progress before he arrived, because Draxx had been staring disapprovingly at him from the moment he entered the room. The droid did so now, while the other Drones held their gazes forward.

"You're late' said Draxx, in a very flat, synthesized voice.

"I thought yesterday was our final meeting before the mission," Jack said.

"That Is today."

"Yes sir....that is today. My mistake. I got confused by the jump."

"That much is obvious, Puppycock," the droid snapped. "Anyone absent-minded enough not to consult their ship's readings after a jump, would lose track of time. Or do you think your Human brain's that much evolved to make such calculations on its own?"

"No sir."

"It's mistakes like these that can put your entire team at risk. You're late for our exercise---you might've well been late for an important rendezvous. Or late to rescue one of your dear friends. Do you see where I'm going with this, Puppycock?"

"Yes, sir. I'll never be late for anything else again."

"For you and your team's sake, I hope so. And I hope you realize that we're pressed for time by your lateness." Draxx didn't bother to wait for Jack's apology, so he continued. "As

I was saying. Your current armor will be of no use to you anywhere in this Sector. The high levels of radiation would eat right through those flimsy suits and cook you alive the instant you set foot on the planet. A new set of armor have been specially designed for you instead. "He summoned a bright holographic display and tapped in some commands on the screen. Seven metallic suits materialized beside him a few seconds later.

Unlike the Drones' current armor, which consisted of billions of nano machines, these suits carried big metal plates that sectioned off where a biped creature's joints should be. They looked more solid in appearance, but less mobile, with armor of the darkest gray. They were smooth, bulky, and round, but not sleek. They had big hands, with 7 flexible digits, and big feet and arms built for strength, but not speed. Their helmets were round, but oval-shaped, with a thin band of blue light stretching across their foreheads for vision. Because they lacked the jaw-mechanism of some droids, a rectangular patch of yellow light sat just below their thin blue visors, where some kind of nose should've been, but served as a mouth instead.

They looked old, and worn---with rust and dents in many places---as if they'd spent centuries locked away in a dark closet. Like everything else on the ship, they were ugly, ancient things of a long bygone era....Very unlike the class-3 armored suits the Drones were so used to.

"This is Armor-Zero," Draxx went on. "Made from some of the most durable metals in our galaxy. It is 100% air-proof, and will keep the Sector's harmful radiation out as long as you have it on. Armor-Zero's fashioned after the most commonly known droid throughout the Plogg

Sector: a nomadic tribe of bots, called the Omegon. They're indigenous to the Sector...one of the original tribes that first settled here, but are now considered the lowest tribe-bots of Strong and are mostly ignored in the world's advanced society--which is perfect for your disguise."

"If we wish to remain inconspicuous, you mean?" Jack asked, with a troubled frown.

"Precisely so, Puppycock," Draxx replied. "You'll be able to walk through any of the Sector's worlds virtually unnoticed."

Jack shook his head with a low, derisive snort.

Draxx paused. "Is something the matter?"

"It's the worst disguise," Jack simply blurted it out, causing the others to turn and shoot foreboding looks at him....

"The worst disguise?" said Draxx, seemingly amused. Perhaps at Jack's ignorance with such matters. "How so, Puppycock?"

"We're in pursuit of the most protected bot in the whole Sector," Jack began. "Surely, if he chose to hide in dumpster...then these...Omegon things might be the perfect disguise. But this is never the case with V.I.Ps."

"With what?" Draxx asked.

"Never mind," said Jack. He noticed that both Ford and Zubkov had already caught on to the point he was trying to make. The others, however, appeared lost. They were too accustomed to switching to different disguises at will, which made most of their missions relatively easy. But this was different.

This mission relied more on the cunning masquerade of infiltration, than on one disguise, which they were to be the outcast in a highly developed society. "It's a Human thing."

"A Human thing?" said Draxx, but this time, his tone changed He appeared more interested in what Jack had to say.

"I've dealt with cases like this all the time on Earth. And I tell you, if the Omegon are indigenous as you say, we'll be very noticeable in the places where we need to be. In the midst of kings, lords, and whatever else you call your celebrities this far out in the galaxy, we'll stand out like 7 sore thumbs....While this disguise might assure that our covers won't be blown, it also asserts that we wouldn't get 1,000 yards of the Technician without being subjected to intense scrutiny....But I guess you haven't thought of everything."

The droid made a weird sound through his vocalizer that could've been a laugh, or a snort. He stalked slowly down the length of the lined Drones ignoring all, before finally coming to Jack. He leaned in close. "And how could you be so sure that we haven't thought of everything, Puppycock?" His voice was now soft, conspiratorial.

"You couldn't possible have known everything if you chose that disguise for us," Jack replied. "We'll have a very hard time getting close to the Technician dressed like bums."

"Like what?"

"Forget it."

"Forget what?"

"It's a Human saying, Commander Draxx," Semhek was all too glad to offer. "It's what the Humans say whenever the subject of their conversations need to be changed...." He looked over at Jack for approval. "Am I correct in this?"

"Yeah," said Jack, with a patient sigh. "That is correct."

"I think I get your point, Puppycock," Draxx went on, choosing not to acknowledge neither the Human's nor the Tekwhaan's custom of dialect. He continued to address Jack's presumptuous assertion. "You're worried that your lowly status might inhibit you from finding the Technician."

"Yes," Jack replied. "The mission may already be a failure because of it."

"Do you even know where the Technician is, Puppycock'?"

"No. None of us do."

That same weird noise came from the droid's vocalizer again.

He leaned away from Jack, and began to head the other way. "General Morlaak, was right about you, Puppycock," he said, over his shoulder. "You do have the instincts needed to find the Technician; which is why he made you Drone-leader for this mission. But you lack the proper insight....I assure you though---your disguise is most suitable for the mission. And you'll realize this once you meet your contacts on the ground---or have you already met them?"

Jack sighed again; an inaudible, but weary gesture, despite the fact that he was made Drone Commander of the mission. "No."

"It seems, Puppycock. That it is you, who haven't thought of everything....Up until 10 days ago, you've never left your own solar-system. Yet, you wish to instruct me on matters far removed from your own understanding.... Regardless of what the General thinks of you, Puppycock. If you come to such hasty conclusions in the future, you might not be able to leave Strong, alive. So I advise you now, to put more trust in the wisdom of your leaders. It may very well save your life."

It was something Jack was used to hearing from his own superiors on Earth. And such speeches were often boring---as it was now. He simply nodded, but said nothing further.

"As I was saying," Draxx went on. "Armor-Zero's designed after the oldest tribe in this Sector. It was even made to look old; but this where the comparison stops. Like the AIGD-2381, its completely coated in a special photochromatic film, making it impervious to all laser fire. Like your class-3 armored suits, it has powerful magnetic boots that allows you to reverse gravity if you desire. Its equipped with both infrared and x-ray vision inside your helmet's visors. Each unit is specially built to suit its Drone, and responds through a direct link connected to your implant.

Every function is yours at a mere thought. There's also another added feature to this unit which is very unlikely to be found on any tribe-rot in this Sector---it is here...."

Draxx made a few steps to the nearest bot and placed a hand gently on its stomach where a fist-sized circle glowed in a soft red light. There, a hidden compartment snapped open to expose a deadly gun nestled inside.

The droid reached in and took the weapon; it was so big it could barely fit in his hand. "Unlike the models you're accustomed to on Oxlor," he said, heaving the big pistol with both hands. "This Jhusrot auto-pistol is specifically designed for Amor-Zero. It uses a rapid 5-round burst to shoot high velocity Jhusrot cluster-rounds. And as you can see "He fumbled at the pistol's banana-sized trigger, trying with all his strength to squeeze it back just a fraction of an inch, but no more. "As you can see, I'm unable to fire the weapon....This is so, because the pistol's handle and trigger are fitted with sensitive grooves that'll only respond to the matching indents in the Omegon's palm. Two fingers, placed here, at the center of the trigger, are all that's required to make it fire."

Draxx pushed the awesome pistol back into it secret place and the compartment slapped itself shut with a muffled clap. He then moved to the bot's side and touched gently, as before, just behind its lower back, pulling what could've been half of a small bazooka. It was only when he crossed to the other side of the bot to extract the other half and snapped the two parts together, could the vicious weapon be seen in full display.

It was all black, perhaps five feet long and 300lbs, with a long line of red dots that ran along the length of its barrel. Sitting directly above the hooked stalk, was a long tubular scope where a fine red beam shot across the room.

"The assembly should be done much quicker by you of course," said Draxx, cradling the weapon in his arms. "This is your long-range Jhusrot rifle, capable of firing compact, high velocity Jhusrot rounds up to three miles. All the functions are the same as the pistol's, and if ever you do use this weapon, the enemy won't know what hit him." He snapped the rifle back in half and replaced them back into their respective slots.

"Your current suits are of no use to you in this Sector," Draxx said. He pulled up another holographic display and tapped a command that caused each of their class-3 armor to whither from their bodies like blown dust.

"Heyyy!" Ford was the first to protest as she stood there in her little naked body. "It's freaking cold in here!"

The others were equally astonished at the suddenness of their denudement, but could do very little in the face of their plight. Their protective armor was gone. And that was that.

They were all stripped bare, save for the identical collars clasped around their necks.

Jack, however, was more amazed at how light the gravity felt inside the ship. Possibly to compensate for the heavy, metal droids living on it. Or maybe the droids didn't have much need for gravity, other than for keeping things on the floor.

"Whether you approve of this, or not," said Draxx, to the naked Drones. "Amor-Zero's the only thing that can keep you alive in this Sector. Once you leave this ship, you can never return, unless---of course---you bring the Technician back with you."

CHAPTER
TWENTY-FOUR

FOR THE PAST 5,000 years, the Omegon tribe-bot named Jaanloch, had been one of the wealthiest space merchants in the entire 2nd Quadrant. Way back then, his fleet of cargo ships handled most of the Quadrant's contracts hauling millions of commercial freight from one Sector to the other. His line of AICS-26ls were well known throughout the whole galaxy. They enjoyed free admittance to any Quadrant; to any Sector; to any world. They were the post-stamp of galactic freighting.

But all that changed when the war began. In one swift, treacherous move, the Drofh seized control of the Quadrant.

An equally swift revolt saw the defeat of the Drofh invaders on the planet, Seezhuk, and other powerful worlds in the Imperial Sector---restoring the Regality. At least, on the outside.

The old Regality's dead! And Jaanloch knows this for a fact....It had died when the Drofh first invaded.

Whatever rebel force that defeated the Drofh in the first war, had somehow taken over. The emperor, and his entire line, had all been wiped out during that war....Imposters now ruled in their place.... Imposters!

Rumor had it that the whole Drofh invasion was just a clever diversion to cover up the real plot on the emperor's throne....Why else would a revolt be over in less than two years, and this...this...mess they have with other Quadrants, be going on for over 500 years? Why else would the emperor declare that his line of ships-that had served the galaxy in good faith for so long an enemy of the Quadrant, then order that his entire fleet to be demolished? Why had so many fled the Quadrant since then, to hide in the core of Oxloraan moons, and other remote Sectors all over the galaxy?

Because the emperor's dead! That's why....Impostors now rule in his place.

This old, beetle-shaped cargo ship, was all that he had left in the Universe. The Plogg Sector was the only place in the 2nd Quadrant he can still call home. The AICS-261 (though the only model of its kind left in the Sector) is still the "King of Freighter" here. Still the fastest, most reliable, most trusted freighter in town. The only cargo ship willing to stand up against the new Regality, while dutifully delivering goods to the citizens of the Sector.

They were all enemies of the Quadrant now---rebels, in their own little way. New things were happening on worlds like Strong, Chramonga, and Claan. Syndicates were merging. New rulers were coming into power on other worlds. Whole Sectors, outside the 2nd Quadrant, such as Oxlor and Dhalkroon, have been coming to their aid for centuries. They all recognized exactly what kind of revolution was taking place. They all saw---as he did---that the Plogg Sector was the future of the 2nd Quadrant.

"No one cared about Strong when we first came here," Jaanloch said to the drones. They were all seated in the magbus that drove them through the lower levels of his ship. A large hooded cape hid most of his head, so the blue light of his eyes threw a dim cyanic haze before him in the dark cab. "This Sector's at the very tip of the Regality's reach; it was the only place we could've went and established what we have now. We were free here. We were nothing but outcasts anywhere else. They didn't care if we died out here. But then things started happening once our towns and cities began to flourish. Outlaws, from other worlds throughout the Quadrant were coming here to escape whatever authorities that had set bounties on them. Then the Merchants soon followed."

He paused here and tapped twice on the back of his big hand, flipping it over as a triangular hologram floated up from his palm. A finger nipped it at the corner and it spun like a top. When it slowed down, a strange symbol appeared in the palms of a warped two hands gripping possessively at each end.

Jack thought it resembled two hands sharing a boomerang.

"Here are your Merchant Keys," Jaanloch said. He gave the relic a light nudge with his finger, causing it to drift from his palm, to the center of the dark cab where it made seven exact copies of itself---one for each drone. "They'll ensure your admittance into the cities. And in the event you should leave Strong for another world, you'll need them there as well. You'll find that the simplest of things are the most handy."

Jack watched as one of the rotating holograms float gracefully to where he sat and found his palm---even though he sat with his fists closed---slipping in between the furrows of his fingers. For an instant, he thought he could feel his armor reacting to the new information.

The mag-bus was slowing down. Jaanloch leaned back to look out the window. "We're here," he said. His head rolled on his shoulders like a loose nut to address the drones once more. "The keys have been uploaded to your implants and shall be available at a moment's thought whenever you need them."

The door slid open.

Bright light from the shuttle-bay spilled into the cab to expose the rust and grime on their armor's metal like festering sores.

The ancient merchant was the last one off the mag-bus. And though they all stood at the same height, he appeared much larger in stature.

Rare, precious jewels, more befitting for a galactic emperor than a lowly tribe-bot, hung from Jaanloch's neck as he strode across the floor of the shuttle-bay at a steady pace. On each of his 7 long fingers were rings, studded with the most priceless gems in the whole galaxy.

Unlike the Drones (following closely behind) his armor was free of dents and rust, and looked polished as it gleamed under the light.

But none of these things stood out more on the wealthy merchant---that bespoke of luxury and elegance---than the red hooded cape that was draped over his shoulders. It was made from a material Jack had never seen before. It appeared thicker and tougher than leather, yet its movements were as graceful and fluid as a shawl's. Though it was covered in fine layers of fur, it was as smooth as silk at the touch. Light as a feather, it fanned majestically behind him as he walked; the large hood billowing over his head like a peeved cobra on the shoulders of a villain.

He rounded a corner where two serve-bots drifted hurriedly out of the way; he swatted at them as if they were pesky flies. He headed down a narrow hallway where a door slid up and the sprawling bridge of another ship lay beyond.

Jaanloch plopped himself down in the captain's seat and made the raspy sound of a lazy bot on the verge of wasteful sleep. He tapped into the control panel before him, and with soft crack, a metal sheet began to slide away from the wide bridge's window. Bright colors of star-dust space poured inside, creeping over the floor and furniture in brilliant waves.

The Merchant leaned back in his seat as if drained from this simple task. He swiveled around, then paused when he noticed the drones, standing dubiously behind him. He might've frowned, if he had the eyebrows to do it. "There's one more thing you'll need once you leave this ship," he said, rising up from the chair, slowly, like an old bot. "Remain here while I fetch some things." Then he went and disappeared somewhere in the back of the shuttle.

When he returned, his arms were heavy with bundled clothing. "With the exception of myself, and a few others," he said. "Omegons are very shy. In public, cover your face at all times. Especially there---" He pointed to the imprint in the armor where their weapons were hidden: the only differentiation in their disguise. "Though most bots do add upgrades to their systems, and modification to their own bodies, they don't go through so much trouble to hide them."

"Cloaks?" said Semhek, stretching the big thing out before him, noticing the few holes and tears in the fabric. "Old and shabby cloaks. Probably smelly too." He draped it over his shoulders, examining himself from the ground up. "It don't help Armor-Zero's ugliness, either."

"It'll help you blend in better," the Merchant said. Having passed all the capes around, he plopped himself back down in his seat.

A faint shudder shook the craft as the cargo ship's docking-port released its hold. Jaanloch used the side-thrusters to push them further away, then climbed to a steep bank, flying up and over the dark expanse of the ship's enormous hull.

He waited till they were miles away before making the jump.

The brown, reddish planet, called Strong, appeared an instant later.

It was a dead world...being so close to its own yellow sun. A giant Venus perhaps; about four times the size of Earth. Its surface was riddled with black spots (many of them were bunched together) like clustered moles on blemished skin.

The shuttle went into a series of swoops and turns in order to avoid the other ships cluttering the planet's orbit. It dove head-first into the thin atmosphere, entering a hot sand-storm that pelted the outer hull with a shower of fine grains, shrouding their vision in thick clouds of dust.

They flew out of the storm in a matter of minutes and emerged in the clear skies on the other side. What had once appeared like little black dots from space, now turned out to be large dome stretching dozens of miles in diameter---made from a kind of stygian material, quite possibly used to harness the energy of the planet's star nearby. And as viewed from space, many of them did cluster and join together.

Some were connected by large tubes, splitting and branching off in different directions to connect all the domes together.

From miles above, they appeared to be nothing more than black spherical lakes, irrigated by an intricate web of canals. But as the merchant brought the shuttle down at a cruising altitude, the enormity of these mountainous domes became apparent. At the very tip, some of them rose up 3,000 feet, where vague outlines of buildings could be seen through the tint. These were where the notorious cities of the infamous Strong were kept---under those dark gargantuan domes. What had once appeared to be the outer spokes of giant wheels, were actually large tunnels that linked one domed city to another.

There were even places where these tunnels snaked around the domes, bending and curving all over the flat barren landscape, like highways.

The sky was filled with every kind of aircraft imaginable. Entire roads flowed over (and around) the domes that reminded Jack of Chicago's skyways back on Earth. There was even a system of lights and signals that controlled all the traffic that would eventually flow down to the wide gaping entrances at the base of each dome. It was like a scene of many fountains, where streams of aircrafts shot up in wide arcs in certain areas, then down in steep descents in other places.

Just a few roads ran straight across the horizon, making long bends that stretched for hundreds of miles. These--- Jack figured---must be the skyways of Strong.

The merchant zipped the shuttle up one of these roads at lightning speed; much faster than any aircraft on Earth was capable of flying. The domes, the tunnels, and the orange landscape...all melted and shot past the shuttle's window in a messy blur. The view through the bridge's window up ahead was like a warped tunnel, created by the shuttle's own speed of travel.

Not even Jack, with all his modified senses, could navigate this vessel at such speeds by hand. He marveled at the tribe-bot's dexterity at the controls, making only slight adjustments here and there; the red hood of his cape raring up at the window---every so often---with mild interest. Cold shivers ran down his spine just then....Another shocking reminder of how far away from home he actually was.

After only a few minutes, the shuttle slowed down. The horizon, the domes, and the orange landscape, all returned as if finally catching up to their elusive world. Though the sun was now on the other side of the planet, the sky remained lit by the bright colors of star-dust space.

The merchant veered off the road and joined the normal traffic, following the line of "skycrafts" down toward the base of a dome. They crawled through a short tunnel at a snail's pace, eventually entering the vibrant city before the merchant shot the shuttle up at the sky-scrapers above.

The atmosphere inside the dome came as a welcomed relief from the brightness that filled the entire Sector. However, the steel jungle of the city brought a certain glamour of its own, No different from any other city that Jack had ever seen on Earth, save for the steepled towers that rose high up in the sky. It seemed like all the buildings were topped with a sharp spire, each threatening to pierce the dome above. Looking straight across---as far as his enhanced vision would allow---he couldn't help but feel as though they were flying through a dense forest of upturned nails.

A sea of colorful lights danced and flickered in every direction. The air was congested with skycrafts of all kinds. The streets were crowed with herds of AI bots.

The shuttle banked around the corners with ease, flying with indifference past the awesome sites of the large city. It parked sideways into a building, where a kind of louvered garage door flapped open.

As the shuttle's cargo door slid up, the sounds of the city immediately filled the bridge. These were the all-too-familiar zing of robotic chatter, and the sputtering buzz of machines flying by.

Two droids approached the threshold of the shuttle's door, gazing over at the Drones with diamond-shaped eyes. They were unlike any other droid Jack knew existed in the Empire, whose limbs and joints still resembled conventional machines, despite their make and model. But these droids, on the other hand, were more sleek and sophisticated in design. They were tall, with slender limbs, coated in black shiny material---like lacquer that reflected their surroundings. They were even clothed, donned in long green robes that resembled tunics. Had it not been for their glowing eyes, Jack might've mistook them for actual living beings. But they were only droids. Beautiful, exotic droids.

"M' lady," said, Jaanloch, still seated in his chair behind the shuttle's controls. He curled out his arm in an elegant gesture of reverence. "Your precious cargo has arrived."

"Late," one of the droids said.

"Took a wrong turn on the Oncran Pass," the merchant said. "Came down the 11th Straight (and so did every bot in wag City) when I should've taken the 4th....My mistake. It's not every cycle I come to Mage City. Last time I checked, the 11th Straight was still the fastest way into the Mage."

"Except during the Piilor Festivities," said the other droid. "The entire Indran Splinter's in celebration. Will you be staying with us, Jaanloch?"

"No," the merchant replied, with a roll of his head. He carried an air of someone who'd seen more than enough of such frolics. And in truth, he has. The battle of Piilor, the first battle which liberated the planet's continent from the Drofh, was fought, and won, well over 300 years ago. He'd delivered most of the rebel's weapons back then. "I'm already late for some important drops I have to make on Brashnore and Tramall....They're all yours. Tell the old Wizard that I send my greetings."

EXPEDITION IV

CHAPTER
TWENTY-FIVE

"NO NO NO no no no!" The silver droid groaned at the spinning cylinder displayed before him. "This is not supposed to happen. I mean, it could happen, because anything in the Universe can, and will happen. But why would this happen just like that? There's no cause for it."

"No cause for what?" Asked a synthesized voice in the dark room.

As the droid turned around, a long band of red light glowed brightly on his shiny face, illuminating the fox-like ears on the sides of his pointy head. "The Scale," he said. A band of yellow light flashed with each word he spoke. "It's predicting ill fate; or some other negative possibility."

The bot rose from his place of rest and emerged from the darkness in the faint green light emitted by the cylinder. He shared the same features as the droid, except that his silver plates weren't as polished. A cape with a large collar hid most of his face, making him resemble the figure on the "King of Spades" playing card.

The bot stared at the cylinder for a long time, studying its barrel-shaped frame where spinning numbers flashed in an infinite amount of combinations. Each group of numbers flashed twice to represent the positive flow of certain calculations, while a single flash represented a negative.

And where no numbers flashed at all, the outcome of a calculation was yet to be determined....It was called: The Probability Scale.

"They're added elements, here," the bot said, after skimming through the thousands of numerical figures that flashed on the spinning cylinder. "Have you added them to our calculations?"

"Yes, Master," the droid replied. "I have. And this is what we have now."

The bot's hand came up to the side of the cylinder and held it in place.

The numbers froze.

With his other hand, the bot punched in a new series of combinations, flicking down to each row as he did so.

Having completed this arduous task, he released the cylinder and allowed it to spin once more while they studied the new stream of numbers that appeared.

They stood there for a long time, replaying the outcomes of days past, days present, and the days that were yet to be. They studied the cause and effects of the deeds done by each citizen that lived in the Indram splinter. But then came the dreadful predictions that represented the events to occur on the planet Strong for the next century. The same set of numbers fell on the entire Plogg Sector. Then the Quadrant. And finally, the entire galaxy. All spelled doom, by a simple line of numbers.

The droid was right!

Something terrible had gone wrong. The Scale had always predicted good fate-till now. Even in the days of the Drofh invasions, it had always been predicted that

Strong would persevere. But now, in times of relative peace, encroaching doom lay in the path of their destiny.

"Same as before," the bot said, apprehension now plaguing his tone. "Here...." He pointed to the blank space at the beginning of the spin. "Then here...." He cranked the cylinder back to a negative row of numbers. "And here...." He cranked it further back to a positive row---the normal pattern to which they were used to seeing.

"A Probability!" said the droid, reading the new set of calculations on the Scale. He felt a tinge of regret for not having discovered the added element that caused the Scale to go off balance. But he wasn't as skilled as his Master, who had created the Probability Scale in the first place.

"Yes Shan," the Wizard said. "An event that can doom us all. And it begins here----in our own Mage City."

"But what change could possibly bring about such a reaction?"

"A change that I helped bring about."

The droid, Shan, turned to his Master just then. Up until now, he'd thought the Wizard to be infallible, impervious to mistakes. "How so?"

"Through certain instructions that I've given. Instructions that aren't being followed. Luckily, we still have a Probability. We can still reverse the negative outcome."

The Wizard left both droid and Scale, to seek privacy in his own quarters. There, he pondered on the events that first occurred over the last century.

From the very beginning, the Sector's civilizations have stood in the face of annihilation and total collapse. Out of an infinite number of possibilities, only a few outcomes ensured its survival, all of which would've been very unlikely had it not been for the Wizard and his invention of the Scale. With this amazing device, the free worlds of the Plogg Sector had managed to avoid one calamity after another. Through precise calculations, they'd veered from the ruling clutches of the Regality, preferring the slack hand of self governance over oppression.

And so, it remained, for eons, until the Drofh came... but even this had been predicted well in advance.

And unlike the rest of the Quadrant, the Plogg Sector was well on its way to reclaiming its former glory.

But the power of prediction is never enough to ensure one's safety for too long. For ill-fate, is just as much an aspect of prediction as a good outcome. And without certain interventions, one's fate may never change.

Such was the fate of the Plogg Sector, 500 years ago, when the Drofh first invaded their worlds. Though their resistance was fierce, their victories remained few. Had it not been for the Drofh's lack of interest in the remote Sector, they might not have been able to liberate the worlds that remained free to this day.

Unknown Probabilities occur very rarely on the Probability Scale. They always came in pairs: one negative, and one positive event. And they were the only things the Wizard was unable to predict.

The last Unknown Probability occurred about 100 years ago, throwing the Scale's calculations awry. It was the year the Technician went into hiding. The last time he was seen or heard from by anyone. It had taken years to set the Scale on somewhat of a neutral ground. In the absence of the Technician, the future of the Plogg Sector wouldn't be great, but at least it still had a future. And as they'd done before, Strong, and the other free worlds, would survive without him.

But now, a new Probability worked to threaten even this. One, in which he feared, was dealt by his own hand.

Through intense calculations, it was discovered that the entire Plogg Sector might regain its former glory if the Technician was to ever return. The Scale even predicted that this was indeed possible, running a long stream of positive figures, explaining exactly why.

Thus, the Wizard sought to find the fugitive, and bring him back. And with the help of the infamous Stendaaran Drones, he thought he might do precisely that.

But now, he saw that even this, was folly...for this added element now threatened to ruin them all. Not just the Sector, but the entire galaxy as well!

It would take years of endless calculations to seek a path around this new problem. Year---he feared---they might not have.

A sudden flash of dazzling lights brightened his quarters from where a tall, thin droid emerged. "Shan said that I would find you here," she said, in the cautious tone of someone knowing they'd just disturbed another. "I have news." She waited for the Wizard to respond---and waited quite a while without getting a hit. "Is this a bad time?"

"Yes," the Wizard replied. He remained as still as a rock from where he sat, hunched over; the band of red light sweeping idly from side to side across his face. He appeared to have been in that same position for days. "It is. But it's a time that can't be helped....What news do you have for me, Morlah?"

"The Stendaaran Drones have already arrived. They're planning to begin their mission as we speak."

"I'm assuming they received their instructions."

"They have," Morlah said. "They've been fully uploaded on all the information we have on the Piilor Syndicate, and Kaypac....The 7 of them---"

"Seven?!" The wizard became so loud that Morlah was startled. His head spun on his shoulders---red eyes glowing as if they might melt. "Did you say 7 Drones?"

"Yes," she said. "The merchant sent 7 Drones, led by one named Puppycock."

"Mortal fools!" The Wizard was furious. "They've ruined us all with their arrogance.!" He fell silent once more, leaving Morlah uncertain of what to do, or say, next. "Leave me," he finally said.

"But father," Morlah began to protest. "I don't---"

"I said leave me!" He shouted so loud, it seemed that he cut off her words, forever.

In silence, the portal returned in a wall of light, and a dismayed Morlah vanished before the darkness came to reclaim the the Wizard's quarters.

From a small gem encrusted on his head, a green haze shot out in a funnel shaped wave.

Seconds later, the bullish head of a Stendaaran appeared in a hologram. His face was like a big purple brick. A pair of thick horns curled to the back of his skull like those on a ram. His squared jaw was firmly set, while his nostrils flared as if he might breathe fire. "Morlaak here," he said, in a low, deep voice.

"How good is your math, General?" The Wizard asked. In this highly advanced society, it was the worst insult he could throw at the dumb beast.

With his brow already set so low, if the General had frowned any deeper, he would've covered his beady eyes. But he didn't. "Good enough to ensure the Drofh would never come close to invading my Quadrant....Why do you ask?"

"So I'll assume you know the importance of numbers in the mathematical laws."

"I do."

"Then why would you send me seven drones, when the Scale only has room for six?"

"I don't care for your Scale, Wizard," the General said. losing patience. "I sent 7, because there's only one drone in my entire fleet that can find your Technician on that waste of a world. But this drone also needs 6 others to assist him.... Did your precious Scale predict that seven---and not six--- would pass the Simulation you designed for them?"

The Wizard's eyes blinked in surprise at this bit of information that added the final piece to the puzzle in which he'd been muddling over with for so many days.... That was where the extra element had been added in the Scale's calculations: the Simulation. Instead of six, seven Drones had passed, setting a new course to an unknown future. "No," he said. "The Scale predicts the outcomes of certain events, but not the events themselves. Your extra Drone threw off the calculations. He created a rare outcome that I like to call, an Unknown Probability....The day he entered your Simulation Chambers, he changed the fate of the entire galaxy....Whether for good, or bad, is yet to be known."

CHAPTER
TWENTY-SIX

THE WIZARD APPEARED from the portal of light with the remnants of his atomized self still trailing behind him like milling fire-flies, swarming to reconstruct his cape as he entered the room. "I'm looking for Puppycock." His words came slurred, and stressed....so dull, it brought no reaction from the Drones beyond his sudden appearance. "Your Commander," he repeated, in a more formal attempt. Where is he?"

"And who's looking?" Jack asked.

High off the uploaded maps, schematics, and the complex grids of the automated world through his implant, Jack had already begun to assume the role of leadership in his company. He met the funny-dressed intruder with a question of his own, asserting he had no right to barge in---at his own sudden whim---unannounced.

"I'm the Senator of this Trisect," the Wizard said. As before, his tone carried no more importance than that of a lowly peasant. "I own this Tetragon."

Jack rose from his place amongst the others, a bit softened by the spirit of authority. A quirk in his genetic design, perhaps. "I'm the Commander of this mission," he said, avoiding the acknowledgment of the distasteful name.

The Wizard stared at Jack for a long time after that. Beyond the thick shell of the tribe-bot disguise, he tried to picture the frail jelly-stick of a Human inside. But he could sense nothing of importance through his limited circuitry. All he had, was his calculations. He knew it wouldn't be wise to disclose the significance of his role. The Human might not appreciate the fifty-odd years of perpetual computing that it took to make their mission possible. The fact that out of millions of negative predictions, a single Stendaaran fleet at the edge of the 4th Quadrant was their only hope, might be brushed aside through sheer ignorance. Jack, the Wizard knew, was better off not knowing his worth. "Have our custom of hospitality met your standards, Commander?" He asked instead. His yellow patch of a mouth glowed to show that he was smiling.

Jack considered their large quarters that occupied three entire floors. For the first time since coming together on Oxlor, the Drones had their own private space. And with the exception of the Rejuvenation Chambers, a small closet of a room in which they were made to sleep standing up) there was hardly any need to complain. "Very much so...uh---"

"I'm simply known as Wizard."

"Ah," said the charismatic Semhek, as though enlightened. "A friend of Jaanloch, the merchant."

"I am he," the Wizard admitted, with a subtle nod. "And I welcome you all to my home. And while you're here, we shall be at your service. You've already met my two daughters, Morlah and Karlah. They will provide any assistance you need...." He made a stiff bow just then, turning around as a bright doorway of light appeared behind him. Without the slightest gesture of farewell, he walked right back through the portal, vanishing, just as mysteriously as he came.

"That..." Ford was the first to comment on what had just transpired. "Was weird."

"I've heard of the famous Wizard," said Ghan.

"So have I," Braak said. "He's revered as some kind of Shlinn "A what?" Jack asked.

"A Prophet," Braak replied. "As such beings are called on your world....Legend has it, that he foresaw the invasion of the Drofh, centuries before the war began."

"You'd think it would've been wise to prevent such a thing from happening,"

Semhek said. "If what you're saying true, of course."

"Maybe it was easier to allow the invasion of the Quadrant," Ford said. "You have to remember, the Drofh can see into the future as well. They would've easily thwarted whatever precautions the Seezhukans had set in place. A planned resistance can end more tragically than a spontaneous one."

"Whatever the reasons for the Wizard's discretion," said Jack. "Is of no importance to us now. Only the mission. And the sooner we find the Technician, the faster we can leave." He didn't like the idea of being on a highly radioactive world, where the surface temperature was as hot as it was on the planet Venus. Certain death laid just beyond his armored suit.

One crack in his infrared visor, and his eyeballs will melt from their sockets, like butter in the face of a drunken flame. "Meerk," he called over to the furry Gamlarrian. "Have you decoded the city's blueprints?"

"I have," said Meerk.

With an armored finger, Meerk traced a small circle on the back of his hand, causing a green hologram of the dammed city to appear in their midst. Like a frail bubble, the dome shattered. The shower of green sparkles dissolved into nothing, exposing the city's steepled buildings like a patch of thorns. It grew in size, tilting upward until it sat completely upright, giving the Drones a topside view of the city. The buildings were the last to go, fading, until all that remained was a large circle filled with hundreds of lines and numbers. A red square glowed in the middle, where the lines began to divide the city like a pie-chart.

Though decoded, and rendered to suit a more basic format, the Gamlarrian's version of Mage City was no less confusing than the archive's original blueprints. "It's the simplest diagram of the city," Meerk said. He did a little trick that made the holographic map spin like a wheel, then froze it in place. "It's a city built by machines. A strict design, with no improvising, or corrections. Every stone, street, and building are all perfectly aligned. These cities, were all put together in a very short period of time; unlike those on most worlds that increase in size as their population grow in numbers. So, to fully understand what we're looking at, we have to take it apart."

The numbers on the map vanished just then, leaving the empty circle and square, with eight lines running through them.

"We'll begin here," Meerk said, causing the circle to break apart in eight triangular sections (like slices on a pizza). "These are called, Trisects. They function as the city's districts. They're 8 districts in all, and we reside here--- "He paused to highlight a single Trisect. "In the Northeast Trisect."

In each Trisect, the lines and numbers reappeared---all perfectly squared. "The blocks in which these numbers are assigned are called, Tetragons. They're what make up the Trisects, and they're essential to navigating the city.

There are 404 Tetragons in this city. And we are here---" Meerk highlighted their Trisect once more. "At the 198th Tetragon, in the Northeastern Trisect."

The trisects rejoined themselves to form a complete circle once more. Meerk highlighted the squared center this time. "This is Tetragon Center," he said. "It's the heart of the city. And it provides the power throughout all the Tetragons in all 8 Trisects."

The needled forest of buildings returned. The numbers faded away, but the lines of the Trisects and Tetragons remained. "These lines all represent different lanes and skyways. All straight lines lead to Tetragon Center, while any curved line will take you through all the Trisects. It's a most genius design of any city's blueprints that I've ever seen. And so simple, it's impossible to lose your way."

The map shrunk, and the green head of an alien creature appeared. Through yellow, cat-like eyes, it glowered down at them with a hard, unblinking stare. Every-so-often, its two elfin ears would quiver, as if shaking off flies it couldn't reach with its unseen hands.

"This," Meerk began. "Is our latest quarry. A lieutenant of the Piilor Syndicate that control the workings of the city's underworld. Her name, is Kaypac."

"Her?" Ford sounded surprised. "You mean to tell me, that thing is a she?" "Yes," Meerk replied. "Kaypace belongs to a very ancient race of beings--now obviously extinct- that once inhabited a swamp-world in this Quadrant, called Loogh."

"But if the species have gone extinct," Semhek. began. "Then this, Kaypac, must be the very last of her kind....And there's another problem I have with this picture, here. Even under the protection of the dome, she wouldn't be able to survive under the high levels of radiation."

"I was just getting to that," Meerk said. "You see, Kaypac here, isn't the last survivor of anything; and the Looghanians have indeed gone extinct, like so many other life-forms throughout the 2nd Quadrant. What you're actually seeing here---" The metallic head of an AIGD-2381, slid out from the side of the creature's head. Only then, did the resemblance of the two holograms became apparent. "As the Earthling saying goes," Meerk continued. "Art imitates life."

"So these were what the Guard Droids once were?" Jack asked, staring at the two different versions of the praying-mantis kind of head.

"All droids are fashioned after their former selves," said Ghan. "As a remembrance of what they once were."

"And a reminder of what they all must return to," added Ford.

"Ah," Semhek began, sarcastically. "The Human girl, with her stories and legends of the Drofh."

"As told by the immortal Drofhs themselves," Ford said.

"Then how is it," Semhek said. "That you're the only Drone in all of the 4th Quadrant, to ever see the Drofh, and live to tell the tale?"

"Maybe they saw something in me that they haven't seen in anyone else in the whole galaxy," Ford shot back.

Jack tried to picture the frail little girl inside her husky armor. He remembered the vicious scar that curled up the side of her cheek. World Smart, yet innocent....Maybe the Drofh did allow her into their world. The only Human to ever do so (or living being for that matter). "Okay," he said, reverting everyone's attention back to the hologram. "So what is this... costume...she's wearing? Why would a Guard Droid for the Technician, want to disguise herself?"

"Oh, it's no disguise, Jack," said Meerk. "Synthetic skins are very popular throughout the entire Sector. In fact, I was just getting to that. See here---"

A wide translucent screen popped up over the droid's hologram. It showed a live feed of the busy Tetragon streets below, teeming with all kinds of alien life-forms.

It was like looking at a city of monsters. No two creatures looked the same. From the shaggy, to the scaly, down to the leathery. Bipeds, tripeds, quadropeds, and octapeds even. Every creature that ever existed in the whole galaxy, right there, under the gloomy dome of Mage City.

Between the throng of silicon skin and plastic tentacles, there were droids who did remain true to their robotic forms. These, Jack noticed, held an air of authenticity about themselves---more so than their "dressed up" counterparts. With less pomp and flair, they carried themselves in a formal manner. The lack of synthetic flesh, made their movements appear less animated and more suitable for life in the robotic world, where they---at least in appearance---were the true robots. He sensed this in Jannloch and the Wizard as well; they were the true pioneers of the Sector, who hadn't forgotten their purpose. The costumed droids, however, weren't natives to any of the world, but mere settlers seeking to escape the rigorous oppression of the new Empire. It was they who brought the fancy trends and fashions to the otherwise bland worlds of the Sector. And the evidence laid right before his eyes, when looking at the two heads of Kaypac's hologram: a visitor, of no more than a hundred years.

It was a positive sign that a system of class existed, even on a world so far more advanced than Earth. He could only imagine the strong sense of identity that a tribe-bot, such as an Omegon must feel. The untainted culture, spanning over tens of thousands of years. He realized then, the Oxloraan's first mistake; and his first assumptions were indeed correct. The Omegon disguise, for all its noble credibility, was all wrong. Despite their convincing appearance, they would stick out like a sore thumb in the midst of the costumed droids, and more so in the company of Omegon tribebots.

"Is there anything the archives can tell us of the Omegon?" Jack asked, causing the Drones to turn in his direction.

"There isn't much to know," Meerk said.

"Did the archives tell you that?" Jack asked. "Or are you just saying it?"

Meerk moved to respond, but then hesitated as he took a moment to ponder the Human's suggestion. He couldn't grasp the man's mode of thinking. How could he discard the information they were receiving now, so suddenly, for such useless data on the tribe-rots? "No," he finally said.

"Then I need you to check the archives for any, and everything, it has on the Omegon....For all the tribe-bots in the Sector for that matter." "But," Meerk began. "There're thousands of different tribes on Strong. Millions throughout the entire Sector."

"I need them all."

"That can take days!"

"We'll never find the Technician without that data. Don't you remember what Jaanloch said of our Merchant Keys?"

"That it's the simplest things that reap the greatest rewards," an enthusiastic Semhek said. "Or something along those lines."

CHAPTER
TWENTY-SEVEN

IT ALWAYS FELT good to rid himself of the armor. Even if that meant being in the only room on the entire planet in which he can do so.

It was their own private quarters. A section in the building that was entirely sealed off. There weren't any windows, nor doors through which anyone could enter; only through teleportation, which placed them in individual cubes that sanitized their protective armor.

It was a plain room, with gray walls and very little furniture. The Wizard obviously didn't get much (organic) visitors from outside the Quadrant. But the room did provide clear evidence that other living creatures could possibly be living in similar---albeit more fashionable---rooms all over the planet.

"This is amazing, Jack," said Zubkov, standing in a brown tunic (not too different from the ones worn by Morlah and Korlah). With the load of archival information uploaded into his implant, he caught a high just thinking of all the new data he had access to at a mere thought. "You saved us all a whole lot of trouble for sure. Who would've thought these tribe-bots were superstitious, and took taboos so seriously?"

"I don't understand it," Braak said. "We must've violated Jaanloch's ship hundreds of times. Yet he allowed us to carry on as if we were right at home. You'd think the tribe-bots didn't follow any customs at all."

"That's because he was following ours," Jack said. "Which is a tribe-bot custom in itself....Listen, we have a lot to learn before we can even think about going out there. All of our previous plans have to be scrapped, and rebuilt."

"Yeah," Semhek said, feeling a bit dejected. "Who would've known that the Omegon is one of the few tribes that never walk in groups....I always thought it strange that Jaanloch was the only Omegon on his ship. But now it all makes sense...ha! Could you imagine how silly we would've looked---all seven of us---walking down the Tetragon lanes?"

"We wouldn't have looked silly at all," said Ghan. "We would've looked---" "Like impostors," a newly convinced Meerk admitted. "Kaypac would've spotted us light years away."

"Okay," Ford said. "Now that we know we can't just rush in on Kaypac, and snatch her up like a gang of Bounty Hunters. How are we supposed to get close to her, without getting our own heads fried off? No offense to you though, Jack."

"None taken," Jack replied. He'd been pacing the room as the data of all the tribes in the Sector were being uploaded into his brain. With each second he gained more insight into the origins of the worlds. And as it turns out, the whole world functioned as some kind of planetary clock, where each citizen reacted in perfect timing with each other. Their behavior, were purely mechanical. Their festivals (and there were many) were done in exactly the same way each year.

Nothing spontaneous ever happened on Strong, which, for the most part, was the Drones' only advantage...to rely on the predictability of these machines.

Such information---as they all came to know now---was not only critical to the mission's success, it was vital.

"It is no coincidence that we were brought here during the Piilor festivities," said Jack. "The Wizard must've predicted that we should get here at this time. It explains why we were rushed through training. But it still doesn't explain the choice for our disguises if we're to get close to Kaypac. And I'm still not sure that the Wizard is one for such dubious mistakes."

"Now that I know what I know," Ghan said. "I doubt the Oxloraans chose this disguise for us. I believe it was the Wizard."

"And I believe the same," added Meerk. "But the question still remains: why?"

"That's precisely what we must find out," Jack said. "And I think I know where to start....Run a file on the previous Piilor festival."

Within seconds, a wide holographic screen appeared before them in which a map of the entire city was displayed. But it looked different this time; no longer being a circular diagram, but a mesh of interlocking lanes that resembled a web. A large hole in the shape of a square, remained at its center: Tetragon Center.

"Since it isn't practical to track every citizen in the city," Meerk said. "I provided only a simple layout of what the lanes look like when there's no traffic. Now, if I added every droid and bot on the streets at that time, then it might look like this---" Colorful dots covered the whole map, save for the dark square of Tetragon Center. "This was where everyone were during the last Piilor festival."

"And where was our Kaypac during this time?" Jack asked.

"I believe...here," said Meerk. All the dots vanished on the map. All, except one: a green dot in the Western Trisect.

"Now," Jack began. "Pull up the location of every Omegon."

Just six blue dots appeared, scattered sparsely over the face of the map. "Now run their patterns, so we can see where they'll eventually end up," said Jack.

The dots all jumped to life just then, moving around the Tetragon Center in tight spirals until they all converged near one place.

"Well, I'll be damned!" Ford exclaimed, staring at the hologram. "How interesting."

"The Oxloraans couldn't possibly have foreseen all that," Semhek said. "No one could," Meerk said. "You'd have to be a Drofh, to predict such a random meeting."

"Or a master calculator, like the Wizard," said Jack. "In a matter of days, 6 Omegon tribe-bots will come within 50 yards of Kaypac, all at the same time. None will be aware of the other's presence....Where is that, by the way?"

The map zoomed in, bringing the city's Tetragons in bigger detail.

"This happens near the 321st Tetragon, in the Southwestern Trisect," Meerk said. "But their path of origin-" He zoomed the map back out to its full display. The dots reversed themselves counter-clockwise until each paused at a different Trisect. "All begin here."

"Then that's where our paths will begin as well," said Jack. "All we need, is Kaypac's head. The secrets of the Technician's whereabouts should be found there. But we'll have to move quickly, and n'sync, in order to immobilize the Omegon without ruining the festival's routine."

CHAPTER
TWENTY-EIGHT

PRACTICING THE PIILOR festival's routine was a simple task. They would only follow one flight pattern, going clockwise around the domed city. From there, apprehending Kaypac shouldn't be too difficult either, supposing the lieutenant of the Piilor Syndicate didn't travel with any bodyguards.

The trick laid in replacing six mobile motorists without disturbing the mechanical dance of the festival. And not only that...it must be done simultaneously, or else cause a glitch in the city's traffic, which functioned as the gears of an ancient, alien clock. Such a mishap would never go unnoticed by the Monitors, who served as some kind of police-force in Mage City. They were very efficient and capable machines, who would no doubt swoop down on the Drone's location before they had a chance to leave the Trisect.

It all came down to timing. The sole outcome of their mission, relied on this one first step, where they all must enter in perfect stride with the rest of the billion citizens of Mage City.

"Ten seconds remaining," came Ford's voice in Jack's ear. Because there were only six Omegon tribe-bots in the entire festival, she was chosen, by Jack, to stay behind and serve as their eyes and ears.

"Everyone get ready," said Jack, crouching low on a shiny jet-scooter, on the sandy desert just outside of Mage City. "This our only shot." A watery portal flapped open before him and he eased the scooter slowly towards it.

"Good luck, guys," Ford said, before counting down. "Four, three, two, one---"

Jack mashed on the scooter's throttle, bracing as it lurched forward and shot into the portal, instantly putting himself on a busy lane, high above the city within the dome.

As much as they'd practiced this transition, it still wasn't enough to prepare Jack for the sudden change when it actually happened. For a brief moment he found himself disorientated, then startled by a craft's headlights that shone close behind him before he realized he was going too slow. He accelerated, quickly widening the gap at a comfortable distance. The dazzling spectrum of the city's buildings whizzed by beside him. "Fighter-1 here, in the Southeastern Trisect."

"Fighter 2," said Meerk. "In the Northern Trisect."

"Fighter 3," said Ghan. "In the Northern Trisect."

"Fighter 4," came Semhek's excited voice. "In the Western Trisect."

"Fighter 5," the big Russian said. "In the Southern Trisect." "Fighter 6," said Braak. "In the Eastern Trisect."

Though not as smooth as originally planned, they did manage to make the transition in unison, creating the effect of flying through a brief flash of light, and nothing more. The unsuspecting---and astonished---tribe-bots, however, will suddenly find themselves skimming over the barren wasteland just outside the dome.

'Don't you think you should let the computer's pre-programmed flight-course navigate us?' This suggestion from Klidaan popped directly into Jack's mind.

The Symbiot was referring to the tribe-bot's recorded flight pattern through the city. Though the lanes ran in and out of the Trisects in a continuous spiral, there were certain stops, and turns, to be made exactly as the tribebot had done.

'There's no need,' Jack replied. The scooter wasn't the fastest thing he'd ever ridden, but it was fast nonetheless, and it handled. with ease. He enjoyed being at the helm of the swift craft, swerving past the slow-moving motorists. 'I have our tribe-bot's flight path committed to memory. The instant we come into range of Kaypac, I need to be sure I can get to her without fumbling at the controls. I can't do that on auto-pilot---it'll only slow me down.'

'And what if you make a wrong turn?'

'I won't. But if you're so worried about the Monitors, why don't you navigate?'

'Make two lefts, then come to a stop at Tetragon 125.'

'I already know that.'

'You made me navigator.'

The further down the city's spirals they went, the more spectacular the festival appeared. Grand displays of light and color threatened to break his concentration on the lane ahead, causing him to rely more on Klidaan's navigating than his own ability to fly. Every so often he'd steal a glance at the celebrations beside him, taking in the sites---if only for the briefest of moments....It must be a wonderful experience for the souls living inside those machines, he thought. Existing for so long in continuous bliss....A pang of envy rose inside of him like a pimple.

"Fighter 6," said Braak. "Now in the Southern Trisect, at Tetragon 318. I need all positions."

"Fighter 1," replied Jack, snapping his thoughts back to the present.

"In the Southwestern Trisect, at Tetragon 270. By the time I head north on 272, we should both be the first to arrive at 321."

"Fighter 3, at the Western Trisect, on Tetragon 326. Should be there shortly after you two arrive."

"Fighter 5, heading east on the Western Trisect at Tetragon 275, in route to 321 on the Southwestern."

"Fighter 2, Southwestern Trisect, at 273."

"Fighter 4, Southwestern Trisect, right behind Ghan, at 327." "Alright, listen up," Jack said. "With the exception of Fighters 3, 4, and 6, the rest of us will be forced to break routine once we cross our designated intersections. The Monitors will be close behind, and Kaypac will most certainly be alerted. But there's no helping it. Fighter 3 and I, will focus on the primary target since we'll be the first to arrive. Make sure to keep the Monitors off our tails until we have Kaypac in our custody. Am I right?"

"Right!" They all responded. It was a language they've all grown accustomed to during the long days of practice.

"Okay, let's go!"

The instant Jack veered off the lane and entered the intersection due north toward Tetragon 321, a Monitor's lights was already flashing behind him. Just one---but enough to alert all the motorists on the entire Tetragon.

'He's ordering us to get back in the routine.'

'What do you think we should do?'

Klidaan caught Jack's sarcasm, so he decided to strike back with a bit of his own. 'I think we should turn back around.'

'And that's exactly why you're just the navigator....'

Jack spotted Braak's scooter hopping over the intersection....Here we go, he told himself, going into a sharp bank onto Tetragon 321. He barely avoided a tubular craft as it grazed right past him. By then, the Monitor was in an uproar at this blatant disregard for the city's sacred ritual.

'He's attempting to fire on us, Jack.'

'I know.'

The laser bolts came moments later; thin streaks of red flashes zipping past him. One entered the back of a rickety craft, blasting off the arm of the occupant inside.

"Kaypac in sight!" Braak said. "Accompanied by a light motorcade!"

After dodging another barrage of laser-fire, Jack keyed in the scooter's auto-pilot, then pressed down on his side where the bulky Jhusrot pistol slid into his palm. He spun around on his seat, getting a good look at the Monitor's sleek black craft behind him. With precise aim and timing, he squeezed off a rapid burst and watched as the indestructible rounds shatter holes in the Monitor's face behind the tinted window. He didn't even bother to see the craft go down as he spun back around to man the scooter. "I'm right behind you! Target the primary subject only! We'll deal with the rest later." With his free hand, he gunned the scooter's throttle, heading toward Kaypac's motorcade at full speed.

Jack noticed something was wrong the moment fell in beside Braak's scooter.

There wasn't any doubt that Kaypac and her entire motorcade had been alerted by the Monitor's alarm. Jack had counted on it. But the laser-fire had heightened the situation a bit more than expected. Though they still had no idea that they were the intended target, he could see they already had their weapons drawn.

Her motorcade was made up of only three cars (including hers), each flashing bright colorful lights along their sides, with hers in the middle.

The other drones were popping into view, some with Monitors hot on their tails.

"Cover me!" Jack shouted, then shot the scooter forward. He headed straight for Kaypac's car, littering the back and side with Jhusrot fire. Something exploded inside. Thick smoke billowed from the back of the car as it began to fall in a steep decline.

Complete chaos erupted after that!

Enraged by the bold assault on the Syndicate's leader, the two remaining cars reared up on their powerful engines and shot after Jack's scooter. They gained on him in a matter of seconds, laying heavy laser-fire in his direction with no regard to the destruction they brought to the other slow-moving crafts and innocent bystanders. They shot past the other Drones, zipping by in the opposite lane; a dozen Monitors in hot pursuit.

"Kaypac just crash-landed on the surface!" Meerk said.

"Fighter 4," said Jack, weaving in and out of traffic and laser-fire.

"Fighter 4, here," Semhek. said, from somewhere down the lane in the thick of the chase.

"Accompany Fighter 2, and secure the target," Jack said. "Don't let her get away!" A bolt zipped right over his shoulder, causing him to instinctively swerve to the left in the incoming lane. From the other side, his pursuers fired on his flank, but the small scooter proved to be a difficult target, dodging and leaping over their bolts with nimble agility.

More Monitors appeared on the scene, but they all flew past Jack to tend to the crippled crafts that had fallen victim to this small battle.

"I'm hit!" Braak shouted. "Going down fast....I'm sorry Jack. I have to land before I fall out of the sky."

"Assist Fighters 2 and 4 in securing the target!" Jack said. "I'll swing back around to pick you up as soon as I can." "Will do," Braak replied."

Jack caught a bright flash from the corner of his eye and dipped just in time as a larger beam from a laser-cannon chewed big chunk out of a building behind him. 'I thought you were supposed to be navigating!?'

'We aren't following the tribe-bot's flight path anymore.'

'What about his mess we have here? I can't shoot and drive at the same time.

'Maybe if you get back in the correct lane, you can use the auto-pilot.'

'I can't. They're waiting for me to do that. That's why they're space far apart....How about the scooter's anterior sensors? Can you link us into the machine and guide us from there?'

'It's worth a try.'

'Then be quick about it.'

'It's done.'

'Okay. Just say when ready.'

'Ready.'

With one hand still on the scooter's controls, Jack turned from the sight of the oncoming traffic to aim at the first car---

'Left!'

He swerved as the blur of a box-shaped car swept by. The sudden distraction threw off his aim, causing him to fire well wide of the target.

More determined than ever, he focused his attention once nore, vigilantly listening for Klidaan's instructions. He managed to avoid two more collisions before squeezing off a quick burst; the vicious rounds ripped right through the first car. He fired again, destroying the windows and robotic parts.

A stream of fire came from the other car behind, hitting a few oncoming cars he was forced to dodge. With steady aim, he riddled the first car a second time, ripping huge chunks of metal from the beaten frame before the injured driver lost control and veered into one of the Tetragon's buildings.

'I have to turn back around. We're way off course.'

'We'll have to jump lanes---'

'No. We don't. We're in a scooter, remember. We'll just have to deal with the other car on the way back....Say when ready.'

'Ready.'

Jack gunned the throttle, throwing the scooter skyward into a great loop.

Sitting upside down, he could see what remained of Kaypac's motorcade below him. With little effort, he righted himself in a single twist, taking sure aim at his target. He squeezed off a long burst, ripping the hood and roof of the car to shreds, sparks jumped all around inside the cabin.

As he ramped down in the middle of the flowing traffic, he spun around to get a look at the shot-up car....It didn't follow.

He rushed back to where he'd shot down Kaypac's car, but on his way back, Zubkov's voice crackled to life in his ear. "Meerk's dead!"

"What!?" Jack nearly lost control of his scooter. "What the hell happened?" "There was a fight," Zubkov said. "Kaypac survived the crash. She managed to injure Ghan, then killed Meerk and sped off in his scooter. Semhek's still in pursuit....Just me and Braak here with Meerk's body. The monitors have us surrounded, but Ford's already preparing a portal for us....In another few seconds we'll be gone."

"Good," Jack said. "Do you know where Kaypac's headed?" He waited for an answer, but none came. They were already back at their quarters. "Ford," he said, after a moment's thought. "I need the location of Semhek and Kaypac."

"Meerk's dead," said Ford, in a saddened voice.

"I know. Is Zubkov and Braak there with his body?"

"They just walked in."

"Okay...we'll deal with that later, Ford. Just give me the target's location."

There was a brief pause as Ford studied the two translucent scooters flying above the Tetragon's hologram...."

Target is headed north, on the Western Trisect, approaching Tetragon."

"Thank you."

"Be careful, Jack."

Luckily, he was already heading north, but he was down on the lower Tetragons, and far behind. He would never catch up to them if he remained on the busy lanes---so he looked up to the dome instead. 'How tall are those buildings?'

'The scooter will stall and fall back to the surface before it can reach halfway up the shortest building.'

'Then what about the gaps in between? Are there any dead ends?'

'None that I see in the archive's schematics.'

Before the Symbiot had a chance to advise him further, Jack banked the scooter over the traffic and slipped through the narrow gap between two buildings. 'Make sure we maintain a diagonal path toward Tetragon 230.'

'I've already set a course. Just follow the crooked lines on the display.'

A green line, like a crack running down the side of an old wall, appeared on the scooter's screen. He zigged and zagged through the dark narrow paths, preferring not to use the scooter's headlights, lest he alert any Monitors close by.

He shot out somewhere on Tetragon 278, relieved that Semhek and Kaypac were still heading down 229. He wound the scooter around the first intersection, gunning up the upper Tetragon toward 230. He avoided a slow-moving procession, preferring to hover near the corner of the intersection instead. Far up the Tetragon, he could see the---

'Jack!!!'

Perhaps it was sheer luck, or primal reflexes, that made him hunch down and lurch the scooter backwards as a hot blast from Kaypac's plasma rifle threatened to vaporize his head before smashing through the buildings behind him. Four more quickly followed---tiny stars, the size of golf balls---at lightning speed, melting the entire front half of the scooter. "I'm hit!" His scooter fell through the sky like a rock; hot plasma still eating away at the metal.

He made an awkward attempt to climb off, but lost his balance. His legs kicked at the air like an amateur skater when slipping on ice.

'Grav-boots!'

'Tuck in your legs.'

As Jack brought his knees up to his chest, he could feel the push of the grav-boots righting his body's position in the air.

The ground was coming up fast. What remained of his scooter had already been smashed to bits on the surface. About fifty yards up, he straightened his legs, relieved to feel himself slowing down. He made a hard, but safe, landing.

"Are you okay, Jack?" Asked Ford.

"I'm fine," Jack said. He looked up toward the dome just in time to see Kaypac's scooter zip through the intersection; Semhek---several Monitors--still hot on her heels.

"I'm opening a portal near your location," Ford said. "Semhek's on his own now. There's nothing more you can do."

Before he knew it, he found himself surrounded by a crowd of curious droids. They appeared to be triba-bots, but not Omegon. An indigenous surfacedwelling kind, known as the Orbdehine. They had cube-shaped heads that spun on their necks, and their beaming eyes regarded him with suspicion.

One was brave enough to approach him on hissing, elephantine legs, hidden beneath a long black robe. Its cubic face dented and rusty with age. "What brought this about?" It asked him. Only half of the lights in its coin-shaped mouth worked. "You made the same run every year for the last three centuries in peace."

The droids were all linked to Tetragon Center at the heart of Mage City. They were all conscious of each other's existence....But Jack was no droid.

A bright light appeared where Ford's portal opened, just three feet from where he stood. The Orbdehines, save for the ones who spoke, took a cautious step back. "You're no Omegon," it said. "Only made to look so....What trouble brews on our world now?"

For just a second, he thought he might give the droid some kind of explanation. Perhaps he ought to tell it that Kaypac, their Syndicate leader, was an impostor, working for the Seezhukans. And the Technician had sent an entire Sector---about a dozen light years in diameter into oblivion....But what good would all that have done?

"No trouble." Was all he decided to say. "The old scooter finally quit on me."

And with that, Jack entered the portal and was seen no more.

CHAPTER
TWENTY-NINE

"I'M HIT!"

The words were shrieking bells in Semhek's ear. He'd seen the whole thing and watched helplessly as Kaypac's rifle dumped raining plasma in Jack's location. From where he sat, it looked as if the man had been vaporized.

But upon hearing his voice those fears were immediately washed away.

He stole a quick downward glance as they crossed the Tetragon's intersection on 230. Jack's scooter had crashed on the surface, but at least he was still alive---and more importantly, out of the sights of Kaypac's rifle. And that's more than what he could say of his present condition. Not only was he left with the task of taking down the guard droid alone (something he doubted he could do), but he had to evade the five Monitors firing behind him as well.

The guard droid moved faster than anything the Simulation Chambers could've prepared them for. She moved so fast, there was barely enough time to react at all. Her entire body blurred as she sprung out from her wrecked car, darting to the nearest Drone (which happened to be Meerk), blasting him from his own scooter before any of them knew what was going on....And now Jack...but he was lucky.

The scooter's sensors alerted him of incoming fire from behind. He dodged and parried with ease, hoping one of the dozen bolts hit Kaypac's scooter instead. But they all bounced harmlessly off her invisible force-field.

They zipped down the Tetragon and approached 232 without a single shot being fired. Semhek thought he'd try his luck to at least even the odds by lessening the number of Monitors behind him. He stole a glance over his shoulder, then fired a quick burst at the first Monitor he saw as it rounded a hovering craft. The indestructible rounds chewed at the curved front of the Monitor's car, exploding out the back with bits of metal and engine parts. The car sputtered, then slowed down as the others flew right by without a care.

As if agitated by his success, the guard droid spun around on the scooter and fired two blasts from her weapon. The bright flashes that spilled from its nozzle was his only warning that eminent death would surely follow if he didn't react within the next fraction of a second.

Right then, he made the scooter hop, just in time as the two plasma balls whizzed by under him, then right through traffic as easy as flying through smoke. Just three of the four monitors were fortunate enough to swerve clear as the vicious plasma skewered the sleek craft of their comrade before continuing to wreak havoc through the rest of the city.

"There's a speedway at the end of this Tetragon," came Ford's voice in his ear. "She's likely to take it if she wants to leave the city."

"I see it," Semhek said, swerving in and out of the slowing traffic. He made another effort to peer over his shoulder, surprised that he wasn't being chased anymore. "What happened to the monitors?"

"These monitors are only assigned to the Western Trisect," Ford said. "Which comes to an end at Tetragon 233. They aren't programmed to cross the speedway into the Northwestern Trisect."

"And let me guess," Semhek said. "There's a whole new squad of Northwestern Monitors waiting for us at the other Trisect."

"At least 23 in all."

"Thanks...." He gunned the scooter past a lumbering carriage, hoping to close in on Kaypac before she could enter the speedway.

As he neared, he took aim, but the shrewd droid whipped her scooter in a series of moves---as she'd done many times before---making the chances of her getting hit nearly impossible. But he still squeezed off some rounds in anger, snarling in frustration when he saw that neither the droid, nor her scooter, showed any signs of slowing down.

Directly up ahead, he could see the speedway, known in Mage City as the 11th Straight. Crafts whisked up and down the wide lanes with lightning speed. On the other side, at least three squads of Monitors awaited them in sleek floating cars. Red lights shone from the top of their hoods, warning the two vigilantes to halt....

They didn't.

"They're going to blast her out of the sky," Ford said.

"For all of our sake," Semhek said, slowing down just a bit. "Let's hope so."

Even from the distance of fifty yards behind, Semhek could see the droid raising her weapon where a bright flash of light suddenly blinked. A ball of plasma went through one of the Monitors' cars.

They all fired on her just then....Scores of red and green streaks of laser shot in the droid's direction. All harmlessly bouncing off her force field, hitting the surrounding motorists instead.

Kaypac swung the scooter around. Bright flashes came from her arm in rapid successions. One by one, the Monitors began to fall; their blurred streaks of laser-fire lessening. And by the time she entered the 11th Straight, there was no one left in the Northwestern Trisect to oppose her.

A disappointed Semhek sped up the scooter and flew through the wreckage of what remained on Tetragon 233. He veered onto the 11th Straight and gunned after Kaypac.

"Semhek," said Ford, sounding urgent.

"I'm listening."

"You have to stop Kaypac before she leaves the city."

"And why's that?" He asked. "I was thinking I might stand a better chance outdoors, where I don't have to worry about any traffic....I need a clear shot to take her out."

"The 11th Straight will take you outside the city, but not outdoors. Once you leave the city, it'll take you into a hundred-mile tunnel that leads to another dome, called Loag City. You might not survive a battle in the enclosed area. And I think she knows that too."

"Glannard!!" The furry Tekwhaan swore in his native tongue. He knew Ford was right. If he entered that tunnel, he would have very little room to maneuver...but neither would Kaypac. So in a way, he thought, the odds were even. The first shooter, wins. He decided to risk it. "I'm going after her!"

"Semhek, no." It was Jack. "Let her go. We can track Meerk's scooter.

We'll find her again." "No...I have her now!"

"I said, stand down! That's an order."

No answer.

"Semhek!"

Still, no answer.

Semhek ignored Jack's command as he flew up the speedway, past the upper Tetragons of the Western and Northwestern Trisects that blew by on both sides. The dark mouth of the tunnel came into view where the traffic narrowed as they entered. A daunting feeling came over him when he saw that the tunnel was narrower than he'd first expected. He knew for certain that if Kaypac got off the first shot---while he was still in the tunnel---he was dead.

She entered first.

Out of wishful thinking, or desperation, he decided that now was a good time as any to fire. He let off a long sweeping burst, not caring for the innocent cars that caught his strays; as long as the vicious rounds made their way into the guard droid's chest (or anywhere else on her for that matter). But none did. Nothing that was fatal anyway, for Kaypac simply swung around and squeezed off a long rapid burst of her own.

The balls of plasma came like a whip from a long chain, fanning out as they left the tunnel, destroying anything that stood in their path.

He moved to skip over the assault as an injured motorist veered into his lane at the same time, cutting off his line of sight. Three balls shot out the back of the craft at the blink of an eye. He felt a searing pain in his left thigh. And when he looked down, he saw that part of his leg was gone!

Through this minor distraction, he hadn't noticed that the car ahead of him had slowed down. He swerved out of the way just in time to avoid a head-on collision, only to be side-swiped by a vehicle in the other lane.

The impact threw him off the scooter, and he fell like a turd through the sky, crashing down to the surface on one grav-boot. Amazingly enough, the scooter still remained in the air; the flow of traffic moved around it, like a stream parted by a protruding rock.

The welcoming light of Ford's portal opened up in front of him. Defeated---but grateful---he hopped towards it to safety.

He appeared in the transparent cube of the Decontamination Chamber that sprayed him down with hot steam and other inoculating gases.

Through the haze, he could see the others eagerly waiting for the decontamination process to be over. Some held medical instruments in their hands.

The next thing he knew, he was falling out of the ruined Omegon suit. Someone caught him....

He could feel his body being lifted, then placed gently on a levitating cot....Something sharp entered his left thigh, where his leg had been severed.

"The radiation's already starting to kill him, Jack." It was Braak. The fat, scaly thing from the planet, Taas. He sounded concerned. "None of us are skilled in medical matters beyond the basics. They'll die here if we don't leave right away."

"We can't leave," Jack said. He was now standing over him, looking down. "All this will be for nothing if we leave now....Seal him up, and put him with Ghan. I'll find Morlah, and see if these droids still know anything about patching up living tissue."

The thin bluish film of an electromagnetic force-field slid over and surrounded the wounded Tekwhaan. He could barely make out Ford's small brown face as she came up beside Jack. The pain was beginning to subside. He felt sleepy.

"They'll fix you up, Panda Bear," Ford said. She once said the creature on her planet resembled him. On one occasion, she even showed him pictures.

He laughed.

"What's so funny?" She asked.

"During Simulation," he began with a soft chuckle. "The same leg always gets blown off."

CHAPTER
THIRTY

THE MED-BOT pierced the soft green silicon skin with a surgical knife until thick, clear fluid welled up on the shiny blade. With a slow, steady stroke, it made a long incision from the top of Kaypac's head to the back of her skull, before cutting completely around her slender neck.

A droid's spindly fingers clamped down on her face, pulling off the silicon skin with little effort to expose the slimy metal beneath. A dry cloth wiped away at the globby mess, often snagging itself on the jagged areas where Semhek's Jhusrot rounds had ripped through. A chunk of her head was missing, and most of her lower jaw had been shot off.

The rest of her body (already stripped of the silicon skin), was in no better shape. A piece of her right foot was gone. The entire left side of her body was in tatters and riddled with holes where she caught most of Semhek's fire at the mouth of tunnel. Only through some strange miracle, did her plasma generator remain unharmed.

At least that's what Zhorg had thought as his pellucid face hovered over Kaypac's broken body. His hologram was larger than life, and his unblinking eyes gave a look of contempt, rather than empathy. "We've already captured the 6 Omegons attempting to re-enter Mage City," he said in a deep, synthesized voice. His thin green lips barely moved. "They didn't put up any resistance. But they refused to tell us what Syndicate they belong to."

Low, grinding sounds came from Kaypac, but none that could form any coherent words. Her vocalizer had been destroyed along with rest of her lower jaw. She'd been laying on the same inclined gurney for most of the hour as the med-bots tended to her battered frame.

A new right foot had just been installed. She curled and wriggled the pointy toes, then turned her half-eaten face to the nearest bot to get its attention.

The med-bot was just preparing to remove Kaypac's leg when it caught the sputtering flashes of her eye. It paused to read the silent message, then spun back around to retrieve a pincer-like tool and a tiny box from a table nearby. It eased up to her mangled jaw and reached into the gaping hole with the pincer. After a few wrenching twists, came a loud snapping sound that made her head twitch. The med-bot extracted a fragment of her throat and let it drop carelessly to the floor. It reached back in, to retrieve the ruined vocalizer. A quick sweep with a magnetic brush removed any loose metal fragments still laying inside. It then placed a tiny new box in the back of her throat. A loud, shrieking whistle immediately followed until she gained control of the new vocalizer that had just been installed.

"Who else could it be, but the Kraaglor Front?" Kaypac said; her voice cracked with new vigor and clarity. A sharp contrast to her old, ripped up body. "They've been sucking us dry since the day of our arrival. All they ever do is make demands. Not once have they offered us anything beyond the few Provinces they had no control over in the first place.

Nol, Pol, Rang, Klaag, Ioag, Mage, Klon City---they were all in the dumps before we came here. But things changed. We brought new wonders from the lungs of the Quadrant. Trade from the generous arms of the galaxy....the living Galaxy...into this dead Sector, abandoned by both the Quadrant and the Drofh. The Piilor Province is now the light Indran Splinter. For the first time, the Province's 9 cities are at peace. So I guess they wish to take things over from here, seeing they have a new lieutenant who's not a native of Strong."

Zhorg remained silent. Conflicting thoughts zipped across his circuits at the speed of light. "It is a strong accusation you make," he finally said. "But have you considered the length of boldness it would take for the Kraaglor Syndicate to make such a move? They already control half of the entire Sector. What is to gain from a small Splinter of a large world? Maybe we should reverse our steps---"

"To where!?" Her new voice peaked to an ear-splitting pitch. The dutiful med-bot yanked off her broken leg with indifference. "The lesser Syndicates? Or maybe that accusation is still too strong. Maybe it's some secret tribe-bot revolt. Tribe-bots with combat training; armed with weapons that can penetrate our shields!"

"That's not what I'm saying at all," Zhorg said. "Then what are you saying?"

"This is no gain for Kraaglor!" It was Zhorg's turn to raise his voice: a throbbing sound that shook the room. He'd grown impatient with the lieutenant's insolence. She was beginning to forget her place. "You're not thinking this through. It's true that the Indran Splinter has grown and prospered under our rule and leadership. But other Splinters have profited off of our success as well; none more so than the Kraaglor Front. It would never be in their best interest to attack you in this way. They would never profit from such a war."

"They would never profit from any war against any of the lower Syndicates," Kaypac said. "But they could prevent losses to their own....They're losing influence, Zhorg. We've both seen it in the Provinces over the last century.

And it's happening on other Splinters as well. Piilor's population have doubled since our arrival. Citizens are now regarding Kraaglor as the old village that was once great. New and exciting things are happening elsewhere....' While others are planning rid the rest of the Sector of the Drofh, Kraaglor's the only Syndicate that has taken the back seat. The citizens are well aware of this. And other Syndicates are seeking the opportunity to gain control of entire worlds as they liberate them from the Drofh. Soon, Kraaglor will no longer be the majority in this Sector. For a long time, the lower Syndicates have been in solidarity. It is only Kraaglor that stands alone."

"Only through their own self-importance. They have no interest in liberating worlds."

"Because of him!"

There came that long pause from Zhorg again. Only this time, he wasn't weighed down by heavy thoughts. He was now burdened with Kaypac's daring implication. "Because of him?" He asked incredulously.

"Yes."

"And what proof do you have of this, other than a hunch of your own devise?"

"The Omegon that were captured outside Mage City," she said, as a shiny new leg was fastened to her hip. "Are indeed the same Omegon from past festivities. But they weren't the same ones who tried to kill me."

"They're only 6 Omegon that are ever recorded in the whole city during that time. And they were out of routine when they were captured."

"But I killed one of them," she said. "And wounded at least two others....If they were the assassins, you couldn't possibly have found all 6 still alive....These bots were different, Zhorg. Highly trained. They must've figured a way to jump into the real Omegons' routine. They had no shields, because they knew nothing can protect them from our weapons. You should've seen the way they avoided my rifle. I would merely point, and they'd go dashing out of the way....Only he can make such droids and devise such a plan, Zhorg. Just look at me! What in all of our galaxy could've done all this?"

"But he would never do that to us---to you. He has no reason to."

"Because we're different from all the others. We don't have to obey him---"

The med-bot brought a clamping device to cover up her mangled jaw. There was a muffled, whirring sound, as internal gears worked to detach the hinges---then a snap...! The bot then removed the device that carried Kaypac's ruined jaw along with it, exposing the entire insides of her throat. A short moment later, the device returned, latching onto her face like a boxy metallic mask. The whirring sounds of internal gears began, a bit longer this time.

When the bot removed the device again, it left a brand new lower jaw on Kaypac's face.

Zhorg noted the stark improvement, though parts of her face were still shredded.

Her entire left arm was replaced. But nothing could've been done for the rest of her face and torso. The bots did their best to fix the dents. A metal plate was brought to cover the hole in her head, then welded in place. The jagged ends that protruded on her triangular head and cheeks were hammered down and sealed back together. The left side of her torso had to be cut out completely then covered with new metal plating that was welded shut.

She was whole again, though many scars still remained: daunting reminders that she wasn't as invincible as she'd once thought.

The restraining straps freed her of the gurney. She rose and headed to the coffin-shaped box, avoiding the tattered scraps of her old limbs (piled high on a nearby table) as she walked by.

The curved metal lid rose slowly with a soft hiss upon her approach. She climbed inside and laid down, waiting, as the lid reclosed itself upon her gently.

No more than five minutes went by before the lid hissed open again. Kaypac sat up, fully covered in new, soft, green silicon skin. A med-bot was already there to meet her with a long white robe to cover her naked body as she stepped out.

Zhorg had watched the whole thing in silence. It was the first time in centuries, that she'd ever had to change her skin. Someone---whoever it was--had really given it to her. She wouldn't forget that. She would make those responsible pay. Of that much, he was certain.

She went right to the table where a piece of her old jaw sat in a metal pan. She reached in and picked it up. "Did you find any weapons?" She asked him.

"No. They were all unarmed when we found them. It's quite possible they could've discarded them to any part of the galaxy by now. I can only assume they wouldn't want us to get our hands on them."

"It would take a photon blast from a battleship's cannon to weaken my shield. With 4 strikes, it can exhaust my plasma field's generator." The broken jaw began to float up from her palm. It spun slowly in mid air. "This is the only part of me where a foreign object is still lodged."

A bot approached the floating jaw, splitting it in half with a fine-lasered tool. From one of the halves, it pulled out a small jagged object.

"So how is it that this alone can penetrate my shield?" Kaypac said, pointing over at the floating shard. "A simple scrap of ore!"

The bot put the shard on full display through a hologram, projected by its own glossy eyes.

Zhorg took a long good look at the little shard that had almost ended Kaypac's life. Had it not been for his silicon skin, he might've frowned in confusion at the projectile that appeared to be no more than a harmless rock. "What is it?"

"The element is unknown," the bot answered.

"That's impossible," said Kaypac, stepping up to the bot. "It's nothing but ore. The galaxy's filled with it."

"It appears," the bot began. "That this particular element, is found nowhere in the entire galaxy. It's an unknown. Which is probably why the assassins chose it as a suitable weapon. And from my readings on its atomic density, this particular element's 100% indestructible. That's why it was able to penetrate your shield without being vaporized. When fired from a powerful weapon, there'll be no defense against it."

"An unknown," Kaypac said, in a pondering tone. "And perhaps, a newly discovered element....Where would anyone begin to find such a thing?"

The bot couldn't find an answer. "Another galaxy, perhaps," Zhorg offered.

"Perhaps," Kaypac said. "If it exists, then it must come from somewhere.

But let's forget about this...thing...for now, and go back to what I was leaning to; for my question is never to seek the how, or the why, but the who. Who in all the galaxy would use this as a weapon? Definitely not the outer Quadrants, for we haven't played any in this stifling war. And who else would find any interest in this dead Sector, but him?"

A reluctant Zhorg hesitated to respond to her bold suggestion. He thought long and hard before he chose his next words. But before he could do so, the bot broke in with news of its own. It was a much welcomed interruption.

"An Organics' been found under the speedway, near the Western Trisect," the bot said.

"An Organic?" Zhorg asked. "What fool would report such a thing?" "Must be one of our Regents from the upper Quadrants," Kaypac said. She turned to address the bot. "What were the circumstances?"

The bot paused to retrieve the data. "Circumstances...a severed limb, nothing more. And it appears that the affliction was handed down by you, Commander."

"An unfortunate case then," Kaypac said. "It was a peaceful festival till someone tried to kill me. Too bad innocent citizens had to suffer for it. Has the Organic been tended to? How many more casualties are there?"

"Just a few dozen or so," the bot said. "Including the Monitors you destroyed."

A harsh grinding sound of derision came from Kaypac just then; her eyes glowing red hot. "Those silly guards fired on me," she said. "What good are they anyway? They can't even tell who's friend or foe."

"They engaged all parties involved in the disturbance," the bot said, without sounding too defensive. "It is how they're programmed."

"And what of the Organic?" Asked Kaypac, not caring to discuss the Monitor's inferior software any longer. "Was it one of our Regents?"

"No," the bot replied. "Readings from our tests suggest one of the lesser known Organics from the 4th Quadrant. A native to a young planet, called Tekw. There's also evidence that the Organic is host to a Symbiot of some kind."

"A Symbiot?" Asked Kaypac, with mounting interest. "Of what race?" "That..." the bot began, a bit regretfully. "Was never determined. There simply wasn't enough evidence in the Organics' blood, other than the low levels of certain nutrients and chemical compounds, to decide on a definite race. The only thing we do know for sure, is that the Organic carries a Symbiot. And judging from the traces of oxygen in the unusually thin blood, I'd say this particular Symbiot's highly evolved."

"How so?" Zhorg asked.

"Most common Symbiots," the bot said. "Extract vital resources from its hosts. Very few are able to survive on their own; and fewer still, can provide their hosts with any nutrients at all. Oxygen, for example, was found in the Organics' blood. And not only that...it was being recycled, which rules out the possibility that it was being fed through an external source. This can only means that a symbiot of some kind is attached to this particular Organic, serving as the creature's lungs. Beyond this...the exact race of the symbiot can't be determined."

Both Zhorg and Kaypac absorbed this new information in the complex circuits of their own thoughts. Both, however, seemed to be puzzling over the same thing. The question was---if their assumptions were correct what would it all mean? If the Organic do happen to be a Meraachzion Drone, then what interest would the 4th Quadrant have in the Plogg Sector? The heat of galactic war never burned in their Sector. And with the exception of a few Drofh strongholds, they remained mostly ignored.

The possibilities implied too much for the leader of the Piilor Syndicate to contain himself. "What protection had this...Tekwhaan, used?" Zhorg asked.

The bot turned around with a cocked head, as if he was about to state the obvious. "Omegon covering," it said, grimly, as if knowing the impact that such an answer would have.

"Your would-be assassin?" Zhorg said, his big green head turning to Kaypac. "So it seems," Kaypac replied.

"What would the Regality of the 4th Quadrant want with you?" He asked.

"I don't see how anyone outside the Sector can profit from your death. Unless, you're secretly involved with the Seezhutan frauds. I seriously hope you haven't betrayed us." His voice took a deadly turn as he said this.

"Of course not!" Kaypac said, becoming angry that Zhorg would even entertain such a thought.

"Then what is this all about?"

"I don't know," she said. "But I intend to find out."

"For your sake, Kaypac," Zhorg said. "You had better get down to the meaning of this quickly. Find these Drones---they obviously have some powerful connections in Mage City, seeing that they nearly succeeded in killing you while the entire chain of the Piilor festival was still in motion.... You nearly escaped with your life this time. But you might not be as fortunate on their second attempt."

"Their second attempt," she said this derisively, while walking back to where she once laid on the inclined gurney. "I'm counting on it." She disrobed, then settled herself into the gurney's customized molds.

The bot turned to face her; the Jhusrot's hologram vanishing as it did so. A green, flickering light sputtered from its eyes and swept over Kaypac's naked body as it scanned and analyzed her dimensions.

"You should be better prepared next time," Zhorg said, though it sounded more like a plea, than just casual advice. In truth, he would hate to lose his second in command to the Meraachzion Drones. But the implications that the 4th Quadrant was somehow involved in some elaborate scheme to take over the Sector, unnerved him. Their involvement would threaten to undo all they've accomplished in the free world's thus far. And not to mention a more daunting possibility of the resurgence of the Drofh in the Sector. If this happens, then all would be lost....The rules, were somehow beginning to change. And somehow it would begin, and end, with Kaypac.

"I assure you," Kaypac said. "When the Drones come after me again, this time, it will be they who'll be the hunted...." The straps released her just then, and from out the gurney's molds, a black shiny fabric billowed out to cover her entire body from head to feet. The black leathery fabric melted down to a chrome-like silver, before shrinking down to a perfect fit around her body.

"And how can you be so sure that you'll know precisely when and where they'll strike next?" Zhorg asked.

"I captured one of their scooters," Kaypac was admiring her new outfit. "I'm certain they're tracking it as we speak. It is only a matter of time before they recuperate and come after me again. And when they do, I'll be waiting."

EXPEDITION V

CHAPTER
THIRTY-ONE

IF HE COULD'VE jumped for joy, he would.

But he didn't know how.

For an ancient droid, living deep in a far away Sector of the galaxy, just plain old satisfaction would have to do---for now.

It was the only feeling that could've stemmed the Wizard's mounting confusion as the tubular Probability Scale predicted one unspeakable horror after another, before finally foretelling the best possible future for Strong and the other free worlds in Plogg. In one final calculation, it laid out a string of numbers that nearly stretched for all eternity. A number that bespoke the best possible future for their worlds, forever.

But as quick as it appeared on the Scale, it was gone--- just like that. Nor did it ever return.

He spent weeks running through the billions of calculations in despair, hoping to learn the events that made such a future possible, but he never managed bring up that magic number again. It might've simply appeared on its own, he thought.

Regardless of whether he'd made an error in his calculations. or not, he did see it. A brief glimpse of a perfect Universe. In the dense clutter of death and destruction,

269

an existence of everlasting peace was indeed possible--- somewhere, in time. Though only foreseeable through a single, but unknown event, it was enough to know that at least there was still hope for all life, however faint of a glimmer it may be. It was enough to put his robotic circuitry at ease.

More pressing matters were at hand for the industrious Wizard, however. A more localized set of calculations that had fallen in harmony with the Scale's initial predictions concerning the involvement of the Meraachzion Drones. And that too, was represented by a number. Though not as infinitely long and incalculable, it represented an important prediction---proceeding a series of events---nonetheless.

"It was always 6," he said to Shan: his loyal, silver apprentice. "The number of Drones that came here had nothing to do with it. Jaanloch could've sent me 100, and it would've still been narrowed down to just 6. An unrelenting prediction. Such is the beauty of the Scale."

"And yet you doubted the power of Its prediction when Jaanloch brought us 7," Shan said.

The ancient Wizard turned from the rotating numbers on the tubular Scale, to give his apprentice a soft stare. Rarely did Shan ever question his mastery. But whenever he did, his judgment was most warranted. As it is now. "Yes Shan," he admitted. "When I first saw the negative readings, then learned of the 7 Drones (which caused the negative readings), it was easy for me to conclude that my predictions had changed somehow. But now, this appears not to have been the case."

"How so?" Asked Shan. "The negative predictions were there, because of the 7 Drones. But the readings clearly stated only one positive outcome will result from 6....So, what changed?"

"Nothing's changed. Once things are set into notion, they cannot be reversed. All the possibilities were read correctly, no matter how many turned out to be positive or negative. The six, or seven Drones, didn't change anything. A positive outcome simply relied on six...and for that, the prediction remained true to its word. The negative readings were simply that; they didn't rely on any specific number of Drones. But once things were set into motion, we had no other choice but to allow them to follow their course."

"Is that what we're seeing now?"

The Wizard's head swung back around to look up at the flowing numbers of negative readings being calculated by the Probability Scale.

"What could possibly be wrong now...?" Shan's voice was thick with apprehension. "We have our 6 Drones. Kaypac's on the run. And the Piilor Syndicate's been shaken to its core....But all that's being predicted now, is doom. There isn't one positive calculation in all the readings. It appears that things have taken a turn for the worst."

"They have," the Wizard said, but he didn't share in his apprentice's fear. "But you must remember, and keep in mind, that once things are set in motion, they cannot be reversed. It is the fundamental law of prediction, and the Scale's readings will never lie."

CHAPTER
THIRTY-TWO

IT HAD TAKEN weeks for Semhek's and Ghan's wounds to properly heal.

Weeks, that Jack watched go by regretfully. But it couldn't be helped.

The Syndicate had locked the entire city down, searching for the would-be assassins of one of their commanders.

Though six innocent tribe-bots had been captured and then molten down to lifeless slabs of metal, a more discreet search went on for other conspirators.

It was thought, that maybe the Piilor Syndicate knew who the true culprits were. But no assaults ever came to the Tetragon where they stayed. In fact, the entire Northeastern and Eastern Trisects remained free of Zhorg's scrutiny.

More discouraging, was the news that Kaypac was no longer on the planet, Strong. Instead, she'd fled to one of the Sector's small rocky worlds, called Langworn.

To Jack, the outlaw droid's escape to another planet was somewhat expected. But the method in which she chose to do so, was a bit too obvious. She didn't conceal the fact of her departure from Strong, nor did she bother to cover her trail that led all the way to her final destination. It almost seemed as if she was inviting them to follow her...to capture her at a more...suitable...location.

For the rest of the Drones, her intentions was all too clear. "She's leading us into a trap, you know," Semhek said, nodding up at Langworn's hologram, which was nothing more than a small gray ball floating in space. Traces of Kaypac's flight-path ran in a long blue line, stretching across the entire planet.

"Seeing that we failed to kill her the first time," said Jack. "Any further attempts from us---at any time---will ultimately head into some kind of trap. She still don't know exactly who's after her, but she'll always be on constant alert. From here on out, she'll always have something up her sleeves. She'll never be caught off guard again...unless...we fall into one of her traps...."

He trailed off, studying the Drones' tense reactions upon the implication that they must follow the droid to the rocky planet. It was a move---he knew---that was a bit too daring, even for Semhek's liking. "She's expecting us. It'll be rude if we keep her waiting."

"Is it wise that we rush into this one so suddenly, Jack?" Zubkov asked, clearly worried that this mission might be their last. "She could have an any of AIGDs waiting for the right gang of fools to take a second shot at her. And not to mention, there's only 6 of us."

"You have to keep in mind, Zubkov," Jack said. "The Technician never made an entire army of those droids; just a few, serve as his personal guards.

And as far as Kaypac having an army; that may be likely. But we're Drones. Six of us are more than enough. And I doubt she'll have that many guards with her."

"And how can you be so sure?" Semhek asked.

"A hunch," Jack replied.

"What's a hunch?" Semhek asked. "Is that some kind of machine that help you see things from far away?"

Ford couldn't help but laugh at the Tekwhaan's response.

"No," said Jack. "A hunch, is just a thought, based on a combination of observation and experience."

"Experience?" Semhek said. "So, you have been in similar situations?" Maybe not with plasma-shooting AIGDs, but with other droids."

"Yes..." Jack began. "And no. But experience tells me that if Kaypac seeks to invite us to this location of her choice, that she is somewhat prepared, but not for a war. We humiliated her the last time, and it's beginning to show in her recklessness It's personal with her this time. She wants to confront us---perhaps to know why we attacked her. But I doubt she's ready to take on an entire Stendaaran fleet. She's taking a huge risk by exposing herself like this, and she knows it."

"So we just go in there, guns blazing, on a planet we've never been to before?" The big Russian didn't seem confident in Jack's plan. "Hardly what I expected from a Detective."

Semhek stood up just then, his shiny new robotic leg hissing softly under his robe. "I have to agree with Zubkov, Jack," he said. "I don't like this. Kaypac's not one to trifle with, in the least. I can attest to that. So can Ghan, here. But none more so, than Meerk....I know the General made you Drone Commander---I respect his decision. But this is no Human Detective game, that Kaypac's playing. She'll kill us at first glance; that much I'm sure about. It is my duty as a Drone, to follow your commands to the ends of the galaxy...to death, if I must. All I ask in return, is that you consider your decisions closely, with the life's of your fellow Drones in mind."

"And you think I haven't considered the dangers of going into Langworn?" Asked Jack, eyes sweeping around the room at the handful of Drones in his command. "Is that what you think?"

None was quick to answer.

"Maybe," Ford began. "We're going about this a bit too hasty." "We don't have a real plan," Zubkov added.

"So what else do you have in mind?" Jack asked them. "Perhaps wait until she goes to Chramonga, or Claan, or maybe she might just return here for the next Piilor festival, so we can attack her the same way all over again....No. How about we just leave her on Langworn. Go back to Oxlor, and forget the whole thing ever happened, and Meerk never existed." He paused, and the silence fell heavily in the room.

No one said a word.

"We can't afford to do any of these things," Jack went on. "The weight of the entire galaxy's sitting on us, on whether or not we can find the Technician. Or have you forgotten why we were chosen? The General didn't just choose me, he chose all of us. We have a mission to complete and we're going to complete it....And for your information, Semhek...I do consider the lives of all of you. Which is why I'm using myself as bait this time.

Kaypac expects us to come after her again. And we shall. But only so that we can draw her out, and she's forced to come to us....And if I do manage to get my head vaporized this time; all the better."

CHAPTER

THIRTY-THREE

ZHORG THOUGHT IT a foolish ploy, that Kaypac should exhibit their location so easily. Nor did he think the Drones would be foolish enough to follow their enemy to the Syndicate's home world. The crimes for which they were guilty of are punishable by death. They would never come, he thought. Her plan would never work.

But when the mid-sized cargo-shuttle emerged from hyperspace near Langworn's room, he found it hard to compute the logic of both friend and foe alike. For Kaypac, her reckless judgment might've been attributed to some strong drive of seeking revenge, or perhaps, the vital need to show strength and leadership in the face of the Syndicate leaders. But the actions of these Meraachzion Drones didn't make any sense to him. For what purpose should they seek to eliminate his lieutenant so feverishly? What was Kaypac's worth that they should come all the way here, to die?

And die, they surely will, once they land on his planet. But first, he needed to know their purpose, which was why he hadn't blown them to bits out in space by now. He would allow Kaypac her moment---her one shot at redemption. But at some point, he would have to take over if he wished to get to the bottom of all this. The Meraachzions shouldn't be anywhere near the Plogg Sector.

"It seems you have guessed your enemy's reactions well," he said, paying close attention to Kaypac as she studied the shuttle's schematics on the hologram displayed before them. He came up beside her to get a good look.

The ship appeared harmless enough: moderate shields, with a pair of rail guns to ward off pirates. But nothing more. It was unlikely they intended to attack her here. And telling from the craft's modest engines, it was unlikely they had any plans on making a speedy getaway by out-running their fighters, either...So, what could these Drones possibly hope to accomplish here?

He became intrigued by these puzzling tactics.

"Advise the Planetary Guard to give them full clearance to enter our world," Kaypac said, to one of the droids that worked the control-panel in the semi-lit room.

"Notice sent, Commander," the droid replied, without looking around.

"Clearance has been given....Marked cargo-shuttle is estimated to arrive at our location in exactly 8 minutes."

"Ready a small platoon," Kaypac said "I need them on the surface, and in position in 5 minutes." She turned to leave, but paused when she noticed that Zhorg didn't make any motions to follow her. "Aren't you coming?" "Preparing for a war?" He asked, concluding that Kaypac's frustration and rage had indeed clouded her better judgment. She was much too bent on her own designs to recognize the enemy's humble approach.

"War's already upon us," she replied. Her tone of voice became very grim.

"It has already crept into our world to destroy us while we toiled. If we don't take serious action, we might not have a Sector to call our home much longer....Why can't you see that?" Without waiting for Zhorg to reply, she spun around and stormed out of the room.

The craggy mountains that covered most of Langworn, were more than just rock and stone. Embedded deep in the caverns, were, sprawling habitations and cities that jotted up and out of the impassable surface, forming their own canyons and gullies in astonishing ways.

From out of one of these, Kaypac emerged, strutting purposefully across the platform that resembled a giant tack, stuck to the side of cliff. More than a dozen armed droids followed her, their long capes whipping wildly about in the hot strong winds as they fanned out to surround the entire platform. They ignored the countless other crafts that whizzed by through the bright sky above them (some landing on similar platforms at nearby crags),choosing to focus only on the fiery bottom-thrusters of the descending shuttle, easing its way down toward them.

The landing pads slipped out from their panels just in time to cushion the shuttle's fall with gentle bounce. Even before the powerful engines began to wind down, two droids were already making their cautious approach, their laser rifles aimed at the bulky cargo-doors on the side of the vessel.

Slow minutes went by without the slightest of movements being made, save for the furious winds, and the indifferent crafts that were zipping by all around them. But eventually, a loud crack sounded, followed by a soft hiss, as the doers parted. open slowly.

An anxious Kaypac craned her neck to zoom through the widening crease. It was all dark inside at first, but then the big rusty head of an Omegon tribe-bot appeared. Then came the hulking body, and the huge hands that carried no weapons. He stood all alone in the gloomy threshold. She couldn't sense the whereabouts of the other tribe-bots anywhere in the shuttle.

She was the first to brake formation, hurrying over to the shuttle. There, the two gazed at each other, both presenting a false representation of their true forms. One, being a life-form, disguised as a bot. And the other, a bot, disguised as a living life-form.

As her artificial eyes met the thin blue band of light that stretched across the Omegon's face, the irony of the moment didn't go unnoticed. She could picture the Drone hiding inside the metal suit. "Step down," she said to him. "I'm assuming you haven't come all this way to strike a pose."

After a deep, nervous breath, Jack walked down the ramp that extended from the shuttle to the platform. The two droids closed in on him as he did so, training their rifles on his head. They grabbed him as soon as he came off the ramp; some kind of magnetic hold that allowed them to carry him just a few inches off the platform through the air. His sole comfort was in knowing that their weapons couldn't penetrate his armor---with the exception of Kaypac---if they did decide to kill him. But for now, they seemed content only on making him their prisoner.

Surprisingly enough, they released their hold when they came before Kaypac. Behind him, he could hear the metallic footsteps of a team of droids as they ascended the ramp and poured into the shuttle.

"What are you?" Asked Kaypac. Her voice sounded leveled, calm, yet still demanding.

"I'm Omegon," said Jack, as he began to recite the bot's attributes from memory. "Tribe-bot of Strong. The original tribe of---"

A bright flash smothered his vision just then, cutting off his words.

He froze, and waited for the pain that would surely come if Kaypac had decided to shoot off one of his limbs. But the moment quickly passed, and no pain followed. His vision cleared. He could see Kaypac still standing in front of him. The strong wind blowing a trail of smoke from the nozzle of her plasma rifle.

Out of sheer instincts perhaps, Jack looked down and saw a fist-sized hole drilled right through the platform where the plasma from Kaypac's rifle had shot through...between his feet.

"You are of no Omegon!" Kaypac growled. In mounting anger, she jabbed his helmet with the hot nozzle of her rifle, causing his head to jerk back violently. "I'm in no mood for lies, Assassin! You are Organic. Flesh and bone. But of what race?"

"Human," Jack said.

"A Human?" She sounded puzzled, unsure of whether she was familiar with the race. "of what planet, and Sector?"

"The planet, Earth. In the Epsilon Eridani Sector."

"Epsilon Eridani?" She raised her rifle and jabbed at his helmet again---all in one swift notion, at the blink of an eye. Too fast for Jack to react if he wanted to avoid the irritating blow. "Epsilon Eridani!? So far in the 4th Quadrant? You're just a baby. Why would the Meraachzions send a baby assassin to kill me? And why me, of all the trillions who call the Plogg Sector their home? And why the Plogg Sector?"

That is just what I came all this way to talk to you about, Jack wanted to say. But droids were notoriously incapable of reading sarcasm. So he got straight to the point. "The Technician," he said. "We don't want this radioactive junkyard of a Sector. We don't even want you. We want the Technician."

"But you tried to kill me."

"Only to find the location of your Master."

At the sound of that last word, Kaypac nearly jabbed him again, but she held the urge in check. Though she'd been wrong about the Technician ordering her death, he still played a role in some Meraachzion scheme. She wanted to know more. "And what interest do the Meraachzions have with him?"

"Three and a half centuries ago, your Master created a machine that caused an entire Sector in the Bhoolvyn region, to fall into a dark void."

"The Bhoolvyn Sector?" She said, incredulously. "There is no such Sector in this galaxy."

"There is...or, more precisely...there was."

"Impossible. I would've heard of such a thing. There isn't a Sector that I don't know in this entire galaxy."

"And yet, you've never heard of a Human."

"I didn't say planet," she shot back. "I said Sector. And there's no Bhoolvyn Sector."

"I can show you."

"A Sector that never existed?" She asked. "I must warn you now, Human. You're not long for this world. If I suspect you're trying to deceive me, I won't hesitate to kill you."

Jack didn't bother to reply to the droid's threat. From his implant, he pulled up a hologram of the lost Sector instead.

It resembled a broken sickle, outlined by a cluster of bright stars. "Here's the border between the 3rd and 2nd Quadrants," he said. "And here's where the Bhoolvyn Sector used to be."

The hologram zoomed in until the cluster of stars grew far apart and a huge gap suddenly appeared, like the shadow of a broken cup. The broken pattern in the stars' constellation became apparent just then, like a patch, torn out from a fabric's design.

Kaypac stared at it, uncertain of what she was looking at. But it was clear to see that something was indeed missing. "Seize him!" She ordered the droids in a sudden change of mood. "Lock him up in the den. Destroy his ship!"

"What?" Jack said, but Kaypac was already walking away. His feet came off the ground just then as the droids regained a magnetic hold on him. He felt the eerie sensation as if his Symbiot had locked his body in place.

"Hey! Wait a minute…! There's more. You haven't listened to everything I've got to---"

"There's nothing more to say!" Kaypac spat, spinning quickly back around to face him. "Organics are notorious liars. Connivers! And I warned you of what would happen if you tried to deceive me."

"But it's the truth!" Jack struggled in vain against the magnetic hold. He thought he had the situation in control, but now, things were taking a turn for the worst. "You saw the map for yourself. The Dark Void is real!"

"Do you mean, this map?" Kaypac pulled up an exact replica of the holographic map from her own uploaded software. The cluster of stars appeared exactly the same. But as she zoomed in, a perfect pattern of stars became visible…

the same constellation that was blacked out in Tack's map. "As you can see. There's no Dark Void."

Jack stood speechless as he gazed at the complete map of the Bhoolvyn Sector. The fear that began to build inside of him disrupted any line of thought that could've formed the simplest of plans in which he might've used to wriggle out of his current predicament. He'd thrown himself at Kaypac's mercy, with the hope that the enlightenment to the possibility of a greater plan would cause her to reveal the Technician's location willingly. But with his best strategy shot to pieces, the game had suddenly changed. "That's not a real map," was all he could think of to say.

"You're such a fool," Kaypac said, in a low, menacing voice. She walked up toward him, coming close. "Your Masters have lied to you. They've planted false things in your little Organic mind, then send you on missions in order to achieve their own ends. But you'll pay dearly for their mistakes....A pity though...you happen to be the most formidable enemy I've came up against thus far."

"I'm not alone," said Jack, regretting he was forced to use this last threat if things went wrong. "You kill me, and my drones will come after you. Kill them, and the whole Quadrant will destroy this entire worthless Sector. So I advise you to let me go, if you wish to avoid a war."

A low rumbling sound came from Kaypac's vocalizer... like a ridiculing laugh. "Spare me those petty Human threats. We'll deal with the Stendaarans, as we've dealt with the Drofh, if it ever comes down to that."

Jack could only watch in despair as Kaypac turned back around and headed down the platform. Her squad of droids falling in behind here, blocking his view. Behind him, he could hear the whirl of his shuttle's engines as one of the droids piloted it off the platform and flew quickly out of sight....

And just like that, he was left all alone on the platform, in an alien world, with two droids holding him prisoner.

As he felt his body begin to move, the reality of his defeat settled in the pit of his stomach. Up above, somewhere near Langworn's moon, his drones were looking down at him, quite possibly planning to break him out of the mountainous fortress. But for now, as his stiffed body floated across the platform, he would wallow in this defeat, knowing he'd played the alien's game, and lost.

CHAPTER
THIRTY-FOUR

"JACK," FORD'S VOICE came as a soft whisper in his ear, fearing the droids might hear her through his thick helmet. She couldn't possibly have known---for certain---that he was all alone, locked away in the dark cave of a cell, hidden deep in the bilges of a Langworn mountain. "Jack."

"Yeah, Ford," Jack said, sitting down and leaning back against the rocky wall. "I'm here."

"Are you hurt?"

"No. I'm fine. For how long, I honestly can't tell you. But I think they're holding me as some kind of hostage."

"I know. We heard everything. And from what was being said, it seems that Kaypac has a lot of questions for you. It's obvious she was lying about the map. She didn't know anything about the Dark Void....! think you might've pissed her off about that."

"I did," Jack said. "But I don't think that I'm the one she's pissed off at. She was lied to by her own Master. She probably threw me in here to save face in front of her men."

"You mean: Droids."

"Yeah---but you know what I mean all the same.... Listen, I want you all to remain where you are for now. Take no action, but pay close attention to what's being said.

I have a strong feeling my captors aren't finished with me just yet. They'll be back...and soon."

"Okay, Jack. But first sign that things aren't going the way we like, we'll scorch half the entire goddamned planet before Kaypac could pull the trigger."

"Don't kid yourself," said Jack, with a soft laugh. "No one's that fast....Just stand by, and make sure you get everything that's being said. Who knows...I might get lucky and pick her brains"

"You mean, her micro-processors."

"Yeah," said Jack. "But you know what I mean. Just stand by. Over, and out."

The long hours dragged by before Jack began to hear the first sounds of movement in the distance. Two pairs of feet, from the sounds of it. Their movements were rapid, approaching fast. In no time, they were at his cell, pausing just briefly as the door slid open.

Jack jumped to his feet as if sensing danger. He made a conscious effort not to draw his weapon, which was still secretly concealed. Both halves of the powerful Jhusrot rifle were still inside their hidden compartments built into the back of his armor. Both weapons had gone undetected by Kaypac and her squad of droids.

As she entered the dark cell with another droid (donned in a similar fleshy disguise), Jack thought he could take them both out at that moment. Kaypac was fast, but he knew he had the drop on her. All he had to do, was draw his weapon and spray them both against the wall. Seeing that laser-fire from the lesser droids couldn't penetrate his armor, an escape might not be too difficult from there. He could have her head, and quite possibly leave Langworn with it as well...!

'They'll kill us, Jack,' his Symbiot warned, gently in his mind. 'That is no ordinary droid she has with her. It's another AIGD.'

'He's different.'

'But deadly in these closed quarters. And from the looks of him, I'm guessing he's the one in charge now. We should hear what they have to say.'

Both Kaypac, and this strange new droid entered the cell. However, they didn't appear to come as Jack's jailers, but rather, like humble inquisitors, seeking his help.

"Human," Kaypac called, from the doorway. "Come here."

As Jack moved toward them, he noticed the droid easing its long fingers to the butt of his rifle. Though it wasn't built into his arm---the way Kaypac's was---Jack never had the slightest doubt that it shot deadly balls of plasma all the same.

"There's far enough," said Zhorg, causing Jack to pause dead in his tracks.

His deep voice sounded tremulous in the small cell. "What is this Dark Void that you spoke to my Lieutenant about? Show it to me."

Once again, Jack pulled up the starry hologram. The image washed the entire cell in a sheen of blue light. The shadows of floating stars drifted along the walls, floor, and ceiling in a stunning kaleidoscope of glowing orbs....The image froze, then zoomed in rapidly.

"There," said Kaypac, the instant she noticed the Dark Void coming into view. "There it is. Just like I told you, Zhorg."

Zhorg stared at the huge gap in the cluster of stars for a bit longer than Kaypac would've liked. In her haste to get to the bottom of the mysterious Dark Void, she'd grown dangerously impatient. And even though it was still too early to tell, he feared she might become inept to the situation. "In what Quadrant is this located?" He asked, a bit more cautious of the strange Human in the Omegon tribe-bot'a armor.

"The Bhoolvyn Sector," Jack replied. "It borders the 2nd and 3rd Quadrants. "It was once a major jump-point in the Dusphloean Regality until the war.

That is...until the Technician caused a great void in apace that swallowed up all the stars there. To this day, it remains impassable."

"You say, Technician," Zhorg began. "By that, do you mean...my Master?" "If we're talking about the same little box that designed you and Kaypac here, then yes. That's who I mean. Your Master. Through lack of a better definition perhaps, the Stendaarans gave him the code-name: Technician."

"You say he created this Dark Void?"

"Yes."

"Why?"

"To stop the Dusphloeans from entering the 2nd Quadrant. The Seezhukans must've been having a real hard time there."

"See..." Kaypac began. "He aids the phony Regality in war. The rumors are true---"

"We still don't know that for sure." Zhorg snapped back. "We know nothing of this Human. He could be a spy for any one of the Orders."

"Then why has the news of this Dark Void been hidden from us?" Kaypac asked. "If it's all just rumors, then why are our maps so different?"

"What?" Zhorg was genuinely confused. "What maps?"

"This," she pointed up at Jack's hologram.

"An easily devised illusion. Anyone could've---"

"Then what about this?" Kaypac brought up a small version of Jack's map through the projectors in her eyes. The hologram zoomed in quickly, and an exact copy of Jack's Dark Void appeared. "In many millennia I haven't had the need to question anything in the whole galaxy," she began, with her spindly fingers spread under the hologram as if holding it up.

"Until now....This is the real map of the Bhoolvyn Sector. And here's the Dark Void. It exists. Its real. So say the galactic archive. For whatever reasons, the maps that were uploaded into our systems were all intentionally swept clean of certain details. Quite possibly with the notion that we may never have the need to venture that far outside of our own Quadrant."

For an instant, Zhorg appeared as if lost for words; struggling with the meaning of his Master's betrayal. "But why?" He finally asked.

"He aides the phony Regality," Kaypac said. "As the Novlor and Delmor Orders have been warning us all along. He has no intentions of liberating Plogg from the Drofh, unless if it means to give it back to the Seezhukans."

"But then," Zhorg began, as the harsh reality of this new discovery dawned on him. "That means that the Kraaglor Front, working for the Seezhukans."

"That is exactly what it means," hissed Kaypac. "Spies! The lot of them!

Why else would he distance himself from us? Leave us on Strong, to run the Piilor Order, while the Kraaglor Front's busy handing over the entire Sector to the Regality---if they haven't done so already."

"Tell us, Human," Zhorg said, now turning to Jack to address a more pressing matter. "If our Master's aiding the Seezhukans, then why have you come here to assassinate her?"

"The Technician's a very important asset to the Seezhukans," Jack said. "From warships to fighter crafts, weapons and droids; they're all of his design. I was sent here to locate your Master and bring him back to the Stendaarans. Our only means of doing so, was through Kaypac, and I hardly think that she would've been willing to comply if we came and asked her politely....Nothing personal, though."

In the semi-lit cave, Kaypac's reaction was hard to read. But Jack could only have guessed she was weighing the options of whether to kill him, or betray her own Master, who...in all actuality...had betrayed her.

She closed her fist and the hologram vanished, prompting Jack to do the same. The cell became dark once more. "And what will the Stendaarans do if they have him?"

"Rid the Bhoolvyn Sector of the Dark Void," Jack said, mindful that she used the word "if," and not "when." "That would be my first guess....I think the restoration of the 3rd Quadrant's natural landscape's a top priority right now."

"And what will happen after that?"

"The war will continue on as it did before the Dark Void. Beyond that, I haven't the slightest idea. I'm just a Drone."

"She wasn't talking about the war, Human," Zhorg spat. "She means, our Master. What will happen to him, once the Stendaarans have what they want?"

"Your guess is as good as mine," Jack said. "Like I mentioned before: I'm just a Drone. As soon as we deliver him, we'll most likely be sent on another mission. It's quite possible we'll never hear from him again." He didn't think it would make much sense to hide this truth. However, he sensed that Kaypac's question wasn't a show of concern for her Master's safety. She saw great opportunity in the Technician's removal, not to mention the dangers of a loaning Stendaaran invasion that would surely throw them in the grip of imperial rule. On this fear, Jack played, for he knew that Kaypac would seek to see the Technician gone either way.

Kaypac turned to Zhorg. Her eyes flashed green, before blinking a string of silent code that only her Commander could decipher.

Zhorg froze as he read Kaypac's incoming message. When it came to an end, his eyes flickered a short reply of its own.

Kaypac gave a stiff nod of agreement upon reading Zhrog's reply. Quickly, she turned back around to face Jack. "Suppose we do help you locate our Master," she said. "Can you guarantee that the Meraachzions will leave this Sector alone?"

"Other than the Technician," Jack began. "We have no interest at all in the Plogg Sector. Once we leave, you'll never hear from us again."

"Whatever plans the Seezhukans made with our Master will be ruined," said Kaypac to Zhorg. "They'll be too busy with the Dusphloeans to keep their eyes set this far in the Quadrant. It's the only option we have at our disposal. If we allow things to continue as they are now, then Plogg will certainly fall. We can't let that happen, Zhorg. This might be our only chance. We have to act now."

"There's no error in what you say," said Zhorg. "In this matter, reluctance will only bring our society to ruin.... We'll be slaves to the Regality....My only regret, is that Master hadn't confided in us. Things might've been different."

"Is it done then?" She asked him one final time.

"Yes," said Zhorg, regretfully. "It is done."

"Good," said Kaypac. "We'll help you, Human. But don't think for an instant that you've gained some kind of victory over me. As much as I want to kill you, a higher purpose stays my hand. And I assure you, when all this is over, you are no longer welcomed in this Sector. If you ever return, for any reason, I will kill you and whoever's in your company. I don't care if the entire galaxy's on the brink of collapse. I will kill you if we ever cross paths again!"

"Sounds fair," said Jack, never doubting for a second that Kaypac would make good on her threat. Not only did he nearly succeed in killing her; he was now attempting to take her Master....He owed her double. And secretly, he hoped never to run into her again. "Once we're all finished up here, you'll never, have to worry about the Meraachzions."

She spun away from him and headed for the door that slid open as she exited the cell.

"Follow us," Zhorg said, as he fell in close behind her.

Down and down they went, leading Jack through the dark twisting tunnels until they emerged at the mouth of a cave that sat at the base of the craggy mountain. To Jack's complete surprise, his shuttle sat just 50 yards beyond; its cargo doors already held open as if expecting his arrival.

"Go back to your Drones, Human," Kaypac said, standing right beside him.

"But don't leave until you hear from us. We'll have to accompany you, if you wish to enter Brashnore."

"Brashnore?" Jack asked, a bit warily.

"A planet just beyond Chramonga," Zhorg said, ignoring the strong winds that yanked savagely at his cape. "Not even a light year away....Now go."

Without another word, Jack did as he was told, leaving the two droids to look after his unceremonious departure as they stood at the mouth of the cave.

He hurried to the shuttle, with a strong feeling of relief that he'd managed to escape a slow horrible death. A good thing the Technician was too smart for his own good. If not, Jack might've still been in that cave. But then again, he wouldn't have been so willing to walk into Kaypac's trap, either.

He hopped the ramp and entered the shuttle, glad to see that it remained untouched, save for the cranked lever that kept the cargo doors open.

"Can you talk, Jack?" came Semhek's impatient voice in his helmet's intercom.

"I think so," Jack said, reclosing the cargo door, then flicking a switch that caused the shuttle's engines to whine to life. "Yeah."

CHAPTER
THIRTY-FIVE

FOR AS LONG as he'd known her, Zubkov had always thought of Ford as immature, smart-mouthed, and a bit of a prankster even. For as long as they've been acquainted, she'd always taken the most casual approach to any situation, regardless of how serious or severe it may be. She treated the world like some unreal thing, as if in a dream, where the rules never applied, nor should they be of any concern. She'd once told him that they'd died the instant the symbiots; took over; the life of a slave wasn't worth having. They belonged to the Quadrant now. Earth had become a mere Province to some alien world from hundreds of light years away. She'd grown numb to most of the horrors that happened all over the galaxy. She's seen entire worlds exterminated by a single blast from Seezhukan war-cannons....And yet, she would show all this fear for the life of one man.

It came as a complete surprise to the big Russian, to see this hardened little girl, just run through the long narrow corridor of the docking-terminal to, embrace Jack as he boarded their ship. It was an awkward display...to see their bulky armor...for the Omegon tribe-bots weren't much for hugging. Their arms were too long; their hands too big, which collided clumsily into each other as they fell into the locking embrace. The emotion, however, was felt all the same.

They were all relieved when Jack had been set free. And now that he was back with them, Zubkov couldn't imagine how they'd continue on if Jack had died. In a way, their clever leader had brought some of their humanity back. He'd couldn't blame Ford for being so happy.

"I thought we'd lose you for sure back there," he heard Ford say, as they neared the couple.

"A good thing these droids have minds of their own," replied Jack. "I was afraid they might've been programmed to ignore reason."

"And what of these new plans that Kaypac and Zhorg have in store for us?" Asked Ghan, bringing a more serious tone back to their short reunion.

"Don't. know," said Jack. "But I tell you one thing: they hate knowing they were so easily manipulated into serving the Technician's own secret agenda. They knew nothing of his involvement in the war. For centuries, he was playing both sides of the fence. But in doing so, he lost their respect and trust. Had I known it was going to be this easy, I might've did things different, and Meerk wouldn't have to lose his life."

"That can't be helped now, Jack," said Braak. "What's the approximate time till we launch for Brashnore. I've already set a course."

"Don't know that, either," said Jack. "These droids aren't about wasting time, though. All that I was told, was that we should wait here."

"Do you think it's a trap?" Asked Semhek.

"I doubt it," said Jack. "If they wanted us, they would've killed me on the planet and blow this ship to pieces. Besides, I think my threat of a Stendaaran retaliation had some kind of effect on them. They desperately want to avoid any involvement in this war. The Sector's still at a very fragile point in its development. The slightest infraction might jeopardize the stability of the free worlds. And the biggest threat to Plogg's stability right now, is the Technician."

"So they're using us to remove him?" Asked Braak.

"As much as we're using them," replied Jack.

For the rest of the day, they settled in their quarters, anxiously awaiting the message from Kaypac and Zhorg. However, when they finally did hear from the two droids, it was hardly the message they'd been expecting.

One could only imagine their deep sense of betrayal upon seeing the two whole fleets of AI fighters flying up from Langworn into space. Within minutes they found their ship surrounded by the sleek, fast-moving crafts. Perhaps Kaypac had changed her mind after all, deciding at the last minute not to betray her Master.

"What are they waiting for?" Semhek said, baffled by the 16 fighters that showed up on the ship's radar. "I hope they don't think they can just take us prisoner. They'll take whatever fire-power this shuttle's got before they take me anywhere."

"Just hold on," said Jack, attempting to calm the jittery Tekwhaan. "They haven't even armed their weapons yet. Something else is going on."

"One's approaching," Semhek said. "I'm guessing its them."

"It might be," said Jack. "Don't do anything just yet. Let's see what happens. But in the mean time, raise shields."

"Shields raised," Semhek said.

"Why all the sudden precautions, Human?"

Jack recognized Zhorg's deep voice through the shuttle's intercom. From a hidden projector on the bridge, his tall hooded image appeared through a flickering hologram.

"We're not quite familiar with the Langworn approach," Jack replied. "It appeared as though we were being engaged."

"Well, you're not," said Zhorg. "This will be the party that will accompany us to Brashnore....You didn't think you could just abduct our Master so easily, did you?"

"Of course not," said Jack, to Zhorg's life-size hologram. "But...I have my own methods. With, or without you, the Technician would've found himself in our custody." It was a brittle lie. One he could afford to recklessly through around.

Zhorg, however, didn't seem impressed by Jack's petty bravado. He was more eager to get down to the business at hand. "A meeting has been arranged." "A meeting?" Asked Semhek, incredulously. "Why not alert the Technician that we're coming to arrest him....For that matter, why not alert the entire planet of our intentions."

Zhorg turned from Jack to stare at the Tribe-bot standing next to him. In their armored suits, they were all identical, impossible to tell apart. But judging from this one's demeanor, he could tell it was a different lifeform from the Human that allowed himself to be captured on Langworn. This one, he surmised, was a doer...but not much of a thinker. This one, might've came to Langworn, and attack an entire army of droids, getting the rest of his party killed in the process....He also noticed that one of its legs was a mechanical attachment, betraying the fact that he was also the same Organic that nearly succeeded in killing Kaypac, while managing to lose his own leg in the attempt.

"We're Drones," Semhek went on. "We use stealth to defeat our enemies.

We never announce our presence. You may have jeopardized this entire mission." "You could never get close to my Master on your own," Zhorg said. "I don't care what you are. Nothing nears Brashnore space without my Master's knowledge. Besides, the meeting's not with him, but another."

"And what does this other droid have to do with anything?" Jack asked.

"It provides a reasonable excuse for where we need to be," Zhorg replied. "The location of my Master's very close to the location of our meeting. You'll need to be swift, fierce...and a bit...stealthy, I suppose." His gaze shifted towards Semhek as he said this.

"And what's your role in all this?" Asked Jack.

"I will accompany you to Brashnore," said Zhorg. "As your guide, of course."

"And what of Kaypac?" Asked Ford, noticing that Zhorg had somehow taken command.

"Already on Brashnore, with our client," Zhorg said. "It was her, who informed me that a meeting's been successfully arranged. A powerful Regent of Strong, in need of a customized fitting, from the very assistants of the famous merchant, Jaanloch."

It came as a surprise to all the Drones that Zhorg had known this.

"And your fighters?" Jack asked, choosing to ignore the mentioning of the merchant. "Wouldn't it look strange, that 2 fleets should accompany a group of merchants to a fitting?"

"They'll be posted just outside of Brashnore space," said Zhorg. "They'll come to my aid the instant they're summoned."

"Well," said Zubkov. "That's good to know. I wouldn't like to be on the receiving end of anybody's fleet in this shuttle."

"There's one more thing I must do before we set off for Brashnore," said Zhorg.

"And what's that?" Asked Jack.

"I must board your ship."

CHAPTER
THIRTY-SIX

WHAAPCO, WAS JUST a lowly serve-bot when the Drofh first invaded Brashnore with their mighty ships that crippled the planet with their bombs and EMPs. Very few had survived the sudden invasion that left the world as dead as a barren moon. Mountainous heaps of scrapped metal had littered the better half of the planet's surface back then; the remains of broken droids; and buildings, shaken to their foundations. Those unfortunate enough to continue functioning were given the arduous task of recycling and rebuilding their own world, under the strict supervision of the Drofh lords and their trusted overseers.

Whaapco, was one such overseer, too concerned with his own survival and well-being to care much for the tight oppression he squeezed around his own kind---his fellow bots. Reduced to nothing but slaves, the surviving citizens of Brashnore had been thrown into an existence of perpetual toil and servitude, working every second of the five and a half decades it took to rebuild the entire planet's infrastructure.

And it was so, every second of the five and a half decades, that Whaapco, charged in overseeing one of the northern continent's larger Provinces, drove his fellow bots under the violent shocks of electric torture. He was known as the "Grinder" back then, for the harsh, unforgiving manner in which he handed down his punishments to any would-be droid, or bot, caught breaking down or malfunctioning under his watch. Too bent on impressing the more fearsome Drofh, he drove them into the ground---literally---to construct mega-towers, hundreds of feet down through the planet's rock, then up a few thousand more into the sky. Through those long, industrial decades, he oversaw the erection and growth of Flawn City: a super metropolis, with an area of over 3 million square miles. It would also become Brashnore's largest city.

But then the blemish of rebellion came. In tiny little pockets at first (in which Whaapco would immediately report to his lords), then in viral chunks that would eventually spread to the whole entire planet to form one of the first known underground Syndicates.

Outnumbered, and soon finding himself in the vengeful sights of the majority, the terrible overseer saw no other alternative but to become a conspirator among his own subjects. He supplied vital information on the Drofh's garrisons, and other secret headquarters that were scattered all over the city. He disclosed the location of hidden tunnels that he himself had seen to completion under the metal muscle of his slaves. He provided the vital codes that controlled all the machines which were used to turn against the Drofh occupiers and liberate their world once more, which, in an ironic sense, had begun to fare better than it ever did before the Drogh invasion.

The Syndicate, once known as the United Order of Brashnore, became very powerful as they rid their world of the Drofh. Not only would they regain their liberty, but they also strengthened their armies as every last one of the trillion-plus citizen droids were reassembled into armed soldiers.

With their hordes of combatant droids, the Brashnore Syndicate sought to liberate the other worlds in the Plogg Sector.

And so they went, from Brashnore, to Strong, to Chramonga, then Claan and Langworn...all up until they pushed the Drofh to the other side of the Kraaglor asteroid field, where the Drofh numbers were at their strongest, and where the battle to liberate the Plogg Sector still rages to this day.

Being on the right side of the Kraaglor asteroid field, more widely known throughout the Sector as Kraaglor Front, the leaders of the Brashnore Syndicate saw it more than fitting to rename themselves after the liberated half of Plogg. Thus, the Sector's first and most powerful Syndicate: The United Order of The Kraaglor Front, was born.

For his vital role in the countless rebellions that aided in the Syndicate's victories, Whaapco, the once feared overseer for the Drofh, was given the envied position of Regent, over all of Brashnore. The Kraaglor Syndicate had since moved their power to Strong---a much larger planet-----by then.

Though Whaapco's new position of power had guaranteed his safety throughout the centuries, it did nothing for the animosity that over a billion droids, who'd suffered under his harsh rule, still held for him. And many of these same droids had risen to power---in one form or another---of their own.

As a result (however ironic it may be), the Regent of Brashnore was denied many services that was easily granted to the lowest droids and tribe-bots. Throughout the entire liberated half of the Sector, the Regent was blacklisted, especially on other worlds where he held no power at all, and the brutality he'd shown toward his own kind during the Drofh occupation had become legend.

On Brashnore, Regent was all he was. Nothing more.

He was scorned, and widely ignored wherever he went. Entire shops, markets, and plazas would spitefully shut down whenever he was spotted anywhere near their vicinities---but then reopen the instant he was gone. As a blatant show of resentment, the droids of Brashnore often turned their backs to him whenever he walked amongst them in public---some showing the charred, black scars where his electric prods once zapped them.

Despite all this, Whaapco was a good Regent to Brashnore; perhaps to make up for all the bad he did in the past. He kept their taxes low, and regulations to a minimum. He pretended to understand their anger and resentment, and reasoned that even he might've treated him the same way, had he been in their position. He'd grown accustomed to the centuries of subtle (and not so subtle) chastisement from his own kind. Through servants, he acquired most of his goods; and being wealthy, he was far from needy.

There were many things that made Whaapco regret his past...but none more so than his denial of being upgraded to a more attractive body. It was the one thing that all the Merchants of Plogg ensured he would never get and so far, they'd made good on their promise.

It was the one thing that worked to fry Whaapco's circuits: being stuck in the body of a serve-bot. A very ugly one at that.

He was nothing more than a silver arrow-head, standing upright on a large disk. Equipped with a magnetic base only, he hovered no higher than five feet above the ground, and flew no faster than a butterfly. His vision split where he'd suffered a crack that ran down the middle of his visor. His voicebox sputtered from centuries of barking orders....He was as old, and rusty, as any scrap of metal in the junkyard.

In a way, he was condemned to live out the rest of his days in the same old covering until his circuits and mechanical parts malfunctioned altogether. A sort of systematic death-sentence in itself.

For years, he'd been offering entire fortunes for any droid to fit him with a new frame. Any frame would do, he didn't care for aesthetics...not at this point. But no matter how high he'd set a price on a new body, none was foolish enough to take him up on his generous offer. The general reason being: one would rather remain poor, forever, than assist him in any way.

He'd long given up on the idea, that is, until he got Kaypac's hail from all the way across the Sector in Langworn. As it turns out, someone was willing to risk their lives to give him a new fitting after all. Some tribebot Merchants, who usually traded outside the Quadrant (not that he cared), on a special run for the famous Jaanloch.

Being outsiders, they had no consequences to fear for aiding him with a new body, as long as they never returned to Plogg. But he promised complete secrecy, as well as a hefty reward for all their troubles nonetheless.

"I don't see why Zhorg has to be involved in all this," he said uneasily at Kaypac's side. The two stood on the landing platform of his gigantic tower, watching Zhorg lead the six tribe-bots from the shuttle. "It's just a simple fitting. These things happen all the time. There's no need for him to be here."

"It was Zhorg who made all this possible, sir," Kaypac said. "These Merchants are new to this Sector. It would be highly suspicious of them to come here by themselves. Especially here," she added emphasis to this last word. "But no one would ever question Zhorg."

"I see," the Regent said. "You have some merit there. And I must admit, Zhorg's presence should add some formality to this meeting, in case anyone care to inquire about the Merchants."

In truth, Whaapco didn't trust the so-called leader from the Piilor Province. He didn't trust anyone who wasn't loyal to the Kraaglor Front, for that matter. As long as there were divisions and factions within an established order, the threat of an insurrection would always exist. Both Kaypac and Zhorg were new to Plogg...like so many others...and hadn't contributed in any way to the liberation of these worlds. Their allegiance to Plogg, didn't stand on solid ground--the way his did. And that was what made them--- and all those like them---dangerous in his eyes. If it was up to him, no outsider would ever hold any position of power, anywhere, within the Plogg Sector.

But he never liked Zhorg for some reason. He felt the droid was too friendly with all the lesser Syndicates, and not cooperative enough with Kraaglor.

There was great ambition in Zhorg, and under his command, his Syndicate had gram well beyond the Piilor Province. Which was what made him nervous upon seeing the droid depart the shuttle.

What role would a commander of an entire Syndicate, play in a simple fitting? It didn't sit right with the Regent, even after Kaypac's explanation, which was highly plausible. He'd survived through too may uprisings and revolts, to let any old scheme just slip by him. The angle was all too familiar. Different circumstances lurked here than just a fitting. Nothing aimed directly at him though, he hoped....

"Welcome!" Whaapco said, as Zhorg and thee six Drones neared. "Welcome to my palace Commander. And I can't thank you enough for this great service that you are doing me."

"Thank you, sir, "said Zhorg, with a curt nod that might've passed for a bow. "An opportunity presented itself where I thought might be of some benefit to you."

"Ah," said Whaapco, thoughtfully. He was already floating back across the platform to his tower, prompting the others to follow close behind. "Speaking of opportunities... you never concerned yourself too much with me. So why the sudden reward now? What would warrant you to come all this way and offer me such a gift?"

"Not me," said Zhorg. "I don't care either way which body you find yourself in. I'm simply returning a favor, for a favor that was done for me....Ask the Merchants. It's they who follow the order to offer you a fitting."

"The Merchants." Whaapco turned to look at the Drones while floating backwards. "Well," he said. "I guess Jaanloch has finally come to his senses. But why now? Has your Master fallen on hard times? Or did he run out his use for the Oxloraans?"

Jack paused when he noticed the Regent wasn't just speaking rhetorically; that he actually expected an answer.

So he gave the best Human response that he could come up with on the spot. "Just following orders, sir," he said. "You're guess is as good as mine."

As insufficient as Jack's reply was, Whaapco seemed satisfied with his excuse. Perhaps because he didn't have a choice, or he simply didn't care what reason they had for coming to his world on such sudden notice. As long as he was fitted in his new body, he wouldn't order them to be scrapped. It was one thing to conspire against the Syndicate; but it was completely another to do it at the Grinder's expense.

The interior of the Regent's towering palace was nothing less than exquisite, for in every direction, the greenish translucent stones---from which the whole palace was made---could be seen. They made up the glimmering walls and high ceilings; the smooth see-through floors; the elegant carvings; and rows of columns that ran down the length of the long hall. It appeared as if the whole palace was carved from one mountainous gem. But it wasn't....The palace's interior was made from actual rocks, imported from the giant world of Ghlaan, just outside the Sector. The dense translucent rock, was ideal for building. And with its blue, greenish hue, it was the perfect aesthetic for the industrious droids who sought to rebuild their world. In fact, mostly all the towers on Brashnore, were built using these crystalline rocks.

There was hardly any place throughout the entire palace where Whaapco considered as private. As a serve-bot, he was never familiar with the concept. And faced with the responsibility of the whereabouts of over a trillion mechanical things, the busy hallways of the Regent's palace buzzed like street traffic.

The large room he finally led them into was fairly crowded as well. To Jack, it appeared like a library---except there weren't any books. Just dozens of droids, moving quietly about; many of them too engaged with their own tasks to pay much attention to their new visitors.

"Okay," Whaapco said, turning to the Drones. "Let's see it."

From the deep well of the Simulation Chambers' archives, Jack pulled up a holographic diagram of a tall, sleek-looking soldier droid.

"Hmmm," Whaapco said, staring at the rotating hologram. He seemed genuinely impressed. "A soldier...very good. What are the specs of this particular model?"

"This model's the very latest in Seezhukan wear," Jack began. "It's equipped with its own shield, mag-boots, and laser-rifle. It is very fast and agile. And it even comes with this---" The hologram shifted into a knifeshaped craft. "You're own flyer. Both droid and machine can be linked to a single line of communication where only you can have access to; and only you can control. No one else would be able to fly this thing, but you."

"You certainly don't speak like a tribe-bot," Whaapco suddenly said.

"No," replied Jack. "I'm a Merchant.'

"I suppose," said Whaapco, dismissively. "I don't like it."

Jack froze---as did all the others---apprehensively, as he tried to decide what the Regent actually meant. "Don't like what?"

"I don't like the fitting," the Regent replied. "The flyer's okay, but I never had much use for a weapon, so I don't see why I would need one now....Show me another."

More relieved than disappointed, Jack gladly pulled up another diagram for the Regent.

"I don't like that one, either," the Regent said. "I told you, I have no use for weapons. I'm a thinker, it is how I survive....I want something beautiful. Make me beautiful."

CHAPTER

THIRTY-SEVEN

THEY MUST'VE RAN through more than 300 different fittings that day; each in which the indecisive Regent, either shunned or turned down completely. He allowed them to rest after the last fitting, and promised to make up his mind when they met again the next day.

Standing in one of the palace's countless rooms, Zhorg peered through a window at the sprawling city of Flawn, and beyond. He'd pondered on many things there; one of them being Whaapco's reaction when he finds out that he wouldn't be fitting into anything anytime soon---at least not from the Drones. He never worried himself on whether or not the Regent might retaliate, though. Outside of Brashnore, he knew the "Grinder" was harmless.

He was more concerned with the Sector's fate, once his Master was removed from the planet. The leaders of the Kraaglor Front wouldn't take it lightly that a Piilor general had aided in abducting one of their own. That, in itself, was an act of war.

He was still thinking of a plan on how to convince the other Syndicates that his Master was a danger to Plogg, when something clicked inside his triangular head. And just as suddenly, his mind went blank.

A sound came. A long staccato of clicks.

"But why, Master?" Asked Zhorg, to the clicking sounds in his head. "I---I can't. I can't do it....Please...don't make me! Don't make me do this...!"

CHAPTER

THIRTY-EIGHT

"THIS IS COMPLETE nonsense!" A frustrated Zubkov said, back in the drone's private quarters. "All of it is. And you know it, Jack. We must've ran through a whole battalion of some of the Seezhukan Regality's most state-of-the-art droids, and this...this...flying dispan...couldn't come up with the decency to at least pick one, considering we're busy Merchants and all. I'm telling you right now Jack, I don't care who this Regent think he is, but I'm not spending another day in this fruity Sector."

"I agree with Zubkov," Semhek said. "If the Technician's anywhere in this palace, then I say we go get him right now, and leave this world. It's not like we're actually giving him a new body. It's all an act, remember? We're just wasting time entertaining this Regent with false hopes."

"I don't see why he can't just choose a body and be grateful," Braak said. "Though he's only a serve-bot Whaapco's one of the most powerful bots on this world. He yearns to be recognized as part of Brasnore's nobility."

"Well," said Jack, with a subtle shrug. "Unfortunately for him, all we have on file are Seezhukan gears of war. But even if we had a model of the emperor himself, it would do him no good, because we can't give it to him.

Sooner or later, we're gonna have to retrieve what we came here for."

"The Regent's no fool," Kaypac said. "Nor would he ever allow you to just storm through his palace, unchecked by any one of the thousand soldier-droids that guard this place. We must follow the plan; trust me, it's the only way."

CHAPTER
THIRTY-NINE

ZHORG, ACCOMPANIED BY over a dozen guard droids, suddenly burst into the drone's quarters in one violent sweep, shooting several bright rounds of plasma over their heads in order to get their full attention. "Seize them!" He said, in the face of the stunned drones.

A furious Kaypac shot up from her seat. "What is the meaning of all this, Zhorg?" she asked. "Was it your plan to betray us all along?"

"I haven't betrayed anyone," Zhorg replied; the blue orbs of his eyes glowing brightly. "I'm simply obeying my Master's wishes. But you, on the other hand. It is you, who have betrayed us for these Meraachzion filth." He raised his rifle and a white flash filled the room as a wad of plasma spat from the nozzle to go flying right through the generator inside of her chest.

Kaypac's metal body collapsed to a lifeless heap on the floor. Hot plasma oozed from the gaping wound in her back, burning a hole in the floor beneath her.

"No one make any moves!" said Jack, into all the drones' intercoms, after witnessing Kaypac's sudden death. "We're out-numbered for now, and they have the advantage."

"What the hell just happened?" asked Ford.

"I don't know," Jack said. "But it looks like some other arrangements have been made....Everyone, do as you're told. We still have a hand to play in this, but now's not the time."

"It appears that you'll be getting to see my Master much sooner than originally thought, Human," said Zhorg, to Jack. "But not in the way you once hoped."

"And that's where you're wrong, Zhorg," Jack said. "I never hoped for anything."

"Doesn't matter," said Zhorg, turning to his squad of droids. "Take them away."

CHAPTER
FORTY

ZHORG STARED INSIDE the cell as a hot laser-grid shot across the threshold to separate him from his prisoners on the other side. He waited patiently till the last of his guards were out of ear-shot, before addressing the drones. "I'm afraid you won't be allowed to leave this time, Human," he said. "Other plans have already taken their course."

"So I'll just assume that none of those plans included Kaypac being alive," Jack said.

"She out-served her purpose," Zhorg replied, in the most casual manner. "She was headed in a direction that would've been disastrous for us all in the end."

"The only thing that'll end up ruining this Sector, is your Master," Jack shot back. "As long as he continues to aid the Seezhukan Regality, the war will eventually spread here, as it did to my home world. They're already beginning to send drones. Stendaaran warships and Oxloraan Planet-Crushers will be next. Their hordes will smother these worlds, including those occupied by the Drofh. You're making a huge mistake."

"My Master don't make mistakes."

"They'll never stop looking for him," Jack said. "Do with us whatever you, or your Master, will. We play a very minor role in this war. We're not even soldiers. Killing us won't stop the----"

"Kill you?" Zhorg sounded amused. "Is that why you think you're here? To stay locked away until your brief little life-spans expire? No, Human. We may be immortal, but we never engage in wasting time. If my Master wanted you dead, you would've died with Kaypac in your quarters. And that would've been the end of that."

"Why cage us up like this then?" asked Jack.

"Your weapons," Zhorg replied. "There's nothing like it in all the galaxy.... and perhaps the entire Universe. It's the only thing keeping you alive. But not for long."

"How so, Zhorg?"

"Because, that is my Master's wish. He wants you to give us the source of the weapon you used on Kaypac."

"And what if we don't know of this source?"

"Whether you know or not, is not for me to decide. No Organic can withstand our truth-serums. If you know anything, you'll tell us one way or the other."

"But we have no weapons," Jack said, splaying his arms to indicate they were all unarmed. "We left them all behind on Strong, as a show of good faith. You know that. You scanned us for yourself."

Indeed," Zhorg said. "And in good faith it truly was. But in time, you'll reveal those too. Along with all that the Stendaarans have planned for us." "I thought you were against the Regality?"

"We are," Zhorg said. "But what's good for the Regality is also good for Plogg. It's the one thing Kaypac never understood. She was willing to aid the enemy, without thinking of the consequences her actions would have on us all. But my Master knew. If the Meraachzion worms win this war, the Plogg Sector will be changed, forever."

"So your Master thinks he can use our weapons to aid the Seezhukans?" asked Jack.

"Oh, more than that, Human."

"But there's one thing you haven't figured out quite correctly," Jack said.

"And what's that?"

"How can you make anything out of an indestructible element?" "What...?"

"Perhaps that's why the Stendaarans, the Oxloraans, and the Meraachzions couldn't use it. Simply because it can't be used for anything else...."

"Huh...but how?"

"....Other than deadly, high-flying projectiles---"

A soft "pop" sounded just then.

Zhorg watched in baffled surprise as his arm dropped to the floor, spewing a wide arch of sparks from the end that had just been shot off. "What---"

Another blast of Jhusrot flew through the cell's laser-grid bars, punching a fist-sized hole through his plasma generator. He fell like a broken scaffold, twitching his last robotic spasms as the power supplied by the precious plasma fled his circuits. He was dead within seconds.

Jack spun around to see Semhek, with his rifle drawn. "I told you not to make any moves," he said.

"No drone has ever allowed himself to be captured alive in the history of this war," Semhek said. "This is because the symbiots terminate their own hosts in the event of such a thing. And I was about to be terminated, Jack."

"Me too," Braak said.

"As was I," said Ghan

And so were Ford and Zubkov.

'Is this true?' Jack asked his own Symbiot. 'Were you about to kill me just now?'

'Only as a last resort,' Klidaan answered.

'Why didn't you tell me about this?'

'It is not something I prefer to discuss with my hosts. It sort of takes their edge away.'

'This is unbelievable!'

'I think all's safe now. The threat's gone.'

"What part of Drone Commander, don't seem to register here?" Jack said out loud, disappointed that his order had been disobeyed. "Now, how else are we supposed to get out of here? The only one who could've freed us, is now dead."

To prove some unspoken point, Semhek snapped his weapon in half and replaced them back into their hidden compartments in his armor. He then approached the laser-grid---meant for keeping prisoners from getting out---and walked right through as the deadly beams bounced harmlessly off the armor's protective coating.

"This is how we get out," Semhek said, then began reassembling his weapon.

In his haste to extract as much information as from Zhorg as he could, Jack had forgotten all about the photochromatic film that covered their armor in order to repel all forms of light, especially lasers. It now made sense to him why Semhek had to put his rifle away before going through the grid; if he hadn't, it would've been sliced to pieces.

Ghan, the tall Lannsillian, didn't waste any time in leaving their prison. The others followed.

"Okay then," said Jack, staring down at the dead leader of the Piilor Syndicate. "Do you think he knew where the Technician's hiding on this planet?"

"Only one way to find out," Ford said, already stooping to a crouch near Zhorg's body. She propped his big triangular head up against the wall, then pulled a pencil-shaped probe from her armored finger, sticking it savagely into his left eye as pay-back for what he did to Kaypac. She stepped back as a blue spherical hologram bubbled up from the end of the probe. The entire layout of the contents inside Zhorg's head hovered in compressed detail before them. "Okay," she said, staring at the maze of complex symbols. "This may, or may not take a while."

"Ghan. Zubkov," said Jack. "Stand guard at the southern corridor. Semhek and I'll stand by the western-end just around that corner. Braak, you stay with Ford. The Technician must know that Zhorg's lights have been put out by now. I wouldn't be surprised if troops are heading to our location right now. So we don't have much time, Ford."

"I'll work as fast as I can," Ford said, just as Ghan's rifle fired off a quick burst that felled two approaching droids at the other end of the long corridor. "Go!"

Jack and Semhek both rushed down to meet the western corridor when a droid's head peeked from around the corner. They were both relieved to see the green streaks of laser-bolts zip right past them. They could also hear more rapid rifle fire coming from Ghan and Zubkov....A battle had begun.

Semhek raised his weapon and squeezed off a burst near the edge of the wall where he knew the droid hid behind. Small chips of metal and rock exploded where the Jhusrot entered the wall. A second later, the broken droid dropped face-first to the floor with a loud crash.

The two Drones approached the dead droid cautiously and peeked around the corner to find a dozen more positioned all throughout the corridor.

Jack shot into their ranks, downing one in the process, causing the others to go scrambling for cover. A barrage of angry laser-fire then riddled the back wall behind them.

Indifferent to the harmless rain of bolts, Jack turned to Semhek. "These aren't the Technician's personal guards," he said. "He must know we're coming. And that could quite possibly mean that he's somewhere in this palace."

CHAPTER
FORTY-ONE

"A MATRIX MIND." The words came out of Ford's mouth as if they meant the end of the Universe. And as she stood there in the corridor---where two small battles raged nearby---staring up at the dozens of holographic cubes and orbs floating above her head, they might as well had.

"What is it?" asked Braak, coming up behind her. He looked up at the holograms projected by the probe, but to him, they meant nothing.

"As our luck would have it, Zhorg turns out to be a walking main-frame of a droid," Ford said, sounding disappointed. "See these things here?" She reached up and touched one of the floating cubes, causing it to expand ten times larger. "It's just one of Zhorg's brains. And if he's as old as I hate to think that he might be, then this one brain could contain every second of information over the past ten thousand years. That's way too much data to sift through, considering what little time we have. And then we have the rest of these." She nodded up at the other orbs and cubes; each one a glowing shape of compressed, ancient data. "If this one turns up without the answers we need....No wonder why the Oxloraans wanted Kaypac; they must've known about Zhorg."

"There's a tracker on Kaypac's body," Braak said. "we can still find her and get what we need."

Ford shook her head. "I already thought of that," she said. "But we would still have to get out of here first, find her, get the data, then find the Technician. All while fighting off all the droids in the palace."

"They can't hurt us."

"That's not the point," Ford said. "It's time that we don't have. The Technician's probably making his getaway as we speak. And by the time we find him again---" She paused, as a sudden thought occurred to her. "Wait...I have an idea." She flicked the cube away and it spun back down to a regular fist-sized box, before, floating back up to join the other holograms. "We might not need Zhorg, or Kaypac, after all."

"What do you mean?" Braak asked.

"The moment we stepped off the shuttle I've been secretly scanning our surroundings, and that includes inside the palace, even as Zhorg killed Kaypac and had us thrown in that cell. So now I have a partial map of the Palace.

I only hope we're not too late." From her own implant, Ford pulled up a holographic map of the palace's interior. She dragged through the maze of corridors and rooms until she found what she was looking for. "Here," she said, stopping at a room that gave them a live feed.

"It's the Regent's quarters," Braak said.

"Yes. I planted one of my cameras when I saw this." She pointed at a large box she thought resembled a pirate's chest.

"What is it?"

"I don't know. I just thought I should keep an eye on it. But this was an earlier feed, before all this...madness...began.

We were probably still in our quarters at that time. If we just speed it up a bit---skip to the present."

Braak gave a distressful grunt when the picture changed. The room was now filled with guard-droids, and what appeared to be the Regent's personal guards. The serve-bot hovered motionless between the crowd. They were obviously preparing to defend themselves in the event the Drones decided to attack them.

But this wasn't the source of Braak's panic. Something else had caught his eye....The box is missing!

"I knew it," said Ford, already flicking to different parts of the Regent's palace where she hid her cameras. But then she saw them: about fifteen AIGDs, the same ones that had accompanied Zhorg to their quarters. They were now heading down the long hallway that led to an outside platform. Four of them were carrying her treasure chest. "Jack!" She yelled into her intercom. "We have to get out of here. Now!"

CHAPTER
FORTY-TWO

THE DROIDS IN the western corridor had quickly figured out that their weapons were useless against the Drones' armor. They retreated as best as they could while Jack and Semhek closed in, picking them off one by one as they turned to flee the Jhusrot rounds that continued to lessen their numbers. Soon, the two Drones found themselves all alone amid the countless bits and pieces of broken droids that littered the floor.

"That was easy," Semhek said, kicking at a severed arm that still twitched at the fingers. He hoisted the rifle close to his face to admire it with some newfound respect. "The Oxloraans sure knew what they were doing when they made this one. It's a bit crude, and ugly, compared to what I'm used to. But it's one of the most destructive weapons that I've ever fired on anyone."

"Jack! We have to get out of here. Now!"

"What is it, Ford?" asked Jack. "Did you find the Technician?"

"He's getting away!" Ford's voice sounded more urgent than ever. "He's on the platform, and he's about to board a ship. We don't have much time."

"Send us his location," Jack said. "And don't wait for us. Just get there and stall him if you have to."

"Okay," Ford said. "Sending data now. I'll gather Ghan and Zubkov to prepare a route to intercept."

A faint beep sounded in Jack's ear as the data was transmitted to his implant. He pulled up Ford's partial map and found the AIGDs hauling a large box across the platform to an awaiting ship.

"You think he's in that box?" Semhek asked, a bit skeptically.

"It's very likely," replied Jack. "His personal guards wouldn't leave without him."

"What's the fastest way out of here then?"

Jack zoomed out from the platform to get a whole display of the map.

Though it didn't show exactly where they were located, he'd gotten a pretty good idea of where they were in the palace. He simply drew an imaginary line from where he thought they were, all the way up to the platform in a diagonal slant. "Here's our fastest and most direct route to the platform," he said.

"We'll have to go through all those walls and ceilings to get there."

"I know," Jack said. "But we have these, remember?" He hoisted his rifle.

Semhek laughed as Jack raised the weapon and took aim. "I haven't thought of that one."

"That's because you're not Human," Jack said.

"And what's that supposed to mean?"

"On Earth, us Humans will remove an entire mountain just to make way for a narrow road." He then fired up into the ceiling.

The Tekwhaan laughed again at the Human's stubborn reasoning before he aimed his own rifle at the ceiling and joined Jack's fire-power, shooting in a wide circular motion until that section of the ceiling collapsed in a pile of dust and rubble.

"Ready?" said Jack, activating his grav-boots.

"Grav-boots ready," Semhek replied.

"Okay then. See you outside." As Jack crouched, the red soles of the boots glowed brighter before sending him up, crashing through the ceiling to the higher floor where he crashed through another ceiling that the Jhusrot had already partially destroyed. And in this way he went, shooting his way up through the walls and floors of the palace until finally making his way to the hall that led to the platform outside.

They shot up through the floor of the hall as if a whale had suddenly spat them out in disgust.

Blind, and covered in dust, they dropped heavily on the ground. "There they go," Semhek said, raising slowly to one knee, shaking the loose dust from his visor. "They're already boarding the ship!" He rushed to the platform, firing and downing the last AIGD before the ship's shuttle-doors slammed themselves shut. He switched his aim to the ship's engines, and was about to destroy it, when an alarm suddenly screamed in his ears. "No," he said to himself dreadfully, reacting instantly to the alarm by darting out of the way before a tossed grenade exploded where he once stood.

"Demolition-droids!"

The Tekwhaan could hear Jack's shout as he went through the air, propelled a few extra yards by the blast.

He skidded across the platform when he landed, drawing fussy sparks from his armor as it went grinding against the smooth, solid stone.

The ship's engines began to stir, but he couldn't be bothered with the Technician's escape just then. A more certain death charged toward him on four metal legs, with a long barrel of a snout pointing down in his direction.

With no time to scramble to his feet, Semhek rolled frantically out of the barrel's line of sight, barely avoiding being blown to bits as the platform exploded. He was so disorientated, he didn't realized that he'd dropped his weapon until he made the conscious effort to fire on the beastly droid, only to find that his hands were empty. However, as despairingly futile as this motion was, it did cause the droid to pause in a hesitative way, as if anticipating the deadly fire from the Jhusrot. It gave him just enough time to reach for the pistol instead, while getting a good look at the giant droid that, gleamed under Brashnore's bright suns. It seemed agitated that it hadn't fired upon, stomping dominantly on the platform, then rearing up on its hind legs to expose an oval-shaped body that appeared to be made of nothing but pipes and gears. A mere boast...that it had conquered its enemy, which it would soon kill, had it not been for the rapid fire from Jack's rifle.

The swiveling head of the Demolition-droid was the first to go, like brittle clay, crumbling under the fierce wind. And with barely anything left to keep it erect, the bomb-tossing barrel fell limp like an elephant's trunk. One of its legs snapped like a splintered board, causing it to fall sideways with a savage scream. Yet, it was far from crippled when the Jhusrot tore into its chest, shattering the gears that kept it mobile...killing it in a sense.

The Tekwhaan climbed to his feet, and with his pistol he fired into the broken droid until it stopped moving altogether. Had they been near the edge of the platform, he might've kicked it over.

"You okay?" asked Jack, coming up beside him.

"No," the Tekwhaan replied, staring across the horizon, where the Technician's ship was making its escape. "He got away." "Oh," said Jack, looking after the ship. "That."

"You don't sound concerned that we failed."

"I'm not," said Jack, raising his rifle to peer through its long-range scope. "And we didn't fail." He squeezed off eight rounds, each hitting the distant target within fractions of a second. Smoke trailed through the sky behind the ship, then an explosion followed as one of its engines erupted in flames....The Technician's ship began to fall.

"Wow!" Semhek was genuinely surprised, and impressed, at seeing the Human make such an incredible shot. But then he saw the other Drones rushing onto the platform and his composure changed. "Nice shot," he said, in a more nonchalant tone. "Would've done it myself if I had my rifle with me."

"What happened out there?" asked Ford, staring across the horizon as she and the rest of the Drones fell in behind them.

"You're late, "Semhek said. "That's what happened. But we already have things under control here."

"We had a slight problem on our way here, Jack," Braak said, pointing back at the palace as the Regent, accompanied by over 100 droids, spilled out onto the platform. His little disk of a body wavered through the air toward them.

"What is the meaning of all this?" the serve-bot asked. "Coming here. Destroying my palace. I should have you all vaporized!"

"Then what's taking you so long?" Semhek asked, gripping tightly to his pistol as he looked past the Regent at all the droids that had them surrounded.

"You must know by now that your weapons have no effect on us," said Jack.

"Which is why you sent your Demolisher after us," Semhek added. "Is that the only one you have?"

"There was never any need for more," replied the Regent. "Brashnore hasn't experienced war since the day we rid ourselves of the Drofh. And that one wasn't in too much of a good condition to begin with. If it had, you'd both be blown to bits by now."

"We need a ship," Jack said.

"I need a fitting," the Regent shot back. "Or have you forgotten why you're here? What happened to Kaypac and Zhorg isn't any of my concern. They're not of Brashnore, nor were they citizens of Plogg. Once I have my fitting, you can leave here in whatever ship you like."

"We don't have time for this," Jack said to Semhek. But then he noticed all the many towers surrounding them, with platforms, and all kinds of flying things. He pointed to the nearest one, where a silver space-ship sat comfortably on its own platform. "There," he said. "We'll use that one."

"we'll jump," said Ghan.

"Jump?" asked Zubkov, warily. "But that's more than 100 yards. The SimChambers never allowed us to---"

"Then you better hope the Sim-Chambers are as adequate in predicting jumps, as they were in replicating Kaypac's speed," said Jack. "We have to get on that ship before the Technician finds another and escape for good this time."

"Wait!" said the Regent, flying in between the Drones. "What about my fitting? You have orders from the great Jaanloch himself."

"I hate to break the bad news to you," said Jack. "But we didn't come here on Jaanloch's orders."

"We didn't come here for a fitting, either," Ford said.

"But---" the Regent began to object, but the Drones were already on their way to the edge of the platform. "You'll never do business on this side of the Sector again"! He shouted after them. "Tell Jaanloch I'll have him exiled for this!"

CHAPTER

FORTY-THREE

JACK COULDN'T HELP but think of a roller-coaster's tracks when he saw Ford's hologram of the twisted arch, floating between the two towers like a strained bow. "Is that supposed to be our planned trajectory?" he asked, thinking he might've been in over his head when he suggested they should jump to the other tower. Staring at the measured readings displayed in bright yellow numbers, he realized that Zubkov was wrong in his estimate of the length between the two towers as well. For it wasn't 100 yards to the nearest tower, but 350.

"If we catch the wind just right," Ford said. "At a 75 to 80° angle, then we should ride the wind long enough to make it."

"In theory," Semhek said.

"Yes," said Ford. "In theory, this can work, considering our grav-boots are powerful enough to give us the boost we need. But if all else fails, the worst that can happen is that we'll be in for a real rough landing on the surface."

"And allow the Technician to get away," Ghan added.

"There's no time to think about that now," said Jack. "The computer said we can make the jump. Prepare to upload the trajectory into your implants, and make sure to set your boots to maximum power."

"There's a problem with that too, Jack," Braak said, using his own logic to predict another bad outcome if things went wrong. "If our boots do turn out be Sufficiently adequate, then too much power might cause us to overshoot our target and go flying off the other side."

"I'll worry about that if it ever becomes a real issue," Jack said. "Set boots to maximum power. Prepare to jump." With a single thought to his implant, Jack could feel the strong vibration under the soles of his boots where most of the armor's power were held poised. He stepped closer to the edge, looking down at the telescopic drop, uncertain of whether his boots would have enough power to soften the fall in the event they fell too short, or too far. But the thought was quickly swept from his mind, however, as he turned eastward to face the winds that rushed by like a great rapid. He braced to a crouch, and commanded his implant to activate the repulsion in his boots, causing him to be launched through the air instantly.

Air-borne, like a man shot from a cannon, he could feel the wind pushing his body sideways as he mounted higher in the sky. He stole a backward glance, and was surprised to see how far he'd gone in such little time.

Three of the Drones had already made their jumps, like black fleas, from the platform where the Regent and the rest of his droids stood by, watching.

There was the brief sensation of weightlessness as Jack climaxed to the peak of his flight, before falling into a steep descent. From here, the wind shifted his body and lined it into the direct path of the other platform, just as Ford's hologram had predicted. But he was no longer jumping, he was now falling at the mercy of gravity....He was coming in too hard.

"So far, so good," Jack said, to the other Drones behind him. "Looks like we're gonna make it, but the landing might be a little bit rough. We'll have to use what little power we have left in our boots to soften the fall."

The platform came up fast. Jack timed the landing as best as he could, activating the repulsion in his boots in short bursts until he felt his body gradually beginning to slow down. As he neared 100 feet from the platform's surface, he allowed his self to fall, landing heavily on the platform like a small car.

Ford, Ghan, and Braak fell next, though their landings weren't as smooth.

"See?" Ford said, calling up to the big Russian, who made his landing with a painful looking tuck-and-roll. "Piece of cake."

"Easy for you to say," Zubkov said. "You don't weigh 307 pounds of solid muscle."

"Yeah right!" Ford shot back you mean, 300 pounds of fat, and 7 pounds of muscle."

Hearing the two discuss their weight caused Jack to worry about Semhek. By far, the little Tekwhaan was the lightest of all the Drones. And as he looked up to the sky, he swore under his breath for having his fears confined. Semhek was flying higher than his planned trajectory. And on his current path, he would miss the platform by at least 50 yards. "Semhek's coming in too high," he said to the others. "He's going to fall over!"

"Oh no!" said Ford, looking up. "Semhek, you have to activate your repulsion right now...Semhek! Do you hear me...?"

"I hear you," Semhek said. He sounded frustrated. "But I don't have any more power. I used it all to make the jump."

"But how?" asked Zubkov. "You're as light as a feather. It shouldn't have taken that much power to get you through the jump."

"I only have one leg, remember." Semhek said. "I'll have to catch him," Zubkov said.

"Not you, Zubkov," said Jack. "Braak's heavier. He has a better chance of catching Semhek and slowing him down than any one of us here." "You'll have to jump from this spot, Braak," Ford said; a holographic display was already in her hand with a calculated read-out of his next planned jump. "Hurry! You have 8 seconds."

Braak ran over to the indicated spot on the platform, taking one look up at the incoming Tekwhaan, before hopping more than 100 yards in the air, directly in the path of Semhek's flight.

The clash of the two armored suits colliding was heard all around the platform, like a distant clap. Though Braak did succeed in slowing Semhek down, he failed to catch him. The Tekwhaan had came in too hard, and too fast, simply knocking Braak out of the way, sending both Drones drifting toward the platform's edge.

Ghan and Zubkov were the first to react, rushing to the edge of the platform as the two Drones fell from the sky, landing hard on the platform with a bounce and a skip before skidding toward them in a violent shower of sparks.

Using what little power he had left in their boots, they fastened themselves to the surface and braced for impact.

Though the tribe-bet's suit enhanced his strength to an incredible degree, Zubkov heard a snap somewhere in his armor as the much heavier Braak slammed into him like a ton of bricks. Only when his feet slid out from under him, did he realize that his grav-boots had become damaged by the strain of the impact. However, he did manage to stop the Drone from skidding on the platform, even though he was now the one sliding toward the edge.

The big Russian pawed frantically at the platform's surface before finally managing to sink a gloved paw into the smooth stone. The platform tore under his grip with a deep grinding sound, pitching small chips of stone in the air as he went. Both legs, and most of his body, had gone over the edge when he eventually came to a grating halt.

"I guess another deserves one hand."

When Zubkov looked up, he saw Semhek standing over him at the edge of the platform. "What...?" he began asked, in a puzzled way. "What did you say?"

The Tekwhaan stooped down and offered him a hand. "I guess another deserves one hand," he repeated.

The big Russian laughed as he allowed Semhek to pull him back up on the platform.

"What did I say that was so funny?" Semhek asked.

"It's not what you said," Zubkov replied. "It's how you said it." "And how did I say it?"

"It's one good hand, deserves another," Zubkov said. "That's not what I said...I said that another deser---"

"I know what you said," said Zubkov. "But you said it all wrong." "How did I say anything wrong, when all I said was that you deserve a hand?"

"But that's not how the saying goes."

"What saying?" The Tekwhaan was now confused.

"You tried to quote a popular Human saying just now."

"That's not so, Zubkov. I don't know anything about any Human sayings. I was simply trying to help you, being as though you saved me from going over the---"

"Are we going to board this ship?" Jack cut in over their intercoms. "Or are we going to keep debating who's the better helper?"

Both Drones spun around to find the others already hurrying up the ship's rear cargo ramp.

"My apologies, Jack," Semhek said, before he turned back to Zubkov. "We'll finish this later. Then we'll find out who's the better helper." He then hurried over to the ship.

For a moment, the big Russian just stood there staring incredulously after the dogmatic alien. He opened his mouth to object but thought better of it and headed to the ship.... It was a battle he would never win.

CHAPTER

FORTY-FOUR

AS SOON AS they boarded the ship, one of the first things Ford did, was run a complete scan of the interior lay-out. She then pulled up a complete diagram of the ship from her implant's galactic archive. She became worried by the information she received. "Jack," she said, coming up to his side as they approached the bridge. "We have a problem."

"What is it, Ford?" asked Jack.

"This is an AICS-734," Ford said, to which the other Drones (except Jack) all gave grievous sighs.

"So?" asked Jack.

"we'll never get this thing off the ground," said Zubkov. "we're definitely on the wrong ship. It won't even power up for us."

"I wouldn't say definitely just yet, Zubkov," said Braak. He turned to Ford. "You say this a 734?"

"Yes," replied Ford. "But do it even matter what model it is?"

"Yes," said Braak. "It does. This is a much older model than what we're used to seeing outside this Sector. And you have to remember, we're tribe-bots now. Not Drones."

"Braak's right," Semhek said. "This is not a war-ship. It's a small vessel, appointed to serve another. With a few convincing words, we just might get it to take us where we need to go."

Thinking back, Jack remembered how well the Tekwhaan handled the AIMC-76, back in the Simulation Chambers. He figured if anyone could get the ship moving, Semhek would be the one to do it. "Okay," he said. "We're running out of time. Better get to work right away."

The ship came alive the instant the Drones entered the bridge. The walls and ceilings lit up with alien symbols and characters all around. On the wide window, a green hologram of a box-shaped face appeared, eyeing the Drones intently as they made their way further onto the bridge. "It's been ages since a tribe-bot set foot in here," it said, in a friendly voice that seemed to catch the Drones off guard. "Are you Spagon's new friends? It's been a while since she's had any."

"Yes," Semhek quickly replied, before anyone else had the chance to foil the plans he already had in mind. "We are Merchants, on a very important errand for Spagon. Time is of the essence, so we would like to depart right away."

There was hesitant pause from the ship as it considered Semhek's request. Though it appeared quite friendly upon first sight, it wasn't ready to just get up and leave so suddenly with a group of strange Merchants. It would need something more. "Then why hasn't Spagon informed me of this before hand?"

"Because Spagon doesn't know," the quick-witted Tekwhaan replied. "We have news that a ship with his...I mean...her merchandise has crashed on its way here. We need to get there in a hurry to retrieve it."

"Here," Jack said, approaching the wide window where the ship's face hovered. "Maybe this might help you understand things a little better." He opened his palm, and out floated Jaanloch's Merchant key, finding its way into the ship's systems through a nearby panel in the wall.

"You're Merchants?" the ship asked, ingesting the information of the Merchant key....It seemed impressed. "Jaanloch's apprentices...what a pleasure. Did you say you lost some merchandise?"

"Yes, "Jack said. "That is true. And we need to get it back to bring it to Spagon."

"Very well, Merchants," the ship said. "Give me the location of this ship. I'll take you there so you can retrieve whatever it is, and bring it back.

When Jaanloch had first given them their Merchant keys, never once did Jack think they'd come to use them on a mission as grave as this one. But as the ship began to rise from the platform, he learned that nothing's too small to be considered worthless in the Plogg Sector.

The ship zipped from the platform to the crash-site in less than a minute.

The wrecked ship laid smashed at the base of a tower in a smoldering heap--its cargo doors held open like a gaping mouth.

Curious on-lookers were already beginning to gather around, and the throbbing lights of the Monitors could be seen blinking in the distance.

"Do you think they're still down there?" asked Braak.

"From the looks of that crowd," Jack said. "I'd say yes, they are." He looked up at the ship's face in the window. "What do you think?"

"It's Jherilon," the ship said.

"What?"

"My name," the ship said. "It's Jherilon. And yes, your fellow Merchants are still presently contained with Spagon's merchandise. But don't worry, they've already called for help."

This was not good news for the Drones. The last thing they needed was more AIGDs to deal with.

"We have to act now, Jack" Semhek said. "Once their help arrives, we don't stand a chance of doing anything."

"We hardly stand a chance of getting the Technician with 15 AIGDs guarding him right now," added Ford. "There's only 6 of us. And considering what Kaypac did to Meerk, Ghan, and Semhek, all by herself, I'd say we're very out-numbered and out-gunned at this time."

"But we have to do something," said Ghan, flexing his robotic arm. "We can't let the Technician get away."

"Ghan's right," said Braak, turning to Jack. "If we're going to do something, then now's the time to do it."

Jack thought of the Taaschlon's words; it took him just a few moments to make up his own mind on whether they should engage the Technician's guards in a head-on battle, or abort the mission altogether. "Jherilon," he said to the ship. "Take us down. We're going to retrieve our merchandise."

"But Jack---"

"Just stay close to me," Jack said to Ford. "We'll do fine. I have a plan." The ship, Jherilon, began to ease them down to the surface.

"And what's this plan, you say you have?" Ford asked.

"We're going to ambush them," replied Jack. "We'll use our rifles. Kill as many as we can; kill-shots only, at the

341

center-mass, where the plasma generators are located. We still have the element of surprise on our side, so we're going to use it to our full advantage."

The instant the ship touched down, its rear cargo-ramp was lowered and out came the Drones, breaking off in different directions through the crowd that had gathered around the wrecked ship. For now, the curious droids would provide the perfect cover until the battle began and all hell broke loose.

But something else was amiss that brought further concern.

"Why don't they come out?" Jack heard Semhek say through his intercom. "They're waiting for help," Zubkov said.

Jack searched the crowd from where he stood, satisfied that he couldn't easily spot his fellow Drones in the throng. Only Ford remained at his side, whom he constantly reminded himself to keep a close eye on once the shooting starts. "Okay," he began, addressing the rest of his team. "This shouldn't be too hard. They're sitting ducks in there. Activate x-ray vision now. Locate your targets, and take them out. But try not to hit the box. We'll have to go in there and get it later on...x-rays ready."

"X-rays ready," they all replied, one after the other. The anxiety of the up-coming fight caused some of their voices to tremor.

"Locate your targets; draw your weapons and fire on my command," said Jack. With both arms, he reached behind his back under the long cape, and came out with both halves of his awesome weapon, connecting them expertly with a loud snap. He ignored the droids nearby, who began to scatter upon seeing the rifle suddenly appear. Through his x-ray lens, he could see the Technician's guards scurrying all throughout the innards of the ship. He regretted they weren't closer together, so he could take them out all at once. But he figured their odds were as good as any---so he just chose a target and gave the final order. "Fire!"

The air suddenly erupted with the thunderous roar of their weapons, firing simultaneously. Out of sheer panic, the entire crows dispersed in wild fright---all droids, bots, and serve-bots alike---fleeing for their precious lives. The wounded ship shook visibly under the heavy impact of the Jhusrot being unloaded into the hull. Inside, the Technician's guards began to fall. The red, liquidly mist could be seen spewing from their shredded plasma generators....

"Look out!"

A flaming ball of plasma came ripping out of the tattered ship's hull, missing a Drone, but chewing away more than half of a serve-bot's body, before sailing off through the wall of a tower behind them.

More balls of plasma came, all flying well wide of the Drones. "They can't see us!"

"They're shooting blind!"

"They're trapped!"

As if hearing this last assertion from the Drones, a droid shot out through the ship's cargo doors in a blur, but was quickly gunned down by Ghan, who had their only exit covered.

No more than a minute went by before the firing stopped and all the movements inside the battered ship had ceased. The entire crowd that had once gathered to witness the crash, was gone. Only the 6 Drones remained in the abandoned area. Through his scanner's readings, Jack saw that all occupants inside the ship were down. The Technician now laid defenseless inside his box....

"Ghan. Braak," Jack called over to the two Drones on his intercom. "Retrieve the box. The rest of us will stand guard."

"Jack!" yelled Ford beside him.

"What is it?"

"Look!" she said, pointing up at the colorful Brashnore sky.

CHAPTER
FORTY-FIVE

IT HAD NOW became clear to Jack, why the Monitors hadn't arrived while the Drones destroyed the Technician's ship. They'd obviously been called off by a much heavier cavalry elsewhere in the Sector.

Jack and the others stared up at this cavalry now: Four silvery spacecrafts, each equipped with tunnel-sized cannons, gleaming under the scorching Brashnorian suns. Their mighty engines bawled like grieving herds of cattle, while they hovered directly above, kicking up thick plumes of dust as they milled slowly through the air.

A godly horn sputtered on within the ships' ranks just then, giving the sound as if holes were being punched through the heavens above. Next, came the synthesized drawl of a droid; his voice booming like staccato thunder all around.

'They want us to surrender,' Klidaan said.

"That's a first," Jack said, sarcastically. "I expected them to come down here and make friends."

The Symbiot didn't bother to reply.

"How's it going in there, Braak?" asked Jack.

"Other than trying not to step in puddles of star-water," Braak replied. "We're fine. We have the box."

"Good," said Jack. "We don't have much time here."

"On our way out," Braak said.

"What're we going to do, Jack?" Semhek asked.

"Nothing," Jack replied. "We're going to take the Technician, and leave." "And what about them?" Zubkov asked, motioning up at the four ships, circling over their heads.

Both Ghan and Braak emerged from the grounded ship just then, hauling the heavy box between them. Both Drones cast their nervous gazes up at the warships above.

"What about them?" said Jack, to Zubkov, with a little shrug.

"They want us to surrender."

"I know," Jack said. "But we're not surrendering. We have the Technician. They wouldn't dare risk destroying him by shooting at us." He then turned to Ghan and Braak. "Let's go."

As if stunned, and outraged, by the Drones' brazen show of defiance, much louder and harsher commands boomed from the ships' horns. Jack could only guess they might've been jumbled orders for them to turn around---and threats, if they didn't. But then dead silence came....

Gone, was the mighty roar of the ship's engines, along with the ear-splitting sounds of the shrieking horns. It was almost as calm as if they'd never arrived, and also the most unnerving thing that Jack had ever sensed. Though the ship's shadows still loaned over them and blocked out the Brashnorian suns, they'd managed to cut off all sound around them. All sound...! He couldn't even hear himself as he attempted to speak through his intercom.

Seeing the others move around in equally confused fashion, Jack realized that they too were affected by the aliens strange weapon. He looked up just in time to see the round objects being ejected from the ships' hulls: insignificant and non-threatening at first, but as they neared the surface, their round shapes extended into fully formed guard droids.

One landed just twenty yards from where he stood, causing a small crater to dent the ground around it.

Long before the droid had the chance to engage them, Jack was already firing his weapon in its direction, blowing chunks. of metal from its limbs and head before finally blasting the plasma generator out through its back.

He didn't care to see the dead droid topple over, nor did he bother with the others that fell from the sky. "Let's get out of here! Now!" He just spun around, and they all made a dash for their awaiting ship.

The vicious rounds of plasma didn't take too long to follow. The thin white streaks zipped past them in blurs that flashed brightly in the corners of their eyes, threatening certain death at the slightest touch. The blasts from the plasma rifles were never heard, nor was the loud crunch of each droid that landed on the planet's hard ground.... It was this lack of hearing that made their desperate flight appear to slow down, though they leaped across the alien landscape at high speeds, and their pursuers were gaining on them with each second that slipped by. It appeared like a deadly dance, this silent chase. A re-enactment of some lost eon perhaps, where every move became a graceful rendition of an ancient history being told. And it was this grace, it seemed, that brought them all back to their ship unharmed---or rather, made the ship go to them with its rear cargo doors open as they all made that final leap into the safety of its dark recesses.

The ship, Jherilon, immediately took to the air once the last Drone scurried up its rear cargo ramp. In no time at all, it would put a great distance between them and the small army of guard droids. However, the much larger crafts had now taken pursuit, bearing down, and attempting to lock in on their position. "Hold on," Jherilon said, calmly, as if he wasn't about to be blown out of the sky. "We're being fired upon."

The first set of laser bolts, shot from the ships' cannons, might've been warning-shots, for they all flew well wide of their target. But it was enough to send Jherilon into battle-mode.

There, shooting up through the clouds at the speed of a comet, Jherilon made a complete spin around (flying backwards as he did so) and spat out a continuous stream---not of laser, or torpedo, or missile, but lethal starplasma into the first craft that came jumping out through the thick clouds.

The front half of the unfortunate ship seemed to cave in, in of metal and glass, as plasma hosed right through it, bursting out though the back like sprayed larva.

Jherilon dipped back down through the clouds, aware that the wounded craft was doing the same, but no longer in pursuit, as it went twirling head-first in a death-spiral on its way back down to the surface.

Seeing their comrade shot down so savagely, the three remaining crafts focused all their fire-power on the smaller ship before them. They were now determined more than ever to destroy---not capture---the outlaws who had so blatantly violated the visages of the Piilor Front.

Struggling to maintain his footing in the ship's rear cargo-hold, Jack couldn't see any of the action, as he would if they all been strapped to their seats on the bridge. But judging from the many shifts, sways, and dips in Jherilon's patterns, he was more than impressed with the sequence---if there were any sequences involved at all. There were too many loops to keep track of, and it didn't last long enough for him to recognize any noticeable patterns. The rocking and swaying gradually slowed as Jherilon's evasive maneuvering came to a stop and the ship leveled to a comfortable cruise once more....In less than a minute, Jherilon's battle with the four menacing ships was over.

By the time the Drones made their way back to the bridge, they found they were already in deep space, and Brashnore was now worlds behind them. There were too many questions that Jack had for this mysterious ship, in which they somehow managed to convince in kidnapping the most valuable asset of the most powerful Syndicate in the entire Plogg Sector. "Who are you, Jherilon?" It was the most sensible question he could think of to begin with. "You're nothing but a luxury ship. How could you have taken out a squadron of warships so easily---all by yourself?"

"I don't know," Jherilon answered. "That is my design: to protect my Master."

"Your Master?" asked Semhek. To him, and the other Drones, it was all beginning to make sense.

"By Master...." Jack began. "You mean, Spagon?"

"No," Jherilon replied. "Spagon, is simply the one I serve. My Master, is the one who created me: Your Merchandise."

"Hmm," said Jack, thoughtfully. They'd suddenly found themselves in the most uncertain situation, for there was no telling how this special ship might react if it ever found out that its Master, was indeed their prisoner. He had no doubts that it would try to destroy an entire Stendaaran fleet, if provoked. He could only imagine the fate of six lowly tribe-bots that ever happened to stand in its way. He could sense the tension in the others as well; their thoughts, very likely quite similar to his. It felt as if the whole bridge had became stiffened with apprehension.

But then, Jherilon surprised them once more, by asking the question that none of them would've ever expected. "What part of the 3rd Quadrant shall we go?"

"What?" Jack could hardly believe what he was hearing. "What do you know of the 3rd Quadrant?"

"Spagon said we are to go the 3rd Quadrant, with our Master," the ship replied.

"Spagon?" asked Ford. "How can Spagon know where we're supposed to go?"

"And what do you know of our mission?" Zubkov added.

"Didn't you all plan this on Langworn?" The ship asked in return. ""To take our Master to the Stendaarans, before that traitorous Zhorg killed her." It seemed to sigh at that. "He was an older model...not designed with the free will that me and Spagon possess."

"Spagon," said Jack, finally catching on to who's ship they were really on. How else could she have gotten there, if not on her own special craft? "Do you mean Kaypac?"

Jherilon gave a hesitant pause; his box-like face breaking into a puzzled frown before he asked them: "Is that what you called her?"

Printed in the United States
By Bookmasters